LEARNING TO WHISTLE

LEARNING TO WHISTLE

A Novel

TESS PERKO

Published in 2026 by
She Writes Press, an imprint of The Stable Book Group

32 Court Street, Suite 2109
Brooklyn, NY 11201
https://shewritespress.com
Library of Congress Control Number: 2025927297
ISBN: 979-8-89636-116-9
eISBN: 979-8-89636-117-6

Interior Designer: Tabitha Lahr

Printed in the United States

This book is dedicated to my mother,
Rose Marie, who taught me how
to love everyone unconditionally.

Traveler, there are no paths. Paths are made by walking.

—AUSTRALIAN ABORIGINAL PROVERB

CHAPTER 1

My mother's memorial service was held in a simple Lutheran church, a mile from our house, a church my mother had admired for years. Near the entrance was a labyrinth. Aunt Patty, Mom's only sister, was walking the sandy circular paths when we arrived. She looked up at us briefly as we passed, but dipped her head forward, pacing in circles with determination. A tear shimmered on her cheek.

Inside the church, blonde wood flanked the walls, and a tree of life rose from the floor behind the wooden altar, its knurled branches twisting upward. Stained glass windows, tinted with a rainbow of vertical rectangles, lit the room and cast polychromatic patterns across the floor and pews. Dad, my brother Zach, and I sat in the front pew with Aunt Patty and Uncle Bill.

As the service started, Zach, usually stoic, sat beside me, his arms clutching his waist, sobs erupting thick and fast, tears streaming down his face. On Zach's other side, my father, his face a portrait of anguish, wrapped his arm around Zach's shoulders and drew him close.

Mom's friends and coworkers shared memories of my mother. They talked about her loyalty, her generosity, her unlimited empathy. I averted my eyes upward to avoid seeing Mom's pearlescent urn and the banks of red roses surrounding it.

Finally, Aunt Patty rose and walked to the podium. Two worry lines had formed between her eyebrows. She sniffed, took a piece of paper out of her skirt pocket, and unfolded it. Then she lifted her head. "Heather was my beloved sister, and Steve was the love of her life. There was a time when she was going to become a psychologist to help people deal with their mental and emotional problems, but she changed her education plans when she met Steve because she wanted to raise a family, so she finished her two-year graduate degree and became a college counselor." Her voice, usually clipped and businesslike, had softened. "She told me once that becoming a mother had made her a better person. I believe it. I've never known anyone with such a well of love for her children."

I saw Dad nod, a slight smile brightening his face.

Aunt Patty continued, "But, Leonie and Zach, she wants you both to spread your wings wider than she did. She loved her family, but she wished she'd traveled before she settled down to get married."

My father squirmed in the pew next to Zach. His jaw hardened, and a scowl crossed his forehead.

Reaching across Zach's lap, I took Dad's hand and squeezed it. He didn't respond.

"We'll miss having Heather beside us, but the love that she shared with all of us made us stronger and happier. The last time we spoke, she made me promise to keep her love close to my heart. Of course, I will. I'll never give her up. Promise her that you won't either." Patty folded the piece of paper, slid it into her pocket, and paced back to her seat, blinking back tears.

AT THE CEMETERY, DAD held the urn as Zach reached for it and caressed its smooth side, his face shining wet in the hot sun. Something about his gesture reminded me of my mother's hands pressed against my forehead when I had the flu. I couldn't eat, so she'd warmed up chicken broth for me to sip. The next day, she added peas to the broth. The next day, she added chicken, and then egg noodles, until I felt completely restored. She always knew how to make life better. No one would ever take her place in my life.

My father held out the urn toward me. "Say goodbye to Mom," he said, his voice breaking like a leaf crunching under someone's foot.

I pushed my pain deep down in my chest as I kissed the urn. With a flood of tears spilling over his cheeks, Zach kissed it too, before Dad placed it inside the niche. Dad moved close to the open niche to whisper something I couldn't hear. I swallowed, the sob rising in my throat. Suddenly, it seemed like a huge piece of the universe was missing. No moon to guide the tides in and out. No North Star. Without my mother, I was a comet without direction.

My father backed away from the niche and stretched his arms around Zach's and my shoulders. I felt dizzy as the cemetery worker placed the marble door over the niche and screwed it on. Zach sobbed again, his body shaking in Dad's arms. We turned away. As we walked back to the car together, I felt my father's body tremble.

CHAPTER 2

In October, Aunt Patty invited me to lunch at a popular Davis restaurant on Third Street. When I arrived, she was sitting at a tiny table by the window that looked out to the street. Nearby tables were full of students who had slung their backpacks over the backs of their wooden chairs. When Aunt Patty saw me, she stood and waited by her chair. She embraced me in a hug. "How are ya doin', honey?"

I dumped my backpack on the floor under the window and wriggled into my chair to get comfortable. "Fine, I guess." It had only been three months since Mom passed, and I was still living in a fog of pain.

She rested her elbows on the wooden tabletop and leaned toward me. As she did, her short light brown bob, lit from the sun streaming through the window, tilted forward. "You know I'm here for you, right?" She had green eyes like Mom's.

I leaned back and looked down at the table. "I know. You've always been wonderful to Zach and me." I raised my head.

Aunt Patty pressed her lips together. "Look, I want to talk to you about something that was important to your mother."

Before she had time to say more, a waitress, dressed in a white T-shirt, torn jeans, and a green apron, approached the table. Her right forearm sported a bird tattoo. "What can I getcha?"

Patty looked at me and said, "You know what you want?"

I nodded.

Pointing at herself, Patty said, “I’ll have the mushroom crepe with a side salad. To drink, an iced tea.”

The waitress turned to me and arched her dark eyebrows. “I’d like iced tea and the Greek Delight crepe with roasted potatoes.”

The waitress checked items on her notepad. “Righto.” She swiveled on the heel of her sneaker and marched away.

Patty sat back and crossed her arms. “Okay, you ready?”

I hunched my shoulders. “This sounds mysterious.”

She shook her head. “Not at all, but to your mother, important.”

My chair squeaked as I adjusted myself. “Okay. What is it?”

She placed her fingers over her mouth. “Your dad won’t want me telling you this. He’s pretty protective.”

I pictured Dad’s face, the stern way he looked while Aunt Patty was speaking at Mom’s funeral. “You and Dad don’t always get along, do you?”

A hint of a smile appeared on her lips. She laughed, not like my mother with a melodic tune, but hearty, full of belly. “We both have strong personalities and were fierce protectors of your mother. Right now, I’m going to make sure you hear what your mother wanted for you.”

The dull throb in my chest grew intense. I rubbed it with my fingers.

Aunt Patty took a deep breath, then let it out. “You heard what I said at the funeral about how much your mom wanted to travel, but missed her chance. She doesn’t want you to make the same mistake. After you graduate, you should take off. Get away. See what’s possible.”

“Before Mom died, she told me the same thing. Even made me promise. But I don’t know if I’m up to it.” My mind filled with pictures of people rushing around in an airport, a plane crowded with passengers, and stores filled with shoppers. The visions blended with each other so that people were smashing into one another, creating chaos. Next, I saw myself walking on a cobblestone street lined with stone houses, lost and sweating in the hot sun. I closed my eyes and sucked in a deep breath. After squeezing my eyes tightly and shaking the images out of my head, I opened them, looked at Aunt Patty, and groaned. A furrow creased the skin between her eyebrows.

The waitress set our plates down, and little clouds of steam rose from the crepes. Aunt Patty picked up her fork and knife. "I was hoping she did. Right after college is the perfect time. You'll be done with school and won't have the responsibilities of a job."

I cut into my crepe, a concoction of vegetables and feta cheese. "Ah, smells like something Mom would make." I looked at Aunt Patty. "Home is too quiet without her. And it's as if something's frozen there now—her unopened books, the weeds in the garden." I took a bite and thought about Mom as I chewed. I pictured her kneading pizza dough on the granite counter in the kitchen, her blonde hair swaying with her body rocking over the dough. "I don't know. Travel. There's so much to it. And I don't have any money."

Aunt Patty set down her knife and pointed her fork in the air. "Your father will come up with arguments to stop you, so don't you pile onto those arguments. If you want to make it happen, make it happen."

I looked away from Aunt Patty and out the window, then back at her again. She let me sit in silence. How strong-minded she was. She reminded me of Mom, but she had a toughness Mom didn't have. Aunt Patty would've never let anyone stand in the way of her dreams.

"She made me promise two other things before she died," I said. "I promised I'd always keep her close, whatever that means."

"That's her way of staying connected to you," said Aunt Patty, resting her hands under her chin.

"I also promised her I'd find other female mentors in my life."

"I'll be one of those," said Aunt Patty. "Your mother was a generous soul. Keep your promises."

Out the window, I pictured Dad stretching his big arms wide to give me a hug, his soft brown eyes holding all the love in the world. I blinked. In his place, I saw Mom's face as we sat in the backyard and she asked me to make her promises.

ELAINE, A FRIEND I HAD met freshman year in Spanish class, and I had been taking Spanish classes together for three and a half years. We studied together every week, and she was part of the group of friends I socialized with on the weekends. A five-foot, six-inch blonde with jade-colored eyes, she was also sweet. She opened doors for everyone and let them enter first. She took time to help people after class. She even tipped the cashiers at fast food restaurants.

In winter quarter of my senior year, I took Spanish, Women's Literature, Economics 1B, and Tennis. Elaine had also signed up for Spanish, which met five days a week so we saw each other often. Professor Arias complimented both of us on our fluency and told us about a six-week Spanish course in Buenos Aires that was starting in June, two weeks after graduation. After the course, we'd have enough credits to count Spanish as our second major.

One day when Elaine and I were studying in the library, she said, "Why don't we do the Argentina thing? I can apply for jobs after that. Don't you think it would be good for you to get away for a while?"

I looked up from my textbook. "I don't know. I'm floating. I don't know where I belong, but I can't go home."

"My mother said when people experience a tragic loss, a new perspective is healing."

"My mom is all over our house. But not, you know what I mean? It's become the sad house."

"So, going to Argentina will get you away from all that. Maybe by the time you come home, your house will be cheerier."

"Six weeks. That's not a long time. Yeah, maybe we should go. Do that Argentina thing."

LATER THAT DAY, ELAINE and I knocked on Professor Arias's office door. She invited us in, and we sat on chairs in front of a wall of bookcases. Professor Arias sat behind her desk. "I'm so glad you're interested in the course," she said, her smile bright and beaming. "You won't believe how much your Spanish will improve—speaking, writing, reading. And you'll be able to explore the city; you'll meet fascinating new people."

She made it sound thrilling. And with Elaine there, I'd be less afraid of all the unfamiliar, all the change. But then I remembered I wasn't from a wealthy family. I said, "I'll need to work. Does the university offer any type of jobs for students?"

Professor Arias's eyes widened with enthusiasm. "You could teach English to the Argentine students at the university. The college is always hiring for those positions."

I shook my head. "I've never taught anything. I wouldn't know where to start."

"The university will train you for two days. You get paid for that too. After the training, you'll know what to do. Since you've studied Spanish for four years of college, you'll be more than qualified to teach English there."

"Two days?"

"And I think you'll love it. As their teacher, you'll connect with people in ways you wouldn't otherwise. You're going to be helping people learn a skill that will change their lives. Doesn't that sound great?"

Excitement fluttered through my chest. I wanted my life to change, but it hadn't occurred to me I could be the catalyst for change in someone else's life.

"I'll go," I said, clapping my hands together.

Elaine jumped in her chair. "Me too. Sign us up."

AFTER OUR MEETING WITH Professor Arias, Elaine walked out of the Foreign Language Building and called her parents to ask for permission. They'd both been on the call and told her they thought it was a great opportunity.

She clicked off the call and beamed, "I'm in! Now you have to ask your dad."

"I can't ask him right now. It feels so, I don't know, selfish."

"Yeah, I get it. But you're going to have to do it soon. The program is going to fill up. And I don't want to go without you, buddy!"

"I'll do it. I promise."

Four weeks later, the quarter ended and Elaine was pushing hard for an answer. "I'm counting on us doing this together, Lee," she said. "You need to let me know if you're not going."

She was right. I couldn't keep hiding.

DAD HAD INSISTED I come home for spring break. Zach's spring break had already passed, so it would be just Dad and me. I took the train from Davis to San Francisco, and then caught a taxi to my house. When I arrived at the house, the hills of the neighborhood were scattered with pale sunshine and dappled with patches of shade. Foggy air ascended from the ocean a few miles away and swirled in between the houses.

When I got inside, I found a note from Dad that said, "Welcome home, honey. I had to go into the office this afternoon. I have the dog with me. See you around 5 p.m. Love, Dad."

I carried my luggage upstairs to my room. It looked like I had never left. Posters of Paris hung on the walls. The pillows my mother had needlepointed for me were arranged on my bed. The afternoon sun cast a weak streak of light through the window as if it had lost interest in shining. I closed the door and went downstairs to wait for Dad.

Memories of Mom were everywhere. In the kitchen, I turned around to take in the whole room. Her cooking utensils were tucked into a crock on the counter. The olive oil decanter was next to the stove. I opened a cupboard and found her Mason mixing bowls stacked inside each other. Her teacups were on display in the china cabinet. The memories hung in the air like ghosts.

In the family room, Mom's soft blue recliner sat empty. I walked over to it and ran my hand across the back of it. Her favorite Tiffany lamp was dark. Her books were neatly lined up on the bookshelf, none lying open to a favorite page. A light dust covered the side table next to her chair where her tiny bone china bouquets of roses and peonies stood as if they were lost without their admirer. My mother wasn't there to cradle them in her hands as if they were jewels. The house was as silent as a tomb.

I opened the French door to the backyard. Outside, the garden where she planted vegetables every spring was a patch of hard dry dirt. Little gusts of wind whipped dust into the air. A few birds pecked at sticks. The bees and butterflies were long gone.

I closed the door and continued to wander from room to room. I breathed in, hoping to smell a hint of Mom's fresh bread wafting through the house. I strained to hear her musical voice calling me to share a story.

My wander around the family home left me like an avocado sliced open with a sharp knife, the pit and creamy pulp scraped from its skin with a metal spoon.

FOR THE NEXT WEEK, I escaped my lonely home by taking long walks around the city every morning with our black Labrador, Rex. From our neighborhood in the hills, I led him down to Taraval Street, which stretched straight out to the Pacific Ocean. We passed block after block of tiny homes, built close together and painted in pastel colors—my mother's favorites—until we reached the shore.

The ocean waves crashed haphazardly onto the sand, squalls of cold wind spraying their salty tears. Rex's paws and my shoes left deep prints in the wet clinging sand. Broken shells and seaweed were scattered across the beach. Over the crashing waves, the milky-blue sky was streaked with ocean spray. As the spray misted my face, I allowed tears to slide down my cheeks. The sky, the ocean, the whole world was crying for my mother.

I walked north to Golden Gate Park, leaving the sand and taking the trail that followed the Great Highway all the way up to Lincoln Avenue. Giant eucalyptus trees soared up from the green forest floor on each side of the road, and, between their gargantuan branches, the pale-blue sky stretched overhead like a tight sailcloth.

I sniffled and wiped my face with the sleeve of my sweatshirt, Rex always ahead of me, searching for squirrels in the trees. Bicyclists, dressed in yellow like striped honeybees, whizzed past me. One had perched his cell phone on his handlebars. It was blasting out a Rolling Stones song, the notes pounding like bullets on a windshield.

Rex lurched for a squirrel that was scooting up a tree about five yards away, almost causing me to lose my balance. "Come on, boy. You'll never catch it," I said, urging him back onto the pavement. A couple, holding hands, was headed west toward Ocean Beach. Rex and I meandered past the polo field, a lake, and a picnic area. I crossed the road so I could see Rainbow Falls, which rushed down a steep bank like a rippling white ribbon. My heart sank as I remembered how much Mom loved the falls. Finally, I turned south toward Nineteenth Avenue, back into city streets and, eventually, our neighborhood.

THAT SATURDAY, DAD, AN architect who loved studying the ancient architects of Greece and Italy, was sitting on the porch reading a book about the Italian architect Palladio. I stuck my head through the doorway and cleared my throat. His auburn hair was streaked with gray threads, and his cat-eyed black-framed reading glasses were perched on the bridge of his nose, magnifying his brown irises. Wearing a navy-blue polo shirt and jean shorts, he was leaning back in an Adirondack chair, his hairy legs propped up on a matching ottoman. When he raised his head, his eyebrows arched up like tiny bushy mountains. "Hey, babe. What's up?" he said.

I sat down on a chair beside him, my feet planted in front of me. "Dad, my Spanish professor is teaching a six-week class in Buenos Aires this summer and has asked me to join her." In my mind, I saw my mother's face. She was smiling at the sound of her daughter speaking of travel.

He tucked in his chin and peered over the rim of his reading glasses.

I perched my elbows on my knees and clasped my hands between them. "This class would give me enough credits to have a second major. I know I'm graduating in early June, but the university will add the credits to my course list after the graduation ceremony." I squeezed my hands together as I waited for him to say something.

Dad cleared his throat, stuck a bookmark in between the pages of his book, and closed it. "I'm worried that you haven't recovered from your mother's death, honey. Staying at home with me and Zach this summer is a better idea."

I felt pressure building up behind my eyes. I sniffed involuntarily. "Dad?"

"Yes, honey."

"Mom once told me that when you were in college, you took a trip to Machu Picchu."

"That's right, I did. I was having a hard time figuring out what to major in. On the hike to Machu Picchu, I discovered that I loved architecture, so I went back to college and majored in it."

I raised my hands in the air and opened them wide. "If travel helped you make an important decision, don't you think it would be good for me? Elaine is going."

He closed his eyes. As I waited for him to speak, I noticed how his lashes twitched ever so slightly.

"Dad, I just think—"

"Give me a minute. I need to give this some thought." He took off his glasses and cleaned them with a corner of his shirt.

I waited and waited. Five minutes of awkward silence. Then I said, "Elaine's going. She's already talked to her parents."

He smiled, and I felt us both acknowledging that I'd played a smart card there. He sighed and said, "If it's what you really want, okay. It's only for six weeks, and Elaine will be there."

I clapped my hands and jumped in my seat. "Oh, Dad, thank you. So, you think the trip will be good for me?"

His eyes started to look misty. "I don't know, honey. I worry that it's too soon after your mother's death." But after another long pause, he opened his arms. I leaned over to embrace him.

When I was younger, I loved his hugs because his long arms wrapped all the way around me, and his hands, thick and soft as pancakes, made me feel warm and snug. That day on the porch, I let myself remember the simple joy of those hugs. But then as I leaned onto his warm chest, I thought about what Aunt Patty had said about Dad being too protective, and I squirmed out of his embrace, jerked up, turned around, and left the porch.

IN SPRING QUARTER, I WENT to the library for travel books about Spanish-speaking countries. While I browsed through the pages of the book on Spain, I imagined myself speaking fluent Spanish to people I met on the street. The book about Argentina had pages and pages devoted to colonial times. The Mendoza area east of the Andes Mountains was a famous Argentinian wine-growing region that reminded me of Napa, north of San Francisco. The section about Peru devoted a whole chapter to Machu Picchu. I read that chapter word for word, picturing my college-age father hiking the trail with the mountains circling around him. A satisfied smile lit up his face.

The night after I graduated, Zach cornered me, knocking on my bedroom door. It was around midnight, and Dad had gone to bed. Zach was a sweet brother, always kind. He was already dressed in his pajamas, a gray T-shirt with a dolphin on the front and shorts dotted with otters. What a nature nut he was.

He sat down on my bed and reached for my hand. In a gentle voice he said, “Hey, Sis, I know you’re torn up about Mom. I am too. Let’s help each other get through this.”

I relaxed my tight shoulders. Blinking away the tears welling up, I sighed. “I miss her so much. I feel lost, like I’m wandering through a maze of streets without a map. I can’t think straight. I lose my concentration all the time. I used to be organized. Now I’m confused. I don’t recognize myself.”

“Hey, I’m with you. I don’t feel normal either. The counselor at school told me that grief does that to a person.”

We sat silently on the bed, the room lit only by a single bedside lamp. The curtains were open. The stars were out there, but I could barely see them, thanks to the city lights that cast a fiery glow. Finally, I said, “I’m going to Buenos Aires to take my last course for my Spanish degree. Dad said I could go, and Elaine’s going with me. It’s a six-week course, and I leave in a week and a half.”

Zach jumped up. “Whoa, I thought we would spend the summer together—the three of us.”

I squeezed his hand. “Don’t worry, I’ll be back in six weeks. It’ll go by fast.”

He hung his head, staring at the bedspread, then leaned over and gave me a hug, a long-protracted caress. With a look of both devastation and love, he stood up and left the room.

When he closed the door, I imagined what it would be like if I spent the summer in San Francisco without Mom. Beach outings without her sun-kissed face. Dinners at home with an empty seat at the table. No one in the garden tilling the soil, planting vegetables and flowers. It would be the most painful summer I’d ever known.

CHAPTER 2.5

A few months before she dies, Mom and I sit outside under the oak tree in the backyard. "Promise me, Leonie, that you'll keep me with you."

Tears slide down my cheeks. I didn't see how I could keep her with me if she died, but I wanted to. "I promise, Mom."

"I have another promise I want you to keep. I hope I've inspired you, but I want you to find other women to emulate. Choose many, in fact. One for leadership skills, another for the art of love, and another for living with joy. She might be one of your professors, a coworker, a girlfriend, a friend's mother, or even a woman you meet only one time in your life. Whatever you wish to be, you can find a woman to use as an example." She rests a hand on my back and rubs it, gently.

"How can you be so strong?" I say, the words interrupted with tiny sobs. I lean harder into her lap and squeeze her to me. I didn't want to find other women to emulate. Nobody could replace Mom. Nobody knew me like she did. Nobody loved me like she did.

"Promise me that you'll find female mentors to teach you how to navigate life."

I rub my wet cheeks with my palms. "Okay, I promise. Aunt Patty is one person I can think of."

Mom chuckles, the sound like a stream's gurgling. "That's right. You're like a daughter to her too." She bends down and rests her hand on my shoulder. "Now, here's the third promise I want you to keep. When your dad was in college, he took a semester off to hike Machu Picchu with a college friend. He told me he was trying to decide on a major, what he wanted to do with his life. His trip was a spiritual awakening—it's how he discovered he wanted to be an architect."

She rubs my shoulder. "I never took a trip like that when I was young. Promise me you will."

I sit up straight. "You think I should?"

"Yes. A journey would be life-changing. You'll learn about yourself, things that you can't learn by staying home. You'll meet people with different views, and you'll grow."

"I promise, Mom, but I won't ever feel happy again if you die."

"You will. You're strong."

Time stops as I gaze at her face, shoulders, arms. "I love you, Mom."

A sheen spreads over Mom's face. "Leonie, I love you. You've made my life incredibly happy."

CHAPTER 3

Pretty quickly, it became clear I was an inexperienced traveler. Elaine and I walked off the plane in Dallas, where we had to wait an hour and a half before catching the flight to Buenos Aires. Signs for baggage claim and connecting gates pointed in all directions. People, dressed in everything from sweatpants to suit jackets, rushed past us, their sneakers, high heels, and hiking boots squeaking and clopping on the linoleum. Bright lights from the airline gates, hallways, and magazine outlets blurred my vision and gave me a headache.

We rode an escalator to catch the train that moved passengers between terminals, then waited with a mob of other people for the train. When it arrived, like an army of unorganized ants, we hobbled our way into the car, smashing ourselves up against other bodies until the doors closed. When the train arrived at the international terminal, Elaine and I had to claw our way from the back of the car, calling out, "Excuse me! Excuse me!" to exit before the doors closed. I felt a whoosh of wind as I finally crossed the threshold.

Our gate was a long way from the train, so we joined a pack of other anxious travelers hustling toward their gates. Coffee stands, chocolate counters, stores filled with perfume and Dallas T-shirts, and a bustling bar with blaring television sets blasted the terminal with lights and noises. When we finally reached our gate, we had twenty minutes until boarding was supposed to begin. Elaine sat in a seat on the edge of the crowd waiting to board, and I rushed to the restroom.

I waited in the very long line, clutching my passport and boarding pass in one hand. After the line inched forward enough for me to be able to peer into the restroom, I could see that there were at least a dozen stalls, all with their doors locked. I glanced back at Elaine, who was motioning for me to hurry. The line continued to crawl along until I could no longer see Elaine, which was a relief because her anxious waving was making my heart thunder. I couldn't bear the idea of irritating her, the travel partner I needed so badly. Ten minutes passed, and it was finally my turn to dash into the next open stall. I hurried in and out, washed my hands, and rushed back to the gate where passengers were already boarding the plane.

Elaine was shaking. "Gee, Leonie! You almost missed the flight."

I slipped into line beside her. "Ah, so many people in there!"

She took a deep breath. "Okay." She looked at my hands. "Take out your boarding pass and passport. You need them to board."

My documents. Where were they? I searched inside my backpack, in every pocket. They weren't there. Where had I left them? By the sink? Did I drop them somewhere? People were clutching the hands of their partners, shuffling their feet forward, foot by foot to the gate. Elaine was looking at me like she was about to scream. I had to do something fast. "I'll be right back. Hold my backpack." I shoved it at her and ran.

I sprinted back to the restroom, passing a line of passengers waiting their turn. Inside, I scanned the counters and sinks and saw only wadded-up paper towels and small pools of water. Twisting toward the stalls, I tried the door of the stall I'd used. It was locked. I knocked as loud as I could.

A woman said, "Busy."

I knocked again. "I'm sorry, but I may have left my passport and boarding pass in there. Do you see it?" I heard the toilet flush and the door opened.

A woman dressed in a leopard jumpsuit opened the door. "I think you did. There's something on the top of the toilet paper holder." Then she walked to the sink. I poked my head inside the stall, grabbed my passport and boarding pass, and dashed back outside to the gate.

The line for boarding had disappeared except for Elaine, who was standing by a boarding attendant, tears streaming down her face. I saw the attendant say something to Elaine, who wailed, "No!" Then the attendant headed toward the jet bridge.

I shouted, "I'm here!" I was short of breath.

"Thank God, Leonie," said Elaine, pulling me toward the door.

The attendant turned around. "Well, you made it after all." She scanned my boarding pass, matched the photo of my passport to my face, and waved us on. We scooted through the aisle past the other passengers, some staring at us with questions on their faces. When I got to my seat, I plopped down and started laughing, covering my mouth with my hand to cover my snorts. The man sitting in the seat in the opposite aisle raised his eyebrows, a smile brushing his face. Elaine, however, sat down silently, secured her seat belt, and hid her face in her hands. After a few minutes, she uncovered her face, wiped it dry, punched me in the arm, and said, "Now I feel better."

THE PLANE DESCENDED OVER the silver-and-blue high-rises of Buenos Aires. It was late afternoon and the sun dipped like a melting orange candle in the west. At the eastern edge of the city, a golden beach stretched for miles, ocean waves lapping at the sand like wet frothy tongues.

"Oh, Elaine, the city is so beautiful," I said, staring at the scene out the window.

She leaned over to see. "Wow, beach, coffee houses, restaurants. We're going to have a fabulous time," she said, her voice almost a sigh.

We followed the other passengers off the plane and through several hallways to the luggage area, where we collected our suitcases. Outside the luggage area near an exit door, a young woman, wearing a gray sweatshirt and jeans with frayed bottoms, held a sign with our names printed in block letters.

We approached her and Elaine introduced us.

The woman, speaking in Spanish, said, "I'm Almara. Welcome to Buenos Aires. I'll be taking you to the university and showing you where you'll stay." Her long thick brown hair was pulled back into a ponytail with a blue scrunchie. She wore gold hoop earrings as big as a Coke can. When she smiled, she blinked, and her dark eyelashes were so long it seemed as if they were waving at us.

"It's exciting to be here," I said.

Almara tucked the sign with our names into a brown leather bag hanging across her chest and smiled, dimples forming in her rosy cheeks. "Welcome to Buenos Aires! Let's get a taxi."

The taxi driver drove us across the city, and as we rode, I tried to take it all in. Almara pointed out famous buildings. "There's Centro Cultural Borges, the center for music, literature, and dance," she said. "I saw a concert there last month."

I perked up. "Which concert?"

"The singer Lola Ponce."

I felt a surge of adrenaline at the idea of hearing Argentine music *right in* Argentina.

Almara spoke with a lisp, which Professor Arias had taught us was a characteristic of Argentinians. "Now we're passing the Museo Nacional de Arte Oriental. Buenos Aires has many art museums representing art from all over the world." I had to strain to understand her accent. Maybe I wasn't as fluent in Spanish as I thought I was.

Almara pointed toward a two-story building with red awnings and a front door with stained glass windows. "There's Don Victoriano, one of Buenos Aires's oldest coffee houses. You know, the city is famous for its coffee houses, not because the coffee is exceptional, but because *porteños* use creative recipes for making coffee. At Don Victoriano, you can order coffee with spices like cardamom or with milk and turmeric."

Elaine's jade eyes flickered with pleasure. "We have to try that place."

Just like the travel books said, Buenos Aires was a gorgeous city: historical architecture, cultural influences from all over the world, elegant foods. I was going to love exploring.

THE RIDE TO OUR DORM lasted almost an hour. The taxi driver stopped the car next to the curb of a white two-story building on a busy street. Pointing out the window, he said, "One block away is the Faculty of Philosophy and Letters, where students study Spanish."

Almara helped us gather our luggage and carry it into the building lobby. "I trust you'll find your way from here," she said. "Sign in at the desk and they'll give you a room."

We were assigned a room in the basement. It was shabby. The doorknob rattled. The paint peeled off the walls, and the oak furniture was marred with scratches and watermarks. In one corner was a chipped white enamel sink with a rough wooden shelf above it. Over the shelf, a small oval oxidized mirror with a chain hung on a nail. Beds, fitted with rough white sheets and covered with faded blue-and-white-striped bedspreads, flanked two walls. A chest of drawers stood between them. Each bed was anchored by a scratched brown desk with drawers and a wooden chair. In the middle of the room, a dull brown rug covered the knotted wooden floor.

I said, "It feels like an old barn, but I'm happy to be here."

Elaine threw her hat on a desk. "Me too."

We tossed our large backpacks on our beds and unpacked them, placing our clothes in piles in the chests of drawers. I set a picture of my mother on the top of my desk. In it, her blonde hair was fluffed back, one side pinned with a pearl hair clip. Her eyelids were brushed with lavender eye shadow that accented her beautiful green eyes, and she wore a soft pink jacket with wide lapels and a lavender printed blouse underneath. I wished she were there with me.

CHAPTER 4

On the first day of class, I found mentorship in an unexpected place.

Elaine and I arrived early to our first class and sat in the second row. Several other students arrived alone or in twos before the nine o'clock bell. Their faces were a beautiful representation of the entire world: brown hair, black hair, ebony skin, pale skin, neatly dressed, casually coiffed. A chorus of excited whispers filled the room.

Just before the bell rang, Professor Arias, dressed in an attractive black wrap dress and black pumps, paced through a side door and set her books on the desk in front of the whiteboard. Her black hair fell in waves around her shoulders, and she wore bright red lipstick. She looked up and scanned the faces in the room, then addressed the class in Spanish. "Welcome to Conversational Spanish. *Me llamo Profesora Arias.* I teach at UC Davis in California, but I'm here teaching for the summer." Her eyes settled on my face for a second then moved to Elaine, a smile brightening her lips. Warmth spread across my chest.

"We'll spend our time conversing about various topics with a few exceptions," Professor Arias said. "Some mornings, I'll be taking you on excursions in the city to learn the culture of Argentina. Culture is a large part of learning a language."

Suddenly, the back door of the classroom opened and banged against the wall. I turned around. A gorgeous woman, about my age, with long, glossy brown hair and skin the color of gingerbread, strode through the doorway. She had long shapely legs, an hourglass figure, and a swanlike neck. As she sauntered between the desks in her white dress and leather jacket, the students watched her. She acknowledged their attention by flicking her hair behind her shoulders with orange-painted fingernails. Finally, she sat at the desk next to me. The door clicked shut.

Professor Arias looked down at a piece of paper on her desk, then at the new student. "Clarisa, is it?"

The pretty woman stretched her elegant chin to gaze up. "*Sí, Profesora. Lo siento, estoy tarde. Problemas con el bus.*"

The professor made a ticking sound with her teeth. "*Vale.* Everyone, your afternoons are free to use as you'd like, and I know some of you have signed up to teach English to our local students. I'll assign each of you to teach two afternoons a week."

Clarisa touched my arm with her flamboyant nails. "*Hola*, I'm Clarisa. Want to form a study group?"

I whispered back, "*Sí.*" I pointed to Elaine on my left. "Can she join too? We're both from California."

When Clarisa smiled, her perfectly spaced white teeth gleamed between her full lips. "Sure. I live in Buenos Aires and am studying to be a high school Spanish teacher."

Professor Arias lowered her chin and glared at us. "I need everyone's attention."

Clarisa fluttered her sensuous eyelashes and flashed that bright smile *again*. I heard a baritone voice somewhere to my left say, "I want to meet her." I thought, *I'd like to be her friend. Or* be *her.*

The professor knocked on her desk to get our attention, then placed her hands on her hips. Her Spanish words resonated through the room. "The first thing I want you to do is form groups of four and introduce yourselves in Spanish using three noun phrases that describe who you are. For example, you might say you're an avid reader, talented dancer, or chocolate lover. Next, I want you to tell your new friends what your current obsession is, such as 'to find the best espresso in Buenos Aires.'"

Sweat formed on my forehead. Who was I now? Without Mom. Elaine and Clarisa stood up spritely. I sat like a mute in my chair until Elaine said, "Leonie, you have to move your desk." I swung my legs to the side and slowly stood, feeling dazed.

A lanky dark-haired guy, dressed in a long-sleeved button-down shirt that hung out over his jeans, poked his head down between us. "I'm Arturo. May I join you?" He glanced at Clarisa as he spoke.

Clarisa flicked her hair back with a manicured hand. "Why not?" she said, her thick brows arching toward us, looking for agreement.

Elaine said, "Sure."

I looked at both Clarisa and Elaine and shrugged my shoulders. "Okay."

The four of us moved our desks into a circle. Arturo sat between Elaine and Clarisa, his smile as bright as a 110-watt light bulb as he kept glancing at Clarisa. I understood. She was beautiful and radiated supreme confidence. I finally knew what *magnetic* meant.

Clarisa folded her hands on top of her desk and said, "I'll go first. I'm Clarisa and a wannabe Spanish teacher, an amateur fashionista, and a hunter of good restaurants. My current obsession is wearing orange nail polish and outfits that go with it."

My hands started to sweat. This woman was poised, dynamic. I felt like vanilla.

Arturo leaned one shoulder in Clarisa's direction. "I love going out to restaurants. We could go out to eat together sometime."

Clarisa blinked her long eyelashes in Arturo's direction. "Thank you for the invitation, but I'm busy right now looking for my first teaching job."

Arturo's smile faded, and he sat quietly back in his chair. Beside him, Clarisa didn't even seem to notice his disappointment. The pleats on the skirt of her white dress were pressed so perfectly, it was as if she had purchased it at an exclusive boutique. After shaking her hair behind her shoulders, Clarisa placed her pretty hands on the desk in front of her and said, "Elaine, would you like to go next?"

Elaine smiled demurely and blinked several times. "I'm Elaine, but you already know that, I guess. I'm a hardworking student, family-oriented, and a loyal friend. My current obsession is to get a full-time job when I return home."

Clarisa clapped her hands. "We have that in common. I want to start teaching as soon as possible. What kind of job are you looking for?"

"Marketing. I want to work and live in San Francisco." She looked pleased at Clarisa's interest in her and glanced at me as she finished her sentence, but I shook my head. I didn't want to be next since I still hadn't figured out what to say. Elaine turned to Arturo. "Why don't you go next?"

Arturo licked his full lips and tousled his dark brown wavy hair with both of his hands. "Okay, ladies. I'm Arturo—a fun companion, quick wit, and excellent negotiator. My current obsession is to . . ." He glanced in Clarisa's direction as he paused, then his eyes flickered as if he was changing his mind. "My current obsession is to find a new nightclub."

Clarisa's laugh was like a song. "A nightclub. Well, when you find a new one, please share it with us. Students need time to relax as well as work."

Arturo's face lit up again. "I will, definitely."

Clarisa wasn't finished with him yet. "I want to know more than that you're fun and a quick wit. What's this about being an excellent negotiator? Is that a skill you plan to use in a career?"

Arturo snickered. "My major was political science, so maybe I'll run for mayor of Buenos Aires. Will you vote for me if I do?"

A snuffle escaped my mouth. This exchange of wit was hilarious.

Clarisa shook her head. "I don't know yet, Mr. Potential Candidate. I'll have to find out more about your character."

This woman was a fortress of self-assurance. If we became friends, I hoped some of it would rub off on me.

Arturo's face turned radish red, and he waved his hand in my direction. "You're next. I don't know your name yet."

I pursed my lips together, then blew out a breath, long and slow. "I'm Leonie." How *could* I describe myself? My head had been so foggy since Mom died. I searched for several descriptors in my mind. Good student? No, too boring. Loving daughter? Too hurtful. Smart traveler? No—I can't even keep track of my passport. I looked down at what I was wearing, faded jeans and a T-shirt. I certainly wasn't a smart dresser like Clarisa.

Elaine touched my arm. "Leonie?"

I thought about the three promises I'd made to Mom. To keep her close. To find female mentors. And the last one I'd already begun: to travel. Maybe I was now defined by those promises. I bit my lips and cleared my throat. Twice. "I'm a strong daughter, a seeker of female mentors, and a pilgrim of life." As the words flew out of my mouth, my eyes opened in surprise.

Clarisa touched her heart with a manicured hand. "What a deep thinker you are. I'd like to get to know you more."

Elaine waved her finger. "And what's your current obsession?"

I knew what I wanted to say for this part, but should I? I hardly knew Clarisa after all, but then again, I was positive that the more I knew about her, the more I'd admire her. I licked my lips as I paused. "My current obsession is to be as confident as you are, Clarisa."

Clarisa smiled like the Cheshire Cat.

CHAPTER 5

Clarisa arrived early to class for the rest of the week. She sauntered through the desks and sat in the second row next to me. I wondered about how big of a closet she had since she wore a new outfit each day—a pantsuit with a leather belt, a wool tunic with leggings and knee-high boots, a midi skirt with a cashmere sweater and ankle boots, and, on Friday, a black jacket and trouser set. Her hair was either pulled back into a thick ponytail or draped around her shoulders, glossy in the classroom's fluorescent lights.

Her face was animated with expectation. "Morning," she said, pulling a notebook and pen out of her small backpack and placing it squarely on the desk in front of her.

Thrilled that she chose to sit next to us, I said, "Great to see you, Clarisa."

When Professor Arias asked us to form work groups, Elaine, Clarisa, and I worked together, spending the three hours of class each day practicing verb tenses and forming sentences with them. By the end of the week, we had reviewed the four basic tenses—present, past, imperfect, and future. By Friday, I felt confident that I had a stronger grasp of the tenses, especially the verbs that took irregular forms.

After class, the three of us crossed the street to the cafeteria, where we bought *bocadillos* for lunch, the Argentine version of fast food—sandwiches made with meat and cheese. We drank lemonade while Clarisa told us about her goal of getting a teaching job. "I plan to be a Spanish teacher. It's a good job that I can have even if I decide to get married and have kids."

Elaine grew excited when she talked about her plans. "I want a job in marketing, but since it might be hard to get one, I'm going to work temporary jobs to get some experience first."

Clarisa's eyes flashed over to me. "Well, Leonie, what are your plans?"

I wiped my mouth with a napkin to hide my grimace while I searched for an answer. "I wanted to go on this trip to have time to think, so I haven't decided yet."

Clarisa looked pleased. "That's exciting," she said, nodding her head and smiling.

"One thing I want to do is see as much of Buenos Aires when I'm here. It looks like an exciting city. My mom died recently, and I'm hoping this trip will help me feel better, if that's even possible."

Clarisa slapped her hands on the sides of her face. "I'm so sorry. I can't imagine how you must feel!"

"She got breast cancer, and the doctors couldn't catch it in time. I'm devastated."

Clarisa blinked like she was trying to redirect the conversation to a happier topic. "I'll be happy to show you around," she said, circling her hand in the air. "It's my home and I'm proud of it."

THE CLASS'S FIRST OUTING was the following Monday. From the university, Professor Arias and our class walked to a historical complex called the Manzana de las Luces. When we arrived, the professor spread her arms to gather us into a group, then announced, "This is the 'Bloque de la Iluminación' and contains some of the oldest buildings in the city, including the baroque church of San Ignacio, a church built by Jesuit missionaries at the turn of the eighteenth century."

A cold breeze swirled around our heads, and I pulled the hood of my coat over my head and stuck my bare hands inside my coat sleeves. "What does 'Block of Enlightenment' mean?"

Professor Arias continued, "The Jesuits—a sect of priests in the Catholic Church—believed in the pursuit of knowledge, not only traditions. Their philosophy was known as the 'Enlightenment,' and since they built their church on this block, this section of Buenos Aires came to be known as the 'Block of Enlightenment.'"

The professor continued, "Besides the church, the Jesuits built a school, museum, and pharmacy on the site, and operated all of them until the Spanish military showed up and took away their power. The Spanish royalty, who followed traditional Catholicism, didn't like the Jesuits."

Buenos Aires was so colorful and diverse—what would it be like to live in an apartment in the city, buying coffee every morning at one of the chic coffee shops? Walking along the beach in the summer? Working in a building that had been built hundreds of years ago?

My daydreaming was interrupted as the students burst into a babble of conversation, hands gesturing dramatically. Professor Arias waved for us to follow, and we walked into the church.

Inside, pillars swept up to the vaulted nave as if an invisible force was pulling them toward heaven. The aisles on both sides of the nave were separated by small Roman arches, which looked like open doorways, places for people to come and go, to meet and congregate. The walls had been painted creamy white, which made the room feel taller and wider than it actually was. The main altar, ornate with teal-blue and gold paint, featured a statue of Jesus and, above him, his mother. The Virgin Mary had a peaceful expression that reminded me of my mother.

I wrapped my arms around my torso and realized I was calmer than I'd been in weeks. Than I had felt for a long time.

Maybe I belonged in Buenos Aires.

Outside the church, I held up my arm to shield my eyes against the winter sun, squinting and squeezing them shut until they adjusted to the brightness. The courtyard was surrounded by ancient stone walls that people were using as a bench. Finding an empty spot, I sat next to an old woman wearing a straw hat that cast a shadow over her face. One cinnamon-colored eye turned to look directly at me, but the other one wandered away to the right. Lines creased her cheeks like streets on a map.

I inched away from her.

The woman raised a blue metal flask to her parched lips, swallowed several mouthfuls, wiped her lips with the back of one vein-lined hand, and exhaled a hearty gust of air. A walking stick, hewn out of white wood and marled with yellow scars, leaned against the wall beside her. I wanted to touch it.

Her voice cackled as she addressed me in Spanish. "You admire my stick."

My face flushed hot. I looked at the ground and said quietly, "Yes, I do. It's so unusual. What kind of wood is that?"

I looked up and she was smiling. She gripped the top of her cane with a brown hand and tapped it on the cobblestone street several times as if to demonstrate how sturdy it was. "When I was about your age, I carved this out of birch wood, a wood that signifies new beginnings." Then she lifted her chin, one eye focusing on the plaza, and the wandering eye scanning my face. "You've begun a long journey. There's a deep wound."

"What do you mean?" Despite the cold weather, my palms felt sweaty.

The woman pressed her hands together in front of her chest as if she were about to pray. Her eyes looked clear and content, but the crinkles around them deepened. "I sense that you have suffered a great loss." She raised her hands and pressed her forehead onto the tips of her fingers. Then she raised her face and looked at me. "But this loss is your friend."

Tears flooded my eyes, and I tried to blink them back, but felt them streaking down my cheeks. Using both hands, I swatted at them awkwardly. "How can anything that feels this awful be a friend?"

The woman took my hand into hers and held it gently. Her hand was rough and warm like a loaf of bread just out of the oven. "Loss is a teacher. Will you tell me of this wound you carry?" She softly rubbed my hand with her thumb and I felt her kindness travel up my arm into my heart.

"My mom died," I said, slumping forward, my chest curving in as I remembered the last time I saw my mother, beautiful even as she suffered from cancer. Her face had glowed with a sunny complexion.

"I will help you," the woman said softly, releasing my hand. "I will give you something to help you heal, help you grow strong." Her wide tiered skirt rustled as she turned to face me. She stuck her hand into her pocket, pulled it out, and opened her palm to display a piece of onyx and a leather string. "Onyx is a protective stone. When a person wears it, it fosters good fortune, personal strength, and happiness." She placed the necklace into my palm. "This necklace is a gift from me to you. Wear it whenever you need strength. It will never fail you."

"Why are you being so kind?"

Her eyes reminded me of a dark seed, so small but containing all the parts necessary to produce new life, a miracle. "Those who help others help themselves. That's the way the invisible part of the universe works. Some people call it karma."

"That sounds wonderful," I said, "but I want my mother back."

"The universe has taken your mother to a better place, and in her new home, she still loves you," the old woman said. "You must not worry about the past, but concentrate on creating a life that is uniquely yours."

A spark of energy entered my chest, lifting my mood. "My father wants me to go home right after this class, but I promised my mother I would travel. I feel conflicted."

The woman smiled, her brown dimples like miniature

canyons in her cheeks. "Your father cares for you, but your life is not his. Follow your *corazón*. Keep your promises."

How could this woman be so sure of herself? If I stayed, I'd be disloyal to Dad. But then I imagined my mother's earnest expression when she asked for my promises. I wanted to be like her. Someone who believed in herself.

After both Zach and I had left for college, Mom had taken a Spanish class even though she hadn't been to school for years. She was always growing, taking steps to make her life the best it could be. "I'm going to keep that promise to my mother. After this class, I'm staying in South America."

The sun poked through the branches of an oak tree. I closed my eyes and felt its rays, its warmth washing over me. I let it sink into my skin as I began to take in the significance of the decision I'd just made.

When I opened my eyes, the woman and her walking stick were gone.

I jumped up from the stone wall and dashed to the right of the wall and then the left, searching for her. I had so many questions—I wanted to ask her where I should go and what I should do to heal. But she had vanished.

A breeze like a soft hand caressed my shoulder. I took a deep breath of the chilly winter air and released it with a sigh, then opened my hand and saw the onyx necklace. I tied its leather string around my neck and tucked the stone inside my T-shirt, then placed my hand against it.

I SEARCHED THE PLAZA and found Clarisa and Elaine sitting together on another section of the stone wall. "Let's go have lunch," said Clarisa, flipping her hair behind her.

Half an hour later, the three of us sat in a small Mediterranean restaurant that served falafels and fresh salads. As I held a crispy falafel ball on the end of my fork, I said, "Something very interesting happened to me today."

"Ya?" Clarisa asked, wiping her lips with a paper napkin. She held her fork like a ballerina holding a wand, wrist elevated, fingers long and extended. Her salad, a mass of lettuce, sprouts, cucumbers, tomatoes, and falafels topped with tzatziki sauce, filled a white bowl in front of her. I sat up straighter in my chair.

Elaine nodded, her mouth full. She was holding a falafel sandwich, a bite now missing from the top.

I swallowed my bite of falafel. "I sat next to a mysterious woman. She had a beautiful cane, and when I admired it, she began talking to me."

Clarisa stopped chewing. "What happened next?"

"She knew about my mother, knew that she died."

Elaine stopped chewing. "How?"

I raised my hands. "She must be a seer of some kind. She also said that my loss would be 'my friend.'"

Elaine set her sandwich down on her plate and placed her hands flat on the table. "Yikes! I'm sorry, Leonie. I'm sure that hurt."

I swallowed hard. "I almost started crying when she said it."

Elaine nodded, her eyes teary.

I crossed my arms in front of my chest. "I've been thinking about what she said. I think she meant that I could learn from losing Mom. Somehow, my loss can teach me to be stronger and wiser."

Elaine said, "My mother said dying is a part of life. People who have lost someone learn to accept it and move on. Maybe that's what your mystery woman meant."

"I think she meant more than that—like I have some kind of responsibility to do something with myself, find myself."

Clarisa arched her eyebrows and slapped one of her manicured hands on the wooden table. "That's it!" she said, her voice like a staccato. "And you've already started doing that by coming here. This is a completely strange place for you. Who knows what might happen in a foreign country?"

I focused on Clarisa's expressive face when she talked—feisty, so self-assured. "That's not all," I said. "She gave me a necklace." I pulled the onyx out from beneath my T-shirt and held it up for them to see.

Elaine reached out and caressed it. "Oh, that's pretty. It glows."

Clarisa pushed her salad bowl aside. "Why'd she give it to you?"

"She said onyx protects the person who wears it. She also said it will help me grow strong and happy, and that I'm supposed to hold it whenever I need courage."

Clarisa batted her eyelashes. "Sounds magical."

Elaine shook her head. "No, I don't think so. It's supposed to be a token to remind you to move on, to get stronger step-by-step."

I took a deep breath. "I'm keeping it. I'm going to wear it, and we'll see about that magic."

CHAPTER 6

As the weeks progressed, our Spanish improved as we studied more verb tenses and conversed about specific topics—travel, cooking, and family. Elaine, Clarisa, and I became comfortable friends, and on the days when we didn't have to teach English in the afternoons, we took walks around the city.

Clarisa insisted that we visit Recoleta Cemetery, the most famous cemetery in Buenos Aires. At first, I was afraid that it would remind me of my mother's funeral, but the burial ground was nothing like the pastoral setting where my mother was buried. Instead, it was a city of larger-than-life statues and tombs made of marble and granite. We visited the mausoleum of Eva Perón and read the story of her life. We marveled at the tomb of a young woman whose parents had recreated her bedroom inside. I was touched by the poems carved on stones that spoke of love and sorrow.

On another afternoon, we walked to the Palermo barrio. We strolled on cobblestone streets past an eclectic collection of urban art, boutique shops, and restaurants. The graffiti reminded me of San Francisco's Haight-Ashbury district, where buildings were also painted with bright-colored social and political slogans. We had lunch at a little café that served pizza by the slice and browsed through the shops that sold creative clothing and art.

One of my favorite afternoons was visiting La Boca, a barrio that used to be the main port of Buenos Aires in the late nineteenth and early twentieth centuries. We walked past flamboyant buildings made out of metal on the Caminito and gawked at souvenir shops that once housed newly arrived immigrants and dock workers. I fell in love with this polychromatic neighborhood, intrigued by its eclectic history and residents.

One Saturday night, Clarisa took us to a nightclub. There, I was introduced to the work of Jorge Cumba, an Argentine musician who played the Andean quena flute with music that combined Argentine jazz and folklore. While the music blared through the room, we introduced ourselves to the throngs of friendly people in the audience, some holding drinks, others standing by the wall, tapping their hands to the beat. I was impressed with how friendly people were and how easy it was to make new friends.

In fact, by the last week of class, I was thoroughly in love with Buenos Aires—its striking assortment of neoclassical, art deco, and art nouveau architecture that gave the city a European vibe; its zany collection of cafés and restaurants that invited people to sit and congregate at all times of the day; and its gregarious people—eager to stop and chat on the street or in a line at the bocadillo kiosk.

I knew I wanted to stay in Argentina after the class ended, but I didn't know exactly how I'd go about it.

ON OUR LAST FIELD TRIP to Almagro, the part of the city known for its flower vendors, I met a woman who taught me about the importance of being content. Professor Arias led us to Calle Sarmiento where flower shops lined the *calle*. I wandered away from the group to admire the lilies outside a shop across the street. While I was reaching out to touch a lily's milky white petal, a woman dressed in a green apron came out of the shop's door and greeted me. I looked up and spoke to her in Spanish. "Your lilies are beautiful."

The woman's voice was warm and animated as she spoke back to me in Spanish. "My family has been selling flowers for generations. My grandfather used to sell them on the calles. Then he sold them in the old *mercado* in Stall 8. Later, he opened this shop. My father took over from him, then I took over from my father." The woman's hands were chapped, the skin crisscrossed with tiny cuts. The creases of her palms were encrusted with dirt. Her sun-kissed curly brown hair was swept up behind her head in a messy bun, and wisps of hair that had come loose trailed down her neck in swirls. Her dark brows, lashes, clear eyes, and broad rosy mouth painted a picture of health.

I moved under the shade of the willow tree in front of the store's window. "My mother planted flowers in the backyard. Because she loved flowers so much, I've come to love them."

The vendor smiled, her eyes bright like topaz. "Me too. I'll sell flowers until I'm old and frail."

I looked into her eyes, amazed that someone could be so sure about what she wanted to do for the rest of her life. "You don't ever wish that you could do anything else?"

The woman smoothed the front of her apron with her rough hands, then rested them in her front pockets. "No, *nada más*. Each day in my flower shop I get to be creative, and that makes me happy. Besides, I like being around beautiful things, and what could be more beautiful than a shop full of flowers?"

"I wish I knew what I wanted to do with my life."

The woman stretched out her hand. "My name is Flora. My father once said I was as pretty as a flower."

Her father was right. She glowed. I took her hand. "*Mucho gusto.*" Her grip was strong, the muscles in her forearm tightening as we shook. "I'm Leonie. I'm here from San Francisco, taking a Spanish class at the University of Buenos Aires."

Flora waved her hand toward the door. "Come in. I'll show you around."

I followed her past buckets of flowers on the floor, vases of flowers on display on shelves, and wreaths of twigs and herbs hanging from the walls.

She pointed to a bucket of delicately petaled lavender flowers. "These are freesias. They smell light and airy, with lingering traces of citrus, jasmine, and rose." Flora drew a single freesia out of the bucket and held it to my nose.

I inhaled slowly. "Mm, a happy scent."

Flora nodded. "Yes, freesias are perfect to give someone who needs cheering up." She walked a few steps and stopped at a bucket stuffed with multi-petaled purple flowers. "This is lilac. Here, you smell it and describe its scent." She pulled a single flower out of the bucket and handed it to me.

I held the flower up to my nose. "It's sweet. Delicate. A fresh and pure scent," I said, savoring its aroma. "I love it."

"I think its scent is feminine," said Flora. "I have a lilac tree in my garden, and when it blooms I sit near it to sweeten my day. Its scent makes me feel feminine too." She shuffled over to a metal pail in the corner.

She took the lilac back from me and handed me a tightly packed purple flower with moss-green leaves. "Here's English lavender. Smell it."

I took a long sniff. "I know this flower. Lavender grows in California. My mother taught me that it's good to plant it with roses to repel aphids."

Flora's eyes brightened. "Ah, you know something about gardening, I see."

I cast my head to one side, imagining my mother kneeling in her garden with a spade in her hand, digging a hole for petunias. "I don't know much, but my mother knew a lot." I looked down at my feet.

Flora cleared her throat. "You're sad."

I didn't speak for several seconds as the image of my mother faded, then blinked away the tears welling up in my eyes. "My mother passed away recently," I said, feeling an ache in my chest.

Flora set a chapped hand on my shoulder. "I'm sorry."

I stood like a statue surrounded by flowers, wincing at the pain in my chest now throbbing like a hammer. Flora dragged two wooden chairs away from the wall and gestured to one of them. "Sit down, Leonie," she said, then sat on the other chair.

We sat in silence for a few minutes, then Flora finally spoke. "What will you do after your Spanish class is finished?"

I dropped my hands in my lap. "I promised my mother I'd travel, explore who I am. I'm going to stay in South America," I said, recovering my composure. "Over the last six weeks, I've fallen in love with Buenos Aires. Maybe I'll make a new life here."

Flora reached out and took my hand. Her voice was gentle. "Buenos Aires is a heavenly place to live, and youth is a good time for exploring. When I was your age, I visited Chile and Peru. Chile is famous for its gorgeous beaches, and Peru is renowned for its Inca ruins. My exploration taught me that South America is rich with history and beauty. I'm happy here." She rubbed my hand with her thumb.

My heart jumped as she said "Inca" and "history."

Flora clasped her hands. "Santiago has beautiful Spanish architecture and sandy beaches. And I think Peru is the most spiritual place in the world."

I imagined hiking on a dirt path up to the ancient Inca ruins. "My father hiked Machu Picchu. What was it like?"

Flora paused before she continued. "I hiked the Inca Trail. I spent four days hiking a worn and treacherous path, stepping carefully, drinking lots of water, and regulating my breaths. It was exhilarating to finally get to Machu Picchu." Her face shone like the luster of a pearl. Radiant. She lifted her eyes to the ceiling. "It's beautiful, the Amazon. The jagged mountains, the dense forests, birds, flowers. Heaven on earth."

In that moment, I realized Flora was one of those mentors my mother had wanted for me. I loved spending time with her in her shop, and her kindness reminded me of my mother. I hoped we could stay in touch with one another.

I looked at my watch. "I've got to go meet my class," I said, squeezing her hand. "This has been lovely. You've lifted my spirits." I stood up to leave.

Flora grabbed my arm. "Just a minute." She hustled to a back room of her shop, and I heard water splashing. Soon she appeared holding a single long-stemmed yellow rose that she held out to me. "This rose symbolizes our new friendship. Friends are one of the most precious treasures of life. From now on, you and I are lifelong friends. I wish you success on your journey of self-discovery."

It seemed like Flora had enjoyed our time together as much as I had.

THAT NIGHT, I WROTE in my journal and looked at Flora's yellow rose. Its petals brightened the shadows of the tattered room. How gently Flora had held each flower and described its characteristics. She had moved among her flowers with grace, touching each blossom with respect and admiration, so content. I wanted contentment.

I would follow my mother's words, take what I'd observed from Flora and try to make it my own.

Mom, I found another mentor.

CHAPTER 6.5

On Christmas Eve of my junior year of college, Mom has her last chemotherapy session. She asks Zach and me to accompany her to her appointment.

The chemotherapy room is large, windowless, and sterile. Blinding fluorescent lights. Beige linoleum floors. Twelve green reclining chairs placed with their backs against the walls around the room.

With a constricted throat, I observe the room's activity, standing behind my mother and brother by the door. In one of the chairs sits a woman wearing a scarf around her head. I look for wisps of hair, but can't see any. Her body fills the chair like a sack of potatoes, lumps everywhere.

In a recliner in a corner sits a man whose body disappears within the folds of his baggy shirt and trousers. His scrawny hands hang over the chair's arms like shriveled leaves caught on the edge of a forgotten lawn chair in the fall. The fluorescent lights light up his bald head, a glowing bulb.

Another female nurse, with long black eyelashes, wearing a net over her hair and dull blue scrubs, leads my mother to a chair on the emptier side of the room. Zach helps Mom take off her coat and sit down in the recliner. He raises the footrest. She looks small, dressed in her pink cotton beanie, pink V-neck sweater, and jeans. How pale her pretty face is. Mom nods when the nurse asks if she wants a blanket, and Zach takes it from the nurse and covers her gently.

Watching deathly pale people hooked up to tubes, smelling disinfectant chemicals, and concentrating on my mother's frail body is not the way I want to spend Christmas. Wasn't college supposed to be one of the happiest times of my life? My mother hadn't visited me at all that semester. Her phone calls were shorter. Dad was more focused on her than on Zach and me. I felt cheated.

A wave of guilt washes over me as I indulge my bitter thoughts. I hang my head and glare at the linoleum.

The nurse in the hairnet pulls two straight-back chairs close to my mother's recliner and invites us to sit. I drag my chair back about three feet, sit, and lean back, acting as if Mom is contagious.

My brother pulls his chair closer to Mom and takes hold of her left hand. When she smiles at him, her eyes water, shining like wet green pearls.

The nurse hangs a bag of chemicals and saline solution on the pole next to her chair. She connects a tube to each bag, then connects the tubes to my mother's port. My mother smiles weakly, her arms limp on the chair arms.

But then she whistles, sounding like a flute as she emits a bright note in a crystal-clear tone and holds it for several beats. As she holds the note, I am reminded of the silky-smooth brown-and-gray cedar waxwings that visit our garden, their shrills distinct from other birds, high-pitched and pure.

"It's been a long fall. Let's get this one completed," Mom says, her eyes twinkling above her pale cheeks.

CHAPTER 7

With one week left in the class, I canceled my flight home. My hands shook as I took the refund money from the ticket agent.

On Wednesday morning, I woke up, disturbed by the noises of engines racing, horns blaring, brakes squealing, street workers shouting instructions. Elaine was still asleep, so I grabbed my shampoo and towel, quietly opened the door, and shuffled in my flip-flops to the shower room a few doors away. I was eager to talk to Clarisa and knew she'd be studying at the street corner coffee shop. When I was ready to leave, I left a note for Elaine telling her I'd be at the café.

Clarisa was sitting at a table in the corner of the café with her laptop open. To the right of her computer sat a cup of maté—a caffeine-rich drink she drank every morning. She was wildly typing, her long fingers bouncing on the keyboard.

I grabbed the back of the chair opposite her, scraped it out from under the table, flung my backpack over the back of the chair, and sat down. "Hey, how's it going?"

In the middle of typing, Clarisa flicked her glossy hair over her shoulder with one hand. "Hey," she murmured.

I rested my elbows on the table in front of me. "I've got to figure out what to do with the rest of my life, but I'm not going home."

Clarisa stopped typing and picked up her drink. Then she put down her cup and drummed her fingernails on the table. She said,

"I think you should travel and meet as many people as possible. They'll give you new ideas, and you'll learn that you have endless options. Maybe somewhere in there you'll find your direction."

That sounded like something my mother would say—a suggestion full of spirit, wildly courageous. I pulled the onyx from beneath my T-shirt and held it in my hand. I could feel its cool rounded edges. "How do I start?"

Clarisa's eyes sparkled. "Just go. Don't think too much. Don't plan too much, and be flexible. I'll email my sister, Luna. She works at the Belmond Hotel near Iguazú Falls. Maybe you can stay with her." She was quiet for a moment as her eyes darted all around the café. Then she blurted, "Yes, Iguazú Falls—that's where you should go next!"

I bit my lip and squeezed my hands together in my lap. "I don't know about traveling by myself. Maybe I'll just stay here and get a waitress job."

Clarisa flipped her hand in dismissal. "You're going, and that's that."

I wanted to be like Clarisa, and I guessed that meant I'd have to start getting used to being uncomfortable. I rubbed the onyx again.

Clarisa winked. "You have until Monday to build up your courage. This is happening." She looked pleased with herself.

I pulled on one of my ears. "I have to tell my father that I cashed in my plane ticket. He's going to blow his stack."

"He'll survive. What did Elaine say?"

"She doesn't know yet."

LATER THAT DAY, I CONFESSED. Elaine was identifying the temp agencies where she would apply when she got home. She asked, "What are you going to do?"

I cringed. "I'm not going home. I'm going to stay here and make a new life for myself."

Elaine's forehead wrinkled. "What? What do you mean *a new life*?"

I stood up from the bed, put my hands on my hips, and avoided her face. "I canceled my return flight and got a refund, so I have enough money to live for a while, and I'll get a job to support myself." My stomach was churning. I cleared my throat and took a deep breath.

Elaine banged her hand on the bed. "I can't believe this. You did this when? Why didn't you tell me? Why didn't we even talk about it? What's your dad going to think?"

My face felt hot. "It's happening fast. I don't know what . . . I . . . I just know. I'm an adult, and I have to make my own decisions."

Elaine's voice rose. "Is this because of your mom? Are you trying to avoid whatever's waiting at home?"

I turned away from her. "I don't want to talk about it."

She took a deep breath. "Death is part of life. Everyone has to experience it and move on."

I heard myself shout. "I know your mother says that! But I don't know anyone else who has lost their mother. Nobody knows how I feel." Then I thought about Zach and how hard he cried at Mom's funeral.

Elaine's voice softened. "Leonie, everyone loses their mother eventually. My mother lost her mother. Your mother lost her mother. Someday, my mother will die."

"How can you say that to me?"

She shrank back. "I'm sorry. I was trying to help."

Closing my eyes, I inhaled and exhaled slowly. Tears welled up. "I need time to think, and I've decided to think in Argentina. I need space to find out who I am."

Elaine rested her hands on my shoulders. "I don't think this is a good idea, but you sound determined. Hopefully, your dad will accept it."

THAT SUNDAY, CLARISA and I went to the airport with Elaine to say goodbye. After she checked her luggage, Elaine turned to me. "Are you sure you're going to be alright?"

Clarisa jumped between us. "If she's with my sister, Luna, she'll be fine."

Elaine rolled her eyes. "I didn't ask you, Clarisa. Maybe it's your fault that Leonie isn't going home." Clarisa shook her head and inched back a few steps, pursed her lips, and shrugged her shoulders.

Holding onto the onyx stone, I smiled weakly at Clarisa and turned to Elaine. "I promise I'll be fine." I hugged her tightly, but inside it felt like a lie. I'd never gone farther than a grocery store alone.

We walked Elaine up to security, and I gave her another long hug. Then Clarisa tapped her on the shoulder and pulled her in for a hug. As Elaine inched toward the X-ray machines, she turned around and looked back at me with teary eyes. She mouthed, *I love you.*

I put my hand on my heart and mouthed *I love you* back. We watched her as she snaked through the switchback passage. Finally, she walked through the X-ray door and was gone.

When Clarisa and I arrived back at the university, I hugged her goodbye and watched as she descended the stairs into the metro. Just before she disappeared, she turned around and shouted, "You're going to love my sister, Luna. Have fun!" Then she skipped down the stairs.

THE DORM ROOM WAS STRANGE without Elaine. Suddenly the entire dorm felt lonely. I shoved my clothes into my large backpack and laid out the next day's outfit on Elaine's empty bed. Sitting down at the desk, I took a deep breath and exhaled slowly, staring at the laptop. With a sweaty hand, I opened the lid and video-called my father, holding my breath as the ring droned on and on. He didn't pick up.

I had planned how I was going to tell him. I'd explain that I wanted some time to think about my next step. I would be responsible and get a job to pay for expenses. But I was so nervous that when I left a message, I blurted out, "Dad, I'm not coming home. I've decided to stay in South America. Don't worry about me. I'm going to get a job and take care of myself. I love you and Zach. Bye." When I clicked off, my breath caught in my throat. I swallowed hard, thinking about Zach. What would this do to him, my backing out on my promise to spend the summer with him? I shivered with guilt.

After brushing my teeth and hair, I got into bed and tried to fall asleep, but my mind was racing. The next morning, I'd take my first trip alone. Would I be safe from bad people? Was my Spanish good enough? Would I be able to navigate transportation by myself? Would Clarisa's sister like me? Where would I get enough money to live? I didn't have any friends except Clarisa—what would that mean to my life? I switched from my back to my side, then onto my back again.

Finally, I fell asleep.

CHAPTER 8

The day after saying goodbye to my friends, as the winter sun turned the Buenos Aires skyscrapers into rectangular prisms of light, I boarded an early morning bus to Iguazú Falls. As I walked down the aisle searching for a seat, I passed middle-aged women carrying shopping bags, men in suits, and twenty-somethings wearing hoodies and jeans. A mass of humanity going north. I chose a seat by the window so I could watch the scenery. As churches, plazas, and government buildings glittered in the sun, I searched the city for clues to my future.

The bus was warm from the heaters that blew from below each seat. Across the aisle from me sat an old woman with a small blue suitcase under her chair and a picnic hamper covered with a dish towel on her lap. Her hands, resting on top of the towel, were wrinkled and worn with sun spots. A thin metal band encircled her left ring finger. Her gray wavy hair, chin-length, was streaked with brunette strands. Her brown face was serene. She patted her bundle occasionally. As if she could feel my eyes on her, she turned and smiled with yellow teeth.

I was flustered by her sudden attention, but said in Spanish, "I like your basket."

She patted the dish towel covering the hamper. "Oh, this old thing. I've filled it with *alfajores* for my grandchildren."

Relieved to find her friendly, I exhaled quietly. "I've heard of alfajores, but I'm not sure I know what they are."

The woman's brown eyes glowed. "They're *galletas*, made of two shortbread wafers with a creamy caramel filling. My grandchildren love them. My daughter lives in Rosario. I visit at least once a month and stay all weekend."

I smiled at her, thinking about my own grandmother who had brought us chocolates when she visited. "It's wonderful for you to be able to visit your daughter."

The woman nodded toward me. "My name is Martina. It's nice to talk to you."

I scooted into the aisle seat so I could hear her better. "My name is Leonie. I'm from San Francisco, but I'm traveling now."

Martina looked over my shoulder out the window. "I've lived here all my life. I was born in Rosario, where my daughter lives, and moved to Buenos Aires when I married and my husband got a job there. I've been traveling back and forth ever since."

Martina pointed to the window near me, and I turned to see where she was pointing. Outside, the banks of the Paraná River with its network of channels created a web of water across acres and acres of land. My mouth dropped open in amazement.

She smiled and lifted her eyes. "It's beautiful, no? I met my husband while I was walking along the banks of the Paraná River in Rosario. When my parents were young, my father worked for the railroad as a hostler, a person who services engines. My parents lived in a tiny house on the side of one of the river channels. A set of wooden stairs descended to the water from the side of the house. After work, Papá sat on the bottom of these stairs to fish. Most nights, he'd catch one or two golden dorados, and my mother fried them for dinner."

I sat back and marveled at her comfortable storytelling, how she opened up so easily to a stranger.

"I was born nine months after they were married. My mother took me to a little white church with a tall steeple to get baptized. She crocheted a white dress and cap for me, and then let the priest pour the holy water over my head. Every Sunday, we dressed up in our best clothes and went to Mass at that white church. We knew all the parishioners. After service, everyone brought out their homemade dishes to the church yard and shared lunch together. When it rained, we crammed our picnic into the church basement. Nobody minded that it was crowded. Even the priest ate lunch and laughed at our jokes and stories."

"Happy memories," I said.

Her eyes were filled with joy. "Yes, I have been fortunate that most of my life has been spent in places with good memories, and I'm a happily married woman and grandmother."

I wrung my hands. "I understand. Places affect my feelings too. After my mother died, I never wanted to go home again. It was too painful to see her kitchen, her chair, and the empty places in the garden where she planted vegetables and flowers. I want to find a new place to make happy memories."

Martina adjusted the basket of cookies on her lap. I felt the empathy in her eyes wrap me in kindness. "Yes, I know what it's like to lose a mother. My mother died last year. She was ninety-two years old. I still miss her, but she lived well, and for that I am grateful. I have tucked her away in my heart."

I looked at my hands in my lap, surprised that I'd just revealed something so personal to a stranger. But it had been easy. I said, "I feel lost and alone." Martina didn't *feel* like a stranger.

A question appeared on Martina's face. "Do you have a father? Brothers and sisters?"

I blinked my eyes as Dad's and Zach's faces filled my mind. "Yes, my dad is an architect and my brother, Zach, goes to college in Santa Barbara, California."

The smile that bloomed on Martina's face was full of love. "So, you are not alone. Your father and brother feel the same pain as you at your mother's loss. It's wonderful to have family and friends who can help us during our sad times. My friend Triana helped me when my mother died."

What did she mean? That I was fortunate to have a family to grieve with? Was I? Why didn't I feel that way?

Martina adjusted the basket on her lap again with her wrinkled brown hands. "When I was ten years old, I met my best friend. It was the first day of school. Triana had just moved to Rosario from Spain, and she was sitting at the desk right next to me. Her head was tilted up, her pug nose lifted in the air, and she had her hands clasped on her desk. I thought she looked snooty, but later, when we started chatting, I found out how kind and interesting she was."

I relaxed and laughed. "First impressions aren't always right, I guess."

The woman laughed too, her voice like a soft gurgle, cheeks rosy and round, face lit like a star. "Triana was from a town in Spain noted for its artists, and she was a skilled artist herself. She had such problems paying attention in our classes. Instead of studying math in class, Triana opened a sketch pad and drew the teacher, students, and the windowsill with its geraniums."

I brushed my hair back from my face and leaned slightly into the aisle. "She did?"

Martina clapped her hands over her basket and, for a second, she looked ten years old herself. "The two of us became fast friends and spent most weekends together. We visited art museums, toured churches all over the city, walked through the Flag Memorial during the day and at night when it was lit up with lights, and watched movies at the cinemas."

I hunched my shoulders, thinking of all the times my mother and I had walked in Golden Gate Park and through the streets of San Francisco. I didn't know how happy I was then. We stopped for coffee sometimes. At home, she taught me how to cook and arrange flowers. "Your friendship sounds wonderful."

When I looked up at Martina, she was smiling at me. "Today, Triana lives in Buenos Aires, a block down the street from where I live. Our husbands worked as bakers for Lucas Rafael Massas e Salgados. While they walked to work and baked bread, we raised our daughters together. She's been my friend for so long she's more like a sister."

"My friends are all from high school and college, so I haven't known them long."

Martina shook her head, her hair swinging gently. "You're young, but as you grow older, you'll want to develop your friendships into lifelong companions, people who know you well, can be honest with you, help you through tough times, be happy for you when you're celebrating."

If I stayed in Argentina, I might never see my friends again, friends like Elaine. I'd miss her terribly.

Martina stretched her wrinkled hand across the aisle and pressed it over mine. "And your family. They're built-in friendships, connected to you forever. I'm not saying that you shouldn't travel, but your home is in the hearts of your family." Her hand was firm and comforting, the hand of a strong and loyal woman.

The bus turned into the driveway of the Mariano Moreno bus terminal, and Martina reached under her seat to get her blue suitcase, protecting her basket of alfajores against her ample breasts. Before leaving, she turned back toward me. The sweet tone of her voice reminded me of Mom. "Goodbye, my dear. Have a safe journey."

"Your story gave me a lot to think about. Thank you." I watched as Martina waddled her way down the aisle to the front of the bus, nodded thanks to the driver, and descended the stairs. Then I scooted back into the seat by the window. When Martina reached the street, she set down her blue suitcase and picnic basket, scanned the windows for my face, raised her hand like a fan, and waved at me. I pressed my nose and palm to the windowpane.

Soon, the bus closed its doors and the driver inched out of the station and into traffic. The wide murky Paraná River filled in the view from my window. A large container ship crawled over its current, and the Rosario-Victoria Bridge glistened in the sunlight—the cables of its giant span twisting like the pleated skirt of a dancer.

Leaning back in my seat, I became mesmerized by the river's lazy current and how the main channel broke off into steel-colored tributaries, flooding the landscape. A few miles down the road, the riverbank was bordered by a wide, paved path. A young mother pushed a blue baby stroller. A man in a suit held the hand of a pretty woman in a black coat and high heels. They were both looking at the river, the man pointing to a sailboat under the bridge. Two young women walked together with their arms entwined, their steps perfectly in unison. People in relationships.

Outside the window, the sky painted itself in blue until the feeble July sun dipped behind the clouds and pulled gray curtains across its canvas. The buildings of Rosario grew sparser and sparser, replaced by ranches surrounded with wooden split-rail fences, corralled horses running free, their manes behind them in the wind. They frolicked and followed each other. Friends.

I thought about Martina's words. *Relationships that last a lifetime.* I leaned my head against the window and closed my eyes.

After napping, I ate a sandwich as the bus plodded north beside the Paraná River. When we stopped in Santa Fé, Rafaela, and Reconquista, several passengers disembarked. More people boarded. The noise of the bus's engine was accompanied by a murmur of voices rising and falling as the hours passed. As dusk settled over the landscape, I nibbled on empanadas and sipped cold water from my flask. The trip continued through the long night, and I fell asleep using my balled-up jacket as a pillow against the window.

CHAPTER 9

Eighteen hours after leaving Buenos Aires, the bus arrived at Puerto Iguazú bus station. The sun hung low in the sky, the air was chilly, and when I stepped down off the bus, I clutched my jacket close.

Still thinking about Martina, I had the urge to call my father. I found a bench under some trees a few yards away from the hubbub of the bus station, sat down, pulled my laptop from my backpack, and video-called him. He was working at home. "You certainly surprised me with that message. I'm disappointed you didn't ask me first." His arms were crossed over his chest.

"I know. I'm sorry, Dad. The idea just kind of sprang up. And it really seems like the right thing for me."

"I disagree, and I'm worried sick."

"I'm okay. I have people looking out for me. Right now, I'm at Iguazú Falls and staying with the sister of a friend from my Spanish class."

His eyes were wounds. "Why are you staying in Argentina, Leonie? It's time for you to get home and find a job." Long rolls of architectural drawings were stacked on the side of his desk, and his favorite white coffee cup stood in front of his desktop keyboard. Behind him, the office door was open, showing Mom's blue armchair in the family room, a depression in the seat.

My voice broke with emotion. "I'm going to find a job, but down here. I can't bear to go home and not see Mom there. You understand, don't you?"

His eyes softened. "Look, Leonie. You'd feel better if you talked to someone about Mom. Zach misses her. I miss her. It's natural that you miss her, but you'll be able to move on someday."

Everyone was telling me that I'd move on. What did that mean? That I should buck up, look to the future, forget Mom? No way. "Dad, you're going to have to trust me. I'll get a job here and take care of myself. And I promised Mom I would travel."

His arms were still crossed against his chest. "You what?"

I gulped in a breath. "I promised Mom that I'd travel. She told me that she wished she had traveled when she was young."

His brown eyes turned sad, upside-down crescents staring into the screen. His deep voice cracked. "You're making a mistake." He looked at me as if for the last time. I was going to have to cut this call short before one of us said too much.

"I love you, Dad, and I'll let you know where I am. I promise. Say hi to Zach for me."

He looked like he had more to say, but stopped himself. "I love you. Be careful." When the screen went blank, I could still see his face, scrunched up in misery. I put my hands over my face and squeezed my eyes shut until my breathing slowed.

I hadn't talked to Aunt Patty since leaving California, but each week I'd sent her a postcard of a different scene of Buenos Aires that I'd discovered. I quickly video-called her then, crossing my fingers that she'd pick up. After a few rings, she logged in. "Leonie! How are you?"

My throat was tight, but I managed to eke out a few words. "I need your help."

"What's going on?"

I massaged my forehead with one of my hands. "It's Dad. I told him I was staying in South America to travel, that I was keeping a promise I made to Mom. I also told him that Mom wished she had traveled when she was young and single. I think he freaked." Already I knew the hurt look on Dad's face was going to haunt me.

Aunt Patty crossed her arms in front of her chest. "I see. Well, I'm not surprised."

"What should I do?"

She raised both hands up to the screen and waved them as if she wanted to reach through and give me a hug. "Honey, keep your promise to your mom, but don't try running away from grief. Use the travel to explore who you are as your mom intended." She paused. "I'll handle your dad."

I swatted the tears from my eyes, and said, "Thanks, Aunt Patty. I love you." I was running away, wasn't I?

When she smiled back, her expression reminded me of Mom. "I love you too. Bye for now."

I closed my laptop, stuffed it in my backpack, and sat for a few minutes, tilting my head and stretching my arms up and down.

FINALLY, I LEFT THE bus station to find Luna's place. Hotel Belmond was the only hotel inside Iguazú National Park, and Luna lived in worker housing behind it, in one small hut in a long row of cabins. Luna's cabin was number 7. I climbed the porch steps to her door and knocked.

A young woman with long shiny brown hair and skin the color of gingerbread opened the door. "Hello, you must be Leonie. I'm Luna." She was shorter than Clarisa but had a shapely figure, big eyes, and rosy cheeks, a cherub. Her style wasn't as flamboyant as Clarisa's either. Her fingernails weren't orange or any other color. They were long and neatly filed. She wore no makeup, but her face shone with freshness and vigor.

"Hi," I said, feeling my face flush with shyness. I lifted my hand to my chest and pressed my onyx stone.

Luna invited me in. Her tiny dwelling was cozy with rose-painted walls and white wood moldings at the floor and ceiling. The kitchen took up one wall. A window over the sink looked out onto the forest behind the hotel. A tiny white table with two chairs stood in front of the kitchen area. A bed and two small armchairs were the only other furniture in the room. An area rug covered the wood floor.

Luna waved toward the chairs. "Come in and sit. Let's get acquainted."

I set my backpack in a corner of the room by the bed, took off my coat, and sat down. "Thank you for letting me stay with you while I'm here."

Luna sat, then leaned forward with her elbows on her knees. "I welcome the company. When I come home to an empty cottage after working all day, it gets lonely. I can go out to socialize, but staying home is comforting."

A warm sensation filled my chest. "You're like me, then. Usually, I like staying at home reading a book or cooking."

Luna's brown eyes glowed as if a candle had been lit inside them. "Clarisa told me you were traveling to discover what you wanted to do next. Is that right?"

"Yes, but my money's not going to last a whole year."

She blinked twice. "So, *chica*, what are you planning to do?"

That word sounded cool to me. *Chica*. Luna had her own style. "I'd like a job where I can work in nature. When I'm around plants and birds, I feel more relaxed and joyful." I envisioned my mother stooping in her garden, plucking green beans off the vines, and pulling tiny weeds from the rich, black soil.

Luna looked out the kitchen window at the forest. "I get it," she said. "Since I moved here, I've spent more time in nature than ever before, and I feel happy surrounded by the forest and waterfalls. I love how the trees perfume the air with their pine scent and how the waterfalls saturate it with moisture."

I wondered what it must feel like to know contentment. Luna

here. Flora in her florist shop. Martina with her grandchildren. What would it mean to know that kind of peace? My whole life, I had always strived for the next goal, the next accomplishment. I'd never focused on being happy in the moment.

Luna turned to me. "I've worked here for over a year. It's giving me time to think about what I want to do for a career. Do you have career plans?"

My heart skipped a beat. "I don't know where I belong, don't know what I should be doing. All I know right now is I want to keep traveling to see as much of Argentina and South America as I can."

Luna sat up. "This is a great place to start."

"Yes. Tomorrow, I'm going to tour the waterfalls. I heard that the park is full of wildlife—birds, butterflies. I want to experience it all."

"And from here, where do you want to go?"

"Mendoza, I think? I hear the vineyards are beautiful, planted all over the mountainsides. There's so much I want to see—I'm really going to need to earn money. I need a job."

A thoughtful expression crossed Luna's face. "Hmm, let me think about that." She stood up. "I have the ingredients for empanadas—you know, pastries stuffed with savory fillings. Let's make them for dinner together."

"Yum. I'd love to help."

She gave me spices and ground beef to mix together for the filling and grabbed empanada dough out of the refrigerator, then turned on the oven. Standing at the kitchen counter, waving her doughy hands, she said, "My aunt and uncle own a winery in Mendoza, and they hire apprentices for one year. I think it's a year commitment because they teach the apprentices about how the seasons affect the winemaking. What do you think?"

Excitement fluttered in my chest. I'd walked through the vineyards at the university in California, spoken to the students working there, and toured the on-campus winery, a building filled with gigantic steel vats and rows and rows of oak barrels, the strong scent of fermenting wine. It was intoxicating. But did I want to spend a whole year doing it? "I've always been curious."

Luna didn't look up from the dough she was kneading. "I could call Aunt Sara and see if they have any openings."

Maybe this was the break I needed. A stable job for a year. Time to explore Mendoza and learn a skill. I squeezed the beef between my fingers as eagerness flooded my body. "I'm not sure I'd be good at winemaking, but I'd like to give it a try. I hope your aunt and uncle are forgiving people."

Luna laughed. "Aunt Sara oversees the apprentices, and she's a sweetheart. You have nothing to worry about." By this time, she had rolled out the dough and cut it into a dozen circles. She showed me how to spoon a tablespoon of meat filling onto one side of each dough circle, then fold the dough over the filling and seal the edges by pressing them together with her thumb and finger. I set each pastry on a metal baking sheet and brushed the top with egg wash, and she inserted the pan of savory pastries into the hot oven.

Luna washed her hands in the sink. "Hey, chica, let's get you started on your wine experience. I'll open a bottle of Aunt Sara's malbec, a robust red wine grown in Mendoza. Argentina is famous for it." She poured rich, red liquid into a globe-shaped wine glass, and held it out to me. "*Salud, mi nueva amiga!* Let your adventures begin!"

Over the tiny square table, we clinked our wine glasses together and took a sip. The rich red wine coated my tongue and throat, and I closed my eyes to take in its full body. There was something about a glorious red wine—as if meaning could be found in it. As the malbec slipped down my throat, I felt the promise of a brighter future.

Several minutes later, Luna set a small platter of warm empanadas in the middle of the table, then used tongs to place three on each of our plates. Steam rose from the flaky pastries.

We let them cool, and when I finally bit into one, I inhaled a toasty concoction of beef and spices wrapped in pastry.

Luna said, "My mom taught me to make these."

"They're delicious. So what do you do here?"

"At the hotel, I work at reservations in the mornings and clean rooms in the afternoons."

I licked a piece of pastry off my lips. "Sounds like hard work."

Luna chuckled. "Ah, but I'm enjoying it. You should see the elegant men and women who come to stay, their clothes so fine, their arms dripping with rings and bracelets. Sometimes I imagine I am one of them, wearing a ball gown, but then I realize that I'm more comfortable wearing blue jeans and kneeling in the dirt while I plant flowers. And there are newlyweds with dewy eyes who come to celebrate their honeymoons." Luna stood up, pulled open a kitchen drawer, removed a dish towel. "The house cleaners fold small towels into different animals." She folded the dish towel again and again until it resembled a turtle.

Luna handed me the towel, and I reached out to examine it. "*Amazing*. You're so artistic." I unfolded the towel carefully to memorize how it was made, but the turtle suddenly fell apart. "Oh, I ruined it," I said, sticking out my lower lip.

Luna folded another towel into a monkey and hung its long arms from the back of her chair. She smiled and said, "It takes practice."

How long would *I* have to practice folding towels to be able to make animals? Why did everything call for hard work?

We sat on Luna's front porch as the yellow sun slipped behind the trees and dusk darkened the sky. Soon the only light left was the pale glow from the full moon casting a silver sheen over the trees, the huts, the trails, and the back of the hotel. The air was crisp and clear, and I looked up to see millions of stars peeking out of the velvet night. Their twinkling reminded me of my mother's eyes, and a throb of pain pulsed in my chest. I sighed, trying to release it. By that time, Luna and I had passed the conversation point of politeness, and the silence under the stars felt comfortable and natural.

"My mother died just over a year ago," I said, feeling the ache in my chest intensify. "I promised her I'd travel, but I think I'm going to take it further. I'm going to start a new life in South America."

Luna's eyes teared up as she listened. "I'm so sorry. I can't imagine how heartbroken you must be."

I looked down at my hands in my lap. "I am."

Luna's voice was gentle and cautious. "What about the rest of your family?"

"Dad and my brother, Zach, are struggling as well."

"Ah, so you have one brother?"

"Yes. Zach is attending UC Santa Barbara. He loves to surf. He also loves animals so he's majoring in zoology and animal biology. He wants to work in a zoo when he's done. My Dad lives in San Francisco. He's an architect. I got my ginger hair from him."

"And your mother? What was her passion?"

"She was a college counselor at San Francisco Community College."

Luna clapped her hands. "A college counselor, an architect, and a zookeeper in the family. Cool."

I hung my head. "Yeah, I'm the one who doesn't have any direction."

The silver moonlight filtered softly through the trees, the leaves rustling in the light breeze. "You're young, chica," Luna said.

I breathed in and blew up my bangs with an exhale. "You're right, I am. But Dad and Zach are pressuring me to go home."

Her eyebrows arched up. "Of course they are, because they miss you. And maybe they worry?"

I turned to face her. "I met a woman in Buenos Aires who told me to follow my own instincts. She knew my mother had died before I told her. Some kind of mystic."

Luna laughed. "I didn't need a mystic to tell *me* to listen to my own voice. My father did. He said that we all have to listen to ourselves. I'm trying to hear mine."

I reached for her hand. "Me too. Let's help each other." We sat holding hands for a while, staring out into the silver landscape.

Luna turned in her chair to face me. "My grandmother told me to spend evenings in soul conversations, and here we are, doing just that."

I squeezed her hand. "I feel like I've known you for years, like you understand me, like we're kindred spirits. Another promise I made to my mother was to find female mentors to help guide me. But friends are just as important, don't you think?"

"I've always had my sister, Clarisa. She's like my built-in friend. But I think it's important to have friends who are not part of your family. People who can see you in a new light."

I dropped Luna's hand, stood, walked a few steps to the end of the porch. "I met an old woman on the bus here who has had the same girlfriend since she was ten, a lifelong friend."

"My father told us that lifelong friendship is like marriage—it's about commitment."

"Commitment? That means dedication. I'd like to start with you. I promise to keep our friendship."

Luna's face glowed in the moonlight.

We left the porch and walked around the circumference of the hotel. The lights from inside illuminated scenes of well-dressed guests chatting and laughing in the lobby. Outside, the moonlight lit the tips of the pine trees with silver. The stars glittered like a thousand eyes. In the distance, the waterfalls sounded like the roaring of a giant rumbling stomach. I let the beauty of the scenery wash over me, filling me with a joy I hadn't felt for a long time.

Late that night, we went to sleep in Luna's queen-sized bed, our backs touching, the bright moon gazing through the window.

CHAPTER 10

The next morning, I woke up smelling coffee and toast, hearing the chittering of birds outside the window and the distant roar of the waterfalls. The brisk shower sent shivers down my spine as I anticipated what I'd see in the park that day. I dressed in jeans and a T-shirt I had bought in Buenos Aires that had a picture of the national flower of Argentina—the Erythrina crista-galli, a tree with bright coral flowers.

Luna had left a note on the table saying that she'd gone to work. After I showered and dressed, I opened my laptop on the dining room table and video-called Elaine.

She clicked on immediately. "Your dad's worried about you. He called my dad last night. They talked for almost an hour."

I sighed and recalled his sad eyes the night before. "I know. I've never been on my own except for college."

Elaine pursed her lips. "Call him, Leonie. Don't let him worry so much."

"I will, but listen. I'm calling with good news. I'm at Iguazú Falls with Luna, who's nothing like Clarisa by the way. Their aunt and uncle own a winery in Mendoza, and Luna's going to call them to see if I can work there. I've always been intrigued by winemaking. Isn't this exciting?"

Elaine huffed out a breath, then sat up in her chair. "Sounds good. You like cooking, and making wine complements food." She didn't look excited one little bit.

"Come on, be excited for me. I'll meet new people and a job will help me get settled here."

Elaine's eyes looked like wheels of sorrow. "You still want to stay in Argentina?"

I felt my facial muscles tensing up. "I can't go home. I can't bear it."

Elaine's face softened. "Let's change the subject. I went back to Davis to visit the Career Center. Now, I'm applying for jobs, including a job at a temp agency. Eventually, I want to get a job with a tech company."

She sounded grown-up, a young adult navigating the world of job hunts in search of a future career. "I'm impressed that you know what you want to do. I'm trying to figure myself out down here."

"What are you doing today? Luna's working, right?"

"Yeah, she is. I'm going to tour Iguazú National Park. See the waterfalls."

"Ah, I'd love to do that. Good luck with the winery job." She looked wistful. "Anyway, I've got to go. Don't forget about your dad and brother. They need you, and you need them."

They *needed* me? I was that *valuable*, important enough to make a difference in other people's lives?

I NAVIGATED MY WAY to the Rio Uruguay tram station, bought a ticket, and waited on a platform for the twenty-minute ride to the park's entrance. I found a seat on the crowded tram between a young man wearing headphones and a buxom woman sitting next to a toddler. Even though it was cold outside, the ride was stifling hot. Sweat formed on my face. The mixed body odors from the riders smelled like dirty laundry.

When I exited the train, the park loomed all around me: trails, cliffs, and the roar of water somewhere in the distance. I raised my eyes, taking in the majestic view. Goosebumps formed on my arms. I looked at the map I'd received from the ticket agent, and, with my finger, followed the Lower Circuit Trail, a route of eight waterfall views. Amazed that I could see so much from a single path, I set out with anticipation. The paved trail soon gave way to a wooden catwalk that traversed over wet granite rocks to the base of several falls. Humidity draped the air with a thick steam, a fresh fragrance, the rush of the falling water like the peal of a thousand bells. My face dripped with mist, and my clothes dampened and stuck to my body like wet sheets. I climbed the steps of the catwalk, searching for viewing spots.

The falls had names like Salto San Martin, Salto Bossetti, Salto Alvar Nuñez, and Salto Dos Hermanas. I knew that *salto* meant "jump," and the water actually looked like it was jumping. Further down the catwalk was the viewpoint for Salto San Martin. Its large arc of water dropped like the lace of a bridal gown over the cliffs, the granite walls, the bluffs just below, and, finally, down a second long precipice to the great Iguazú River at the bottom.

Suddenly, pressure behind my eyes caused a flood of tears to burst down my face. I leaned against a railing and let the mist wash over me like a baptism. Feet flat on the ground, I let the drops of my sorrow drain away drip by drip into the solid ramp. Blinking my eyes and washing the mist from my face with a wet hand, I took a step away from the rail, then looked up the trail, letting the wild beauty of the park surround me with protection. When I started hiking again, I felt energetic—renewed, like I'd discovered a seed, a tiny kernel of personal power that took the place of my grief. I felt better prepared to move on, to turn toward a new future.

My skin drank in the cool vapors. *Vencejos*, flying like dark-feathered crossbows—with forked tails and long, narrow wings—flew above the falls as if appealing to me for attention. I could barely hear their monotone cries amid the roar of the water. Suddenly, I wanted to fly like the birds, to shout, "This is happiness!"

For the rest of the morning, I was filled with a new exhilaration and anticipation of what I would discover as I traveled around South America. The beauty of the waterfalls and stark contrast of the cliffs seemed to promise that I'd find more beauty and meet new people to help me figure out who I was.

By the time I finished hiking around the Lower Circuit Trail, my stomach was rumbling. A food stand near the trailhead was selling bocadillos, so I bought one for lunch with a cup of steaming maté. I sat down at a picnic table and watched the other tourists as I ate.

Tourists stood in groups of twos and threes, taking pictures. They laughed and wrapped their arms around each other, their chins and elbows dripping with mist. Smiling and laughing. People standing on the trail, holding their faces up to the steam, letting the vapors bathe them. Children playing in the puddles on the pathway, splashing the water over themselves with screams of joy. Couples, kissing in the showers. Solitary figures, gazing at the cascades with flickers of smiles on their faces. It was as if no one there had ever known sadness, had ever lost a mother. Some of them must have lost someone they loved, right? Maybe it was the waterfalls, surging over the cliffs in a continuous flow with supernatural strength, flowing through the obstacles of nature with unbounded energy. Maybe in the presence of that kind of natural majesty, we all felt grand, our potential unlimited.

AFTER LUNCH, I BOUGHT a train ticket to see Garganta del Diablo, the park's biggest and most spectacular waterfall. In the train's carriage, spirited tourists scrambled for seats. I found a spot in an empty row next to a window. Water covered massive areas of the landscape, waterfalls dropping like a curtain of rainbows, the sun casting prisms of color over wet granite walls. When the train reached Estación Garganta del Diablo, the tourists hustled out of the train, whooping and cheering, their arms waving gleefully in the wet mist.

I followed the throng onto the Paseo Garganta del Diablo, the path that led to a view of the mighty waterfall, Devil's Throat. My heart pumped with excitement, expecting a precipitous and dangerous drop, but instead, I walked into a surreal landscape.

On the platform, butterflies were waiting for us. Hundreds and hundreds of yellow, blue, green, gray, and white wings shimmered on the rails of the wooden bridge in front of the falls. They flickered their wings and nodded their antennae, warming in the sunlight. The tourists respectfully kept their distance, pointing here and there in astonishment.

As I watched the iridescent insects, I felt someone staring at me and turned around. An elderly woman, dressed in a flamboyant wrap—a fabric of a complex pattern of miniature wings—stood within two feet of me. Her dark hair fell in ringlets around her face, her skin like a smooth leather wallet, her dark eyes cavernous and glowing with stories.

The woman spoke to me in Spanish. "*Mariposas* are a symbol of transformation. They begin as ordinary caterpillars, brown and unimpressive, then break out of their chrysalises, transforming from larvae into flying beauties. They become extraordinary." Her voice lifted and softened like the notes of a lullaby: sweet, tender, and maternal.

"They are gorgeous," I replied, looking at her and smiling. Why was she looking at me so intently?

The woman reached down and took my hand into both of hers. As if I had entered a private room with her, I no longer heard the voices of the other tourists around me. Time seemed to stop. Her voice was musical and vibrant. "You will undergo a transformation like the mariposa. You will travel far to find your wings and make friends who will teach you how to fly. Your growth, ah, will be extraordinary. You will work hard, journey to sacred places. These experiences will teach you who you are and what you can be. Someday, I see, you will help other people discover their potential."

Like my mother? Maybe become a counselor? I imagined myself walking along the path of a college campus toward the Student Services Building. I smelled the cut grass and trimmed hedges. Students passed me and said hello. I turned toward the woman and blurted out a response. "How would I do that? I'm confused. All I know is that I need to explore South America."

Her smooth face glowed like dark honey. "Someone who loves you is looking after you on this journey. You will grow, but first, you must heal. Not all life is easy. We must accept pain, blend it into our lives until it becomes strength." She closed her lips and a sweet smile lit up her face.

I tried to figure out what she meant, why she was here. Someone was looking after me? Mom?

She gently let go of my hand and backed away a few steps. The voices of the tourists rose around us, a cacophony of exclamations in various languages. The sun was now high in the sky. Suddenly, the butterflies launched into the air like thousands of flower petals blown by the wind. Bodies floated. Wings glittered. The skirt of the sun's yellow warmth dazzled with a rainbow of flying forms. I raised my head to admire them, my mouth dropping open in awe. Never had I seen such a magnificent display of color and life. A wave of exhilaration surged through me, and I silently thanked my mother for pushing me to travel.

When I turned to look back, the woman with the colorful wrap was gone. In the air where she had stood, butterflies flitted together in a synchronized dance of blues, greens, browns, and yellows. Then, one by one, each pair of wings broke away from the cluster to join the throng fluttering above the people's heads. I watched the creatures for a long time, the mist kissing my face.

What had she said, the woman in the colorful wrap? *You will undergo a transformation. But first, you must heal.* I could feel my breath enter and leave my body like a peaceful stream. My transformation was beginning.

Finally, while the butterflies still swirled in the air, I silently wished them goodbye. I looked over the viewing platform to concentrate on the landscape. All around rose a subtropical forest. The upper Iguazú River streamed out of the forest and dropped like a colossal curtain of water, hundreds of feet across and hundreds high, the water surging over the cliffs, dense clouds of vapor rising from the riverbed below. The forest was deep green, the river below was azure, the earth crimson, and the foam of the falls white. Standing in the presence of this incredible beauty, hope began to rise in me. My thoughts of possibilities started swirling in patterns as wild and beautiful as the dance of the butterflies. I was about to find my own inner flame.

CHAPTER 11

Around five o'clock that evening, I arrived back at Luna's cottage. I made myself a cup of tea and sat on the porch. Looking out to the forest, I reminisced about my last conversation with Mom under the oak tree. When Luna stepped onto the porch, I placed my cup on the deck, stood up, and hugged her. After I released her, she sat down in the other Adirondack chair.

She pulled her wool hat off her head. "I have good news for you. Aunt Sara has an opening."

I clapped my hands together. "Really? What good luck!" I danced in my chair, but deep inside I felt a little apprehension. What if I didn't do a good job? Wouldn't that be embarrassing for Luna and Clarisa? Devastating for me?

Luna laughed. "One of their apprentices had to go back to Buenos Aires unexpectedly. You can start as soon as you get there."

I gasped. "But she hasn't even met me. What if she doesn't like me?"

Luna flapped her hand at me. "Aunt Sara has heard about you from Clarisa and now me. She knows as much as she needs to know."

"Thank you, thank you, my friend. I can hardly wait to get there."

Luna raised the bag she'd been holding in her lap. "Not so fast, chica. Before you do, we have another whole night for soul conversation and barbecue. I bought steaks. Let's bundle up and toast to your new adventure under the stars."

While Luna went inside, I lit her tiny gas barbecue and brushed the grill with oil, then joined her inside. Luna chopped up parsley, cilantro, onions, and garlic, and mixed the herbs with red wine vinegar, salt, pepper, and chili flakes to make chimichurri. She peeled a red onion and cut it into thick rounds, then washed the little steaks, sprinkled them with salt and pepper, and placed them on a platter. Being in a kitchen with Luna reminded me of cooking alongside Mom. My heart was warm with companionship.

We stood on the porch wearing parkas as we barbecued, sipping wine and watching the July sun sink behind the trees. When the steaks were ready, Luna hustled into the kitchen and came back with the chimichurri sauce and *fainá*—a large flatbread made with chickpea flour, water, olive oil, salt, and pepper. We ate our dinner sitting in the Adirondack chairs.

After finishing my steak and chewing my last bite of fainá, I said, "Tell me about your family."

Luna wiped her hands on her napkin. "My family. You know Clarisa, of course. She is my older sister by one year, and we've always been close. My parents live in Buenos Aires too. My father is a chemist and my mother teaches English at a university. While we were growing up, they took us on family vacations at least once a year. We visited Aunt Sara, my mother's sister, in Mendoza and my Uncle Miguel, my father's brother, who lives on the beach in Uruguay. Aunt Sara let us take walks through her vineyards and pick the produce from her garden. When it wasn't too hot, we had big family dinners outside under the olive trees."

I imagined Luna's family sitting at a large table under olive trees with plates of food set in front of them as the sun set in the distance. It sounded wonderful. "So, you're close to your aunt Sara?"

"Yes. She's not just a winery owner, but wise too, like someone who has seen the life paths of many people."

"She sounds like a second mother for you, yes?"

"Yes, but my mother also had those qualities, and my father too. Clarisa and I grew up surrounded by good advice and kind people."

That sounded like my family. Mom was the parent willing to hold my hand whenever I had a problem. She always looked at me with a deep respect, so when she gave me advice, I listened. Losing her was like a physical amputation, as if she was cut out of me with a hatchet, and now I was reeling, the gaping hole still huge. Aunt Patty was like my second mother, and that meant that I wanted to reach out to her the same way since Mom was gone.

I turned to Luna. "My mom gave wise advice. For example, whenever I had trouble with my girlfriends, my mom helped me sort out my feelings. Before seeing the waterfalls, I didn't know if I could ever recover from losing her. But today I felt joy for the first time since she died. But right now I feel the burning and longing again. I have so much regret about not spending more time with her. And sometimes I'm actually angry at her for leaving me. Without her I'm a comet that's lost its orbit."

Luna reached for my hand and squeezed it. "Chica, I have a story I want to share with you. It might help."

"I'm listening."

Luna sat up straight and clasped her hands in her lap. "My grandmother told me this story when I was about ten, and I've never forgotten it." A faint smile lit up Luna's face. "When my grandmother was little, she lived with her parents on a farm. Every day after working in the fields and barns, her father came home, then the whole family ate dinner together around their large kitchen table. First, they thanked God for all they had, and then they ate. Most of the food was from their farm and gardens, and most nights they had fresh rolls that her mother had baked that day.

"After dinner, after the kids washed and dried the dishes and cleaned the kitchen, her father sat in the sitting room in front of the fire and read fairy tales from a huge red book to the children. They asked him questions about the stories and he took his time to answer each one thoroughly and kindly. Later, when they went to bed, he came in and helped them say their prayers and hugged them in his strong embrace until they couldn't breathe."

I interrupted, thinking of home, my mother sitting on the edge of my bed, a book open in her hands. "I loved it when my mother read stories to me." I could feel my heart beat contentedly.

Luna continued. "When my grandmother was older, her father taught her how to ride a horse, milk the cows, collect eggs from the chickens, chop the wood, and grow a garden. She remembered how his big, puffy hands held the tiny seeds before dropping them in the earth and covering them with a fine layer of soil. She felt safe, loved, happy—like life would always feel like a sunny spring morning full of promise.

"One day, when her father was working in the grain silo, he fell off the ladder into the grain and was buried beneath several feet of corn. He died of suffocation."

I gasped and squeezed my eyes shut, trying to wipe out the image of a man suffocating in a vat of corn. "Oh, how awful."

Luna held up her hand. "Her mother managed fine enough. Her brother owned the farm next door, and he helped the family run their homestead, but my grandmother was devastated. She didn't want to go to school. Didn't feel like eating. Even though she'd once loved to read, she stopped reading and spent hours sitting on the porch steps with her head in her hands.

"One day, her mother sat down next to her, pulled my grandmother's little hands away from her face, and kissed her on her forehead. 'I know you miss Papá. I miss him too, but we must go on.'

"My grandmother looked up into her mother's face. 'I feel lost without him. Nothing makes me happy because I can't tell him about it. My heart is broken, Mama.'

"Her mother hugged her. 'Once we have someone in our life, we never lose them. You can tell him about what you do. He'll hear you. What you must do is continue to live as if he was still here like he was before. That's what I do, and feeling him beside me makes me happy again.'"

I leaned toward Luna, waiting for more.

Luna spoke again. "So, Leonie, chica, that's what my grandmother did. From that day on, she lived as if her father was just out in the fields, in the barn, in the garden, beside the fire, sitting on the porch, waiting for her to tell him all about her life. She kept him close and that allowed her to be happy again."

The dark silhouettes of the trees were pasted against the deep blue sky. I imagined my mother sitting beside me.

Luna sat up straight. "Why don't you live as if your mother had never died? And when you want to tell her something, just tell her. Keep her love close to you, and continue loving her."

I could feel myself looking at Luna as if I had been startled. What a unique way to view death. "I love this idea, this story. And my mother understood what you're talking about. She said she'd always be with me, but I forgot that until just now. Thank you, Luna. You have helped."

Luna watched quietly as the sky pulled back its curtains to let the stars peek through like millions of diamonds. She tipped her head back and drank the last of the wine in her glass. "I know you'll love Aunt Sara. She's a special woman."

I raised my eyes to the glory of stars. Would Sara be another magical gift? Was she to become another mentor?

CHAPTER 12

The flight to Mendoza from Puerto Iguazú was three hours long, and then I had to find a driver to take me from the Mendoza airport to San Rafael, the southern wine-producing region of Mendoza. During the long but beautiful drive to Bodega Romero, Sara's winery, we crossed over the Diamante and Atuel Rivers. To the west, the ice-capped Andes Mountains arched up to the cerulean sky, their lower slopes lined with acres of bare vineyards, dormant fruit orchards, and olive groves.

The driver talked ceaselessly as he drove me through the city of San Rafael. At one point, he pointed his left thumb out the window. "Here are the ruins of the old fort. Look at the colorful tiendas. They fill up the plaza, except for the church, of course." He drove around the plaza.

Trying to keep my eyes open, I yawned so big I was sure I looked like a hippo, then I clapped my hand over my mouth. What would my mother say to these poor manners in this foreign country? I leaned forward in my seat. "So, this is Plaza San Martín." A white marble church named Catedral San Rafael featured figures of saints in its stained glass windows. Larger-than-life marble statues of Roman goddesses and clay figurines of local historic leaders stood around the plaza. It was a town as beautiful as Buenos Aires.

Once out of the city, the driver turned toward the mountains to follow rural roads that ascended into the foothills. The winery eventually appeared in the midst of high-altitude vineyards and olive groves—a well-kept garden dominated by a white stucco building with wooden doors made of rough planks and iron hinges. The sun had already taken refuge behind the mountains and dusk had painted a brown tobacco glaze over the buildings and gardens.

A robust woman with black hair walked out of the wooden doors toward the car. A white Mallen streak started from her part and curved down to her chin. "*Buenas tardes*!" She passed some bills to the driver and patted him on the back. "*Gracias*. Drive safely, please." I opened the door and climbed out.

The woman, about fifty years old, turned toward me and smiled. "I'm Sara. Welcome to Bodega Romero, where we are all following our own spiritual journey." She reached out to grasp my palm with the hand of a farmer—weathered dry skin cracked with cuts and hardened with calluses.

I tried to smile, my eyelids barely open. "Thank you." When I leaned down to pick up the handle of my large backpack, I wobbled.

Sara reached out for me. "Poor girl. You're exhausted. Let's get you inside to the kitchen for some hot food, then I'll show you to your room, and you can get some rest tonight."

Sara picked up my backpack, slipped her other arm into the crook of mine, and turned us to the building. Above the two matching wooden doors, engraved in metal, was a sign that read "Bodega Romero," and underneath was the phrase "*un lugar para viajes espirituales*." Just as she'd said—this place took its spirituality seriously. I wondered what that was all about, but kept quiet and obediently accompanied Sara into the kitchen.

After I drank a big glass of water and ate two empanadas, Sara showed me my room in the workers' quarters, which were down a dusty path behind the great hall and Sara's house. The window of the room was propped open and the fragrant scent of rosemary wafted inside.

Sara pointed in the direction of the door. "The bathhouse is further down the path. Bath towels, soap, and other toiletries can be found in the cabinets there. Help yourself to whatever you need."

A little bed covered with a fluffy green-and-pink-flowered comforter was pushed against the opposite wall, and next to the bed was a small bookcase with a lamp. Next to the bookcase, a desk with a chair.

Sara pointed to the bookcase. "I put books in every dorm room. You can find some about winemaking. I hope you enjoy them." She had a warm smile.

Under the open window was a walnut dresser with porcelain knobs painted with flowers. On top of the dresser, someone had placed a yellow pitcher of red, pink, and white carnations.

"Thank you for dinner and this charming room," I said. "I love it. Good night."

"Good night, dear girl. I'll see you tomorrow."

Before I went to sleep, I sent Dad an email telling him about my new job in Mendoza. Too tired to say more, I promised I'd follow up soon and ended by asking him to say hi to Zach. When I rested my head on the pillow, I fell asleep quickly.

I SLEPT FITFULLY, WAKING up to the sound of a brass bell ringing somewhere out in the yard. After finding the bathhouse and showering, I dressed in jeans, a hoodie, and hiking boots. I braided my hair into a single braid down my back and grabbed a hat before leaving my dorm room to find the breakfast room. At the end of the row of dorms on the edge of one of the vineyards, I found a rectangular wooden building. Inside, the room was filled with two long communal tables, made of pine with matching chairs, and three smaller pine tables by the windows along one wall. Several young adults were seated, eating and talking. As I entered, their faces turned toward me. A few of the women waved.

On the opposite side of the room from the door, a long rectangular table held large stainless steel buffet chafing dishes with covers. Beside the dishes were platters of tropical fruits and breads. At the end of the table, a banquet-sized coffee urn stood next to a decanter of cream and a bowl of sugar.

I skulked the perimeter of the room to reach the buffet table, gingerly took a coffee cup, and flipped the spigot on the urn to release the black liquid into my cup.

A booming voice with a strong Argentine lisp from a side table caused me to spill my coffee. “Eat hearty, mi chica! You'll need more than *medialunas* today. Get yourself some eggs, tortillas, sausage, and fruit so you last all morning. It's going to be hard work and cold out there.”

Still facing the urn, I took a big breath, then grabbed a napkin and sopped up the spilt coffee. Then I turned around to see a robust man, his burly elbows on a table, with a heaping plate of food in front of him. He held his fork like a shovel. I gingerly approached him, pushing my shoulders back and lifting my chin.

I stuck out my shaking hand. “I'm Leonie, the new apprentice.”

He gripped my hand and shook it, the vibration climbing up to my shoulder. “I know who you are, mi chica. Sara told me all about you early this morning. Welcome to Bodega Romero. I'm Bolade, the wine master. Today, you'll start your spiritual journey with the rest of us.” He released my hand.

There it was again. A reference to the spiritual. What was this place? Were all wineries like this? I said, “‘Bodega Romero—*un lugar para viajes espirituales*.’ What exactly does that mean?”

Bolade's black hair framed his brown face in waves. Two thick, untidy eyebrows sliced across his forehead, and a shadow of a black mustache covered the skin under his broad nose. His lips were red and plump. “Romero is an ancient name from Roman times. It means ‘pilgrim’ or a person who is visiting a shrine. Sara and Santiago named their winery with this name to signify that everyone who works here is following their own personal spiritual journey. We keep that in mind as we work, and it gives our work significance and purpose. I also like to think of this winery as a shrine that I am visiting on my way to a higher place." He looked pleased.

I blinked, wondering how to respond. "The message inspires me. Okay, I'll see you out in the vineyard soon."

I piled my plate with eggs, sausages, potatoes, and fruit and found a place to sit down at one of the long pine tables near a woman who had already finished eating. I introduced myself in Spanish. "Hi, I'm Leonie. This is my first day here."

The woman had dark brown hair, a ruddy complexion, rosy cheeks. A French braid reached down to her shoulder blades. "I'm Hanna." As she extended her hand to shake mine, I noticed her long slender fingers—they would look beautiful over a set of piano keys. Her handshake was confident, and she smelled like a cotton sheet. I liked her immediately.

Hanna introduced me to the other apprentices around the table, and as I ate my breakfast, she described the layout of the winery and explained the apprentices had been uprooting old grapevines during the last few weeks. Today, they would start planting the new ones.

About fifteen minutes later, Bolade treaded over to the table and placed his giant hands on his hips. "Time to plant, mis amigos. Put away your dishes and meet me in the south vineyard." After scanning the room, he strode out the door like a gladiator.

Soon, all the apprentices had gathered at the edge of the south vineyard where baskets of roots had been set out on a rough wooden bench. We wore long sleeves and pants, warm vests, and work shoes. Most of us also had hats to protect our faces from the winter sun.

Bolade pointed to a pile of work gloves, and each apprentice took a pair and put them on.

He pointed to the baskets on the table. "Each take one," he said, at a lower decimal now, but deep and throaty. He waited as we grabbed the baskets. "Gather 'round, muchachos, so I can show you how it's done." He gently pulled a root and a small knife out of my basket, squatted over the dirt, and used the knife to trim the root. "Don't trim too much. You need to leave the life source inside the root, so be careful." Then he placed the root about two inches deep into the loamy soil between his knees. "Plant each root one to three inches deep, then cover it with dirt at the base of its stem. After that, drench the soil all around it." Heads and hats nodded. Then the apprentices dispersed and chose rows to plant.

The soil was covered with a thin frost, and the dirt cracked as I dug into it with a spade to make a hole for each root. As the sun rose higher, it warmed up the frozen ground, and by midmorning it had spread a thin layer of gold over the whole vineyard. The plants looked delicate in my hands, at the mercy of how carefully I placed them in the soil. If I trimmed them too much or didn't water them enough, they would die before having a chance. My chest warmed as I held each one in the palm of my gloves. My mother had spent so many hours kneeling in soil as I was now. I concentrated on the work, poking holes in the soil, setting tiny plants inside, then patting the soil around the base of the plants so they stood up straight. I was my mother's daughter.

Bolade strode up to my row. "The weather is getting warmer, and these grapevines will need the sun to thrive. We're planting them on a southern slope so they'll get maximum sunlight and be protected from frost."

I looked up, the brim of my hat shielding my eyes from the winter sun. "What kind of grape are we planting?"

His voice came from deep down in his throat. Low, warm, strong, rumbling notes. "Viognier."

I stood up to hear him better. "Can you say that again?"

He repeated the word slowly like a baritone practicing lyrics. "Vee-own-ÑAY. This grape was originally from Dalmatia, which is now Croatia, and brought to Rhone, France, by the Romans.

It can be hard to grow, but when you pass this aromatic vintage over your tongue, you know it's worth the effort. It's my favorite varietal."

A laugh, a peal of chimes, erupted from my mouth. "You're an encyclopedia of wine. I'm learning already."

Bolade perched his swarthy arms on his waist. His dark eyes twinkled. "That's because you're working at Bodega Romero, my dear." Then he strode away to talk to the next apprentice.

After three hours of hard work in the vineyard, a bell echoed out across the fields to summon us to lunch. I walked down the long line of newly planted vines between the tightly strung wires that would eventually support them, back toward the workers' lodges and the rectangular cafeteria. When I reached the end of the row at the base of the sloping yard, I surveyed the expanse of the field now delicately gleaming in the midday blanket of pale sun. I examined the rows of new vines we had planted that morning, and pride filled my chest.

At the foot of a row several yards away, a statue of some kind stood on a cornice facing down and back toward the vineyard. Something glimmered from around its neck, so I trudged toward it through the cakey dirt.

From the base of the statue, I gazed up at a life-size Virgin Mary, dozens and dozens of rosaries strung around her neck—glass gems with ornate metal crosses, blue plastic beads with plain crosses, wooden globules and beads shaped into roses, strung like strands of pearls around her veil and over her blue gown. Her countenance fell serenely over the vineyard like the loving and peaceful gaze of a mother over her child. The trace of a smile lit up her rosy lips. A few of the other apprentices passed the statue on their way to lunch, making the sign of the cross, then continuing on.

The sun warmed my arms, and suddenly I felt my mother nearby. I felt a slight breeze caress my shoulders and neck and imagined Mom's face tilted up to the sun, her eyes closed, her eyelashes making crescents upon her cheeks. Looking around, I almost expected to see her walking through the vineyard, waving her arms in joy. But the rows were empty. Dropping my head and folding my hands, I prayed, "Mary, please help me fix my broken heart and find out who I am. Help me to keep my promises to my mother." I stood silently for several seconds as the winter sun warmed my head, then made the sign of the cross.

THAT NIGHT WHEN I got back to my room, there was a message from my father. "I just called to see if you're okay, Leonie. Call me back."

Facing the screen, I pulled my fingers through my ginger hair, rubbed my eyes, and called him. He clicked in almost instantaneously. His face filled the screen.

"Look, Dad, don't worry," I launched in right away. "I got a job at a winery in Mendoza. Luna's aunt Sara owns it."

Dad cupped his left hand over his chin and mouth. His eyebrows arched up like curved fuzzy caterpillars. "So, you're really not coming home then."

"No, Dad. I told you. I'm going to sort myself out down here. Trust me, won't you?"

He shook his head at the screen, took a deep breath, and blinked away the tears in his eyes. For the next few moments, neither one of us spoke.

"I'd rather you came home, but maybe this will be good for you."

What a relief it was to hear him agree with me. The winery job was a great place for me to explore, find out what my strengths were. "The people I'm meeting are intriguing, Dad. I'm learning a lot, even after only one day."

His eyes flashed like an internal slideshow. Then he sat back in his chair, looking like he had decided to avoid an argument.

"I'd better go, Dad," I said, "or I won't get enough sleep. This wine work is physically challenging."

Dad laughed, his eyes suddenly lighting up. The worry lines in his forehead relaxed. "Ah, the life of a working woman. That's good to hear. Be careful, my darling, and keep in touch. By the way, Zach misses you. I hope you'll call him too."

As I closed my laptop, I pictured my brother's tears at Mom's funeral, and I swallowed hard. I slowly closed the lid of the laptop and dropped my chin. Hot tears welled up and rolled down my cheeks. I wiped them away with the back of both hands, then lay down on my bed. I needed to talk to Zach, but wasn't ready to face his disappointment at my refusal to go home. I sat up, reached for my laptop, pulled it to the bed, and opened my email.

Dear Zach,

I hope you can forgive me for not coming home after my Spanish class. I know we were going to spend half the summer together, but I've decided to work down here. I'm trying to find some direction for my life and hope you understand.

I've gotten a job at a winery in Mendoza, a popular wine region of Argentina. My boss, Sara, is charming and friendly, and she made me feel at home right away. I'm an apprentice and will be learning all about how to grow grapes and make wine. I'm having fun already and making friends.

I'm doing my best to get a new footing, and I know you are too. We're sharing the same feeling, but in different places.

Ever your sister,

Love,

Leonie

I closed my laptop and stretched to put it back on the desk. I scanned the books in the bookcase beside the bed. Blinking away tears, I read their titles and found one about wine varietals. I had a lot to learn.

CHAPTER 12.5

I'm fifteen years old. Mom and I stand side by side in the kitchen at home. The ingredients for pizza dough are scattered around a large Mason mixing bowl. Mom's hands are inside the bowl, turning a lump of dough over and over until it is smooth as I watch her. She sticks one of her hands into a bag of flour and sprinkles the flour on a clean spot on the granite counter. Then she places the dough on the sprinkled flour.

"Now, you knead the dough," she says. "Turn the dough over and push it onto itself until it becomes smooth and elastic."

I flour my hands and place them on the dough. "Like this?"

"Let your hands tell you where the dough needs smoothing. You'll find that the dough will want to be pushed in one direction and then another before you're done." While I work the dough, the music from the kitchen's radio is the only sound in the room besides the slapping of the dough as I turn it on the counter.

"That's it. See how smooth the dough looks now? Let's coat the bowl in olive oil and place it there to rise for an hour. Here, use this brush to coat the top of the dough with oil as well."

That night at dinner, Zach eats three big pieces of the stuffed pizza Mom and I make out of my first batch of pizza dough.

CHAPTER 13

I hadn't known that hard, manual work on a vineyard would build back some of my confidence. But after three months of stooping in the dirt, digging holes, cradling the new vines in my hands, and placing them tenderly in the soil, I felt renewed and accomplished.

By the end of September, we had planted three new vineyards with three different varieties of grapes. As Bolade tramped along the rows of plantings, his voice resonated across the vineyard. "These grapes were brought to Argentina from Europe. The high elevations, rich soils, and intense sun of the Mendoza region are perfect for wine production. The rich soil and the sun intensify the flavor of the grapes and produce hearty fruity wines."

Every night, Hanna and I soothed our chapped hands and dry feet with the workers' thick hand lotion. We sat with the other apprentices outside around a campfire where we roasted a dinner of meats and *papas andinas*, a variety of locally grown potatoes. Often, Sara brought out a pot of chimichurri for seasoning our meat, her version made from mint, parsley, and other herbs from her garden—herbs as fragrant as flowers.

The apprentices were from all over the world. Franz had come from South Australia, where his parents owned a winery in the Barossa Valley. He was strong and robust with sandy hair and giant hands. His accent was a blend of cowboy and proper English, and his laugh a hearty guffaw. One night around the dinner campfire, he shared his story with me, speaking in English. "I plan to return home to one day manage my family's business and become the wine master," Franz said, chortling like a horse. Everything was funny to him. "My family's vineyard was passed down to my mother from her parents. It has been in her family ever since her ancestors immigrated to Australia from Poland in 1840. My ancestors brought their winemaking skills with them. Our place is famous for its shiraz vintage, the most popular vintage grown in Australia."

Hanna came from Hungary, where her family owned a winery in the Szépasszony-völgy in Eger, a region known as the Valley of the Beautiful Women, just north of Budapest. Another night around the campfire, she shared her story with the apprentices. "A popular red wine from my valley is known as 'Bull's Blood.' According to legend, Hungarian soldiers fortified their strength by consuming a blend of wine and bull's blood. Today, the wine known as 'Bull's Blood' is actually a blend of three or more varietals."

Hanna waved a hand in the air to the east. "Most of the two hundred wine cellars are within walking distance of one another. Every year, we hold a festival called the Bikavér Feast in July, which is summertime in Hungary. The local wines are paired with the region's best dishes." Hanna looked from Franz to me. "After finishing my apprenticeship, I'm going to travel to Buenos Aires, then return home to work at the winery."

These two knew exactly what they were going to do after they finished working at Sara's winery. I ached for that kind of certainty.

NIGHT AFTER NIGHT, WE rested around the campfire, perching our feet on the wide stone frame of the circular hearth. As I listened to the apprentices talk and laugh, I discovered that I could read their energy by observing their body language. Franz, with his straight back and squared shoulders, possessed an air of authority, while Hanna, with a ready smile, expressiveness, and often open arms, exuded warm hospitality. Everyone shared stories, except for me. I listened but kept my arms folded across my chest.

The apprentices spoke in both Spanish and English, some more fluent than others, and some with versions of Spanish that originated in countries other than Argentina. Clara was from Valencia, Spain. Isaac was from Israel. Felicity and Helene were from Provence, France. In all, there were sixteen paid apprentices working under Bolade's supervision. I was saving most of my money for when I left the winery to travel to Chile and Peru, positive by then that I wanted to follow in my father's footsteps by hiking to Machu Picchu. I helped the other apprentices understand the various Spanish dialects. My own Spanish improved a little more each day, and I slowly became more confident talking with my new friends.

In October, the beginning of spring, Sara started scheduling us to work in the tasting room, the grand hall just behind the winery's large wooden double doors. Hanna and I worked in the tasting room on Saturdays from 11:00 to 5:00. We stood behind the semicircular waist-high counter and poured wines for a handful of customers who chose their tastings from the wine menu. With their glasses in hand, they wandered around the grand room looking at the family photos on the walls or standing in the middle of the empty space chatting with their friends.

Behind the tasting room was a storage area where we grabbed more wine as needed, and behind the storage room was Sara's family's great kitchen. Since the apprentices' shifts carried over through lunch, Sara provided an assortment of appetizers the apprentices could eat when we had time. My favorite foods were the empanadas that came steaming straight from Sara's commercial oven. Each day, the pastries contained new flavor combinations based on the fresh vegetables from the vineyard's garden and the local meats and cheeses of Mendoza.

As Hanna and I served wine to the customers and sneaked back to the kitchen for food, we discussed which wines would taste good with which appetizers. I said, "Let's see, what's in this empanada? The crust was flaky and delicious."

Hanna's lips were coated with buttery flakes. "Beef and mushrooms."

Sara's aperitivos reminded me of my father, who enjoyed food more than anyone I knew. When my mother cooked a roast for dinner, he dished up his helping without speaking. Then he cut into the roast, raised a forkful to his mouth, and chewed silently as the rest of us at the table chatted away. Finally, after several bites, he identified which spices my mother had included in the dish. "Ah, rosemary," he said, nodding. "Dijon mustard and garlic."

I felt a tug on my heart thinking about these family dinners. I had inherited my father's love for food, always thinking about the flavors I was eating and recipes I would like to cook.

Often, as the winery's customers gathered their belongings and headed out the door, they said, "Let's find a place to eat."

That got me to thinking, and one day I asked Hanna, "Wouldn't our customers enjoy eating appetizers with their wine? We're being treated better than they are."

Hanna thought for a minute, then said, "Hmm, I'm surprised Sara doesn't serve some food with the wine. My family's winery back in Hungary serves cheeses, nuts, and dried fruits to our customers."

As the customers we'd just served collected their coats and hustled out the door to find restaurants, I turned to Hanna. "Should we see if Sara would be receptive to serving appetizers?"

Hanna smiled. "Let's find out."

That night when Sara was in the kitchen preparing dinner for the apprentices and her family, Hanna and I approached her. We had just cleaned the tasting counter in the great room and stowed the open bottles of wine in the storage room's cooler. We gently knocked on the kitchen door, opened it, and stood across from Sara at the island counter.

I said, "Hanna and I have come up with an idea to increase the winery's business."

Sara was stirring a pot of steaming rice over the stove. One hand went to her hip, and she flipped her Mallen streak back from her face with the other. She pursed her lips. "Not sure I'm ready for this, but let's hear it."

I smoothed my hand over the cold granite counter. "If we served food to go with our wine, our customers would spend more money and stay longer. We might even attract *more* customers. The foods you make in your kitchen for the apprentices are so delicious. We could create a menu with some of those."

Sara stopped stirring the rice. "I've never done anything like that before."

Hanna stepped closer to Sara. "Would you let us experiment with recipes in your kitchen?"

Sara moved the spoon slowly through the pot of rice, then laid it down on a saucer next to the stove. She covered the pan with a lid and turned the heat to low. "I don't know. Where would the customers eat this food?"

I jumped at the answer. "There's empty space in the tasting room. Could we set up some tables and chairs? The customers could sit and enjoy their wine and food there."

Sara soon began nodding, her eyes bright with ideas. "You know, we have some round tables and chairs in the barn from our daughter Olivia's wedding a few years ago. We could use those."

Hanna chimed in. "What about putting tables out on the patio as well? Then, you could serve even more customers. The huge olive trees provide plenty of shade."

Sara wiped her hands on a waffled dish towel and stuck the towel in the waistband of her apron. "A great idea. You can use my kitchen to experiment with some recipes, and then we can talk again. This will be a big change for me, so let's go slowly."

During the weekdays Hanna and I were busy working in the vineyards, and on Saturdays we served wine in the tasting room, so Sunday was the only day we had for experimenting with recipes. On the first Sunday after we'd asked Sara's permission to use the kitchen, Hanna and I scoured the cookbooks in Sara's kitchen for authentic Argentine recipes that would pair well with wine. We sat at the island's granite counter, sipping viognier and malbec wines while turning page after page of thick cookbooks and nibbling on empanadas as we filled our notebooks with ideas. The ability to be creative energized me, filling me with a joy that I was sure my mother had felt when she was cooking in her own kitchen.

The next two Sundays, we visited the gardens. There we found fresh onions, sweet potato bushes, kale, and young tomato plants. We tramped to the back of the garden into the orchard and discovered quince trees hung with bright yellow pomes. Beyond the quince orchard, olive trees towered to the sky with gnarly branches full of scars and decades of history. I felt like a woman with a mission—to choose the freshest ingredients, to create the most wonderful appetizers that would lure Sara's customers into spending more time and money at the winery.

By the fourth Sunday, we were mixing flour, salt, oil, and water in large mixing bowls to form balls of empanada dough. We kneaded the dough on the cold granite counters until it was smooth and pliable, rolled it into Ping-Pong-size balls, then used a rolling pin to flatten each roll. We also experimented with rolling the dough into long rectangles and cutting out empanada discs with a dough cutter. We altered the dough recipe, sometimes using oil and other times using butter to change the richness and flavor of the dough to complement various fillings.

That day, we also took buckets out to the orchard to collect quince. As we stood among the branches and plucked the golden-ripe orbs, I imagined I heard my mother whistling. Abruptly, I stopped picking and listened, and I heard the hum of the breeze wafting among the branches. After pausing to picture my mother's face, I resumed picking fruit.

When our buckets were full, we carried the fruit into the kitchen to make quince paste. First, we peeled and cored the fruit, then gathered the peels and cores into small bags of cheesecloth and boiled the quince flesh with the gauzelike bags so that the pectin trapped in the discards would leach out and thicken the quince. After removing the cheesecloth bouquets and passing the quince flesh through a canning sieve, Hanna and I added sugar to sweeten and further thicken the mixture. Finally, we poured the quince into glass baking dishes to let it stiffen in the refrigerator.

Hanna closed the refrigerator door. "This afternoon, let's go to the markets to find cheeses to complement the quince." We took tastings of quince with us and found that the local goat cheeses paired deliciously. Back in the kitchen, we practiced filling empanada dough with the quince and goat cheese mixture and with other combinations of garden vegetables. We sealed the edges of the mini empanadas and discovered that we needed more practice in folding the edges so that the empanadas looked attractive to eat. Laughing, we ate the ones that didn't look good enough to serve to customers.

ONE DAY AT THE END of December, as the vines in the vineyard displayed glossy pale-green leaves and miniature jewel-like bunches of grapes, Hanna and I walked up to Sara in the tasting room and handed her a menu. I said, "We've come up with a menu of appetizers that we believe will be perfect complements to the wines. We can't wait to see what you think."

Sara's dark eyes flickered over the menu like butterflies hovering next to milkweed. "Listed in both Spanish and English. Smart."

BODEGA ROMERO

LOS APERITIVOS

Empanadas rellenas de membrillo y queso de cabra
Quince and goat cheese empanadas

Empanadas rellenas de cebollas y queso de cabra
Onion and goat cheese empanadas

Empanadas rellenas de papas y lentejas
Potato and lentil empanadas

Fainá con oregano y tomates
Flatbread with oregano and tomatoes

Calabacínes rellenos con jamón y queso
Zucchini stuffed with ham and cheese

Chipitas de queso
Cheddar cheese buns

Her eyes flickered over the menu, then she said, "Wow, I think all three of these empanada types will taste wonderful with our wines. Well done, girls!"

I stood proudly with my hands behind my back. "Thank you. We liked the empanada idea, but we added the traditional fainá for people who love pizza. We created the stuffed zucchini and chipitas for really hungry people."

Hanna held up six long fingers. "We limited the menu to six delectable aperitivos—an elegant collection, like the wine."

I stood straight and proud. "And to keep the menu fresh, we can change the fillings for the empanadas to feature whatever vegetables and fruits are in season."

Sara looked up. "Have you thought about pricing?"

Hanna handed Sara a sheet of paper. "We have. Here's a suggested list of prices for each appetizer."

A smile spread across Sara's face. She rushed to the door and yelled to Bolade, who was standing outside the two massive wooden doors, his hands folded behind his back and his gaze stretching over the vineyards. "Let's get a group in here to move some furniture."

Bolade's deep voice purred. "This sounds exciting." Then he strode away to find some help.

When Bolade and six apprentices, including Franz, walked into the tasting room, Sara organized a transformation of the tasting room and patio. "Bring the tables and chairs out from the barn, clean them, and set them up inside and outside."

Fifteen minutes later, Franz and another apprentice carried a round table into the tasting room and set it down.

IN THE WINERY'S BUSINESS office, Hanna and I printed menus on elegant five-by-seven-inch cards and inserted them into holders for the middle of each table. Sara called out instructions to apprentices directing them to fetch and decorate the table with napkins, small plates, and flower vases. Hanna and I wandered through the vineyard, clipping wildflowers and roses to fill the tiny vases for the center of each table.

I held my hand up in the air toward Hanna. "Splendid work, my friend." She gave me a high five. Her face was beaming.

When we were back working in the kitchen, Sara walked in. "I'm proud of my new chefs."

Franz poked his head in the door. "I want to be sous-chef."

Sara pulled him into the room and patted him on the back. "You're hired. Be prepared to chop, dice, and stir."

THE FIRST CUSTOMERS TO see the tables on the patio and in the tasting room were delighted that they could sit down while enjoying their wine. When they bit into the empanadas filled with quince and goat cheese, their eyes opened wide. Once they finished their first aperitivos, they ordered more dishes—savoring the earthy fillings and delighting in the opulent flavors of the traditional fainá.

In a few weeks, one group of customers turned into dozens of parties. Instead of customers spending an average of forty-five minutes at the winery, they spent two or three hours, sipping wine with our new appetizers. Sara assigned more apprentices to work in the tasting room serving wine and food, and when the room was full of customers, she paced between the kitchen and the tasting room, making sure orders were filled quickly and customers were satisfied. All the tables were filled with laughter, cheers, gesturing hands, raised glasses, plates of food, and scraping chairs as people moved back to the tasting counter for more wine.

At the end of the day, customers walked out the double wooden doors carrying bags and boxes of viognier and malbec wines. As Hanna and I watched them leave, we knew we had transformed Sara's business. Blinking the tears from my eyes, I placed my hand over my heart, feeling more accomplished than I had ever felt in my life.

On the last Sunday of January, after the great wooden doors had closed behind the last of the day's customers and Hanna, Franz, and I were filling the dishwashers, scouring the cooking sheets, and wiping down the granite counters, Sara joined us in the kitchen. "Good job as usual, Franz. I'll see you at dinner," she said, motioning for Hanna and me to wait behind. Franz removed his apron and left.

Sara reached over the granite island counter and handed an envelope to me and another one to Hanna. "I'm giving you both a bonus. In the last two months, we've made more money than we used to make in a year, and it's all because of your ingenuity and creativity. Muchas gracias!"

Hanna and I had done something extraordinary. This time, tears rolled down my cheeks. I grabbed Hanna and hugged her, holding on for a long time. Sara came around the counter, spread her arms out, and hugged us snugly. Then she kissed each of us on each cheek.

THAT NIGHT, I VIDEO-called both Dad and Zach at the same time and told them about my contribution to the success of Sara's business.

Dad looked over the top of his screen reflectively. "So, you're as good a cook as your mom was." He looked lost in his thoughts. "Ah, your mother made the most delicious roast lamb."

Zach rubbed his belly. "My favorite was her chicken and dumplings."

I felt a flood of tears building behind my eyes as I envisioned Mom at the dinner table, happy that we loved her cooking. Oh, how I missed her. I looked up at the screen and Dad and Zach sat silently blinking. Clearly, they expected me to say something. My voice cracked like a static radio. "Guys, I've got to go. Work starts early tomorrow." Right before I clicked off, their surprised faces turned to disappointment. As the screen went black, heaving sobs erupted from my throat. I buried my head in my pillow and cried harder, losing my breath in between sobs. Eventually, I fell asleep on a wet pillow, still wearing my clothes.

CHAPTER 14

During the summer months of January and February, Bolade and the apprentices worked in the vineyards, twisting the grapevines around thick wires to support the produce and pruning some of the grapes from the vine branches. Towering over us as we stooped in adjacent rows, Bolade shouted, "We prune the branches to produce less fruit. That way, the remaining grapes have a higher concentration of flavor."

Pruning in heat and humidity was intense and repetitive, but I was driven with fervor. Like Bolade, I had developed pride in my work, and felt good working hard to produce delicious wine. I wore a brightly colored hat with a wide brim and a long-sleeved shirt to shield myself from the blazing sun. Still, it was so intense that sweat rolled down my face, and I had to use a bandanna to wipe it off every few minutes. Sometimes I wrapped a wet bandanna around my neck to keep cool, but sweat still collected under my armpits and trailed down my back. To rest, we sat in the shade of the olive trees nearby and drank water from flasks kept cold in an ice chest. We ate peaches and plums that Sara cut up for us. As I sat under the trees with my comrades, I felt like I knew how my mother had felt after planting flats of flowers in her garden, creating something beautiful for her family.

Every Sunday night, I talked to Dad and Zach about work. "Today, we pruned back the vines. That was hard work. But working with plants is rewarding. I understand why Mom loved her garden so much."

Zach tipped his head back and chuckled. "Working at a winery sounds almost as much fun as working with animals." Behind him, his blue surfboard with an orange stripe down the middle leaned against the wall by the door, his wet suit hung on a hook nearby, and a pile of unfolded laundry was piled on his unmade bed. "My oceanography class went on a field trip to the Channel Islands National Marine Sanctuary. A totally dope trip. There are shipwrecks out there."

I imagined Zach climbing the rocks on the Channel Islands with his classmates, the waves crashing against the shore like angry gods. I missed the wild waves of California beaches. The water was freezing, but the shores, craggy with rocks and brittle with pebbly sand, were magnificent. Above the agitating sea, the endless blue sky was almost always clear of clouds. I ached to see California again but took a deep breath, focusing, instead, on my promise to Mom to continue to travel.

ON THE LAST SUNDAY in February, Argentina celebrated the National Grape Harvest Festival. The winery workers took baskets into the vineyards and picked the ripest grapes from the vines. In the orchards, we picked baskets of stone fruit, then brought the fruit to the vineyards where the Virgin Mary statue stood among the vines. Father Joseph from the local church came out, and while Sara; her husband, Santiago; and the workers watched, he blessed the fruit, the vineyards, and the orchards in appreciation for God's abundance.

Sara leaned over, the brim of her hat touching mine, and said, "We ask Father Joseph to bless our winery every year on this day to ensure that our harvest will be plentiful." She folded her hands in prayer and a single tear streamed down her cheek. The baskets of fruit placed near Mary's statue shone like jewels in the summer sun, the scent of their ripeness perfuming the air. Bees silently flew among the gathered people as if they, too, knew it was a sacred day, a day for gratitude. Sara, Santiago, and many of the workers made the sign of the cross with the priest as he finished his blessing. They stood quietly for a moment, then gathered the baskets and walked into the great hall.

Inside, everyone sat around the tables that had been decorated with vine branches. Sara stood up. "Thank you all for your months of labor, the icy winter, the gentle spring, and the brutal summer." Heads nodded. Sara continued. "This day, we honor and recognize the workers—that would be you and everyone here—who made the harvest possible. The rest of the day is a day of rest, but also a day of merriment to enjoy the bounty of our labor."

A raucous eruption of cheers and clapping broke out in the hall. Santiago brought out several bottles of wine from the storage room and recruited Franz to help him open them. Hanna and I brought trays of empanadas out from the kitchen that we had made the day before. Bolade took his guitar out of its case and started playing. Once everyone had wine in their glass, Sara led a toast. "In gratitude for our hard work and the bounty of our land." The celebration lasted into the evening.

THE SUMMER RAINS AND sun washed and heated the vineyards, and the grapevines sprouted leaves and blooms, their branches curling around the wire trellises, grape leaves covering the fields like millions of pale-green dresses, and bunches of grapes dangling like rubies. Soon, it was March, harvest time.

One chilly morning at the edge of the vineyard, when the air prickled my cheeks in the sleepy morning sun, and we were gathering our buckets and tools for grape-picking, a tall dark-haired man with stunning brown eyes, a shadow of a beard, and a lanky frame loped over to the bustling activity and stood quietly off to the side, watching us gather our equipment. Bolade walked up and slapped the handsome man on the shoulder. He hollered over our bustling. "This is Mateo. He's going to help us get the harvest done faster."

I paused to study the new worker. His eyes were as brown as chocolate truffles, and when he finished gazing across the group of us and paused on me, I stood numb, and the universe seemed to stop breathing. I felt threads of magnetic energy pulling me toward him and wondered if he felt them too. Mateo blinked, and his brown irises were lost behind his thick, dark lashes. He bent his head down and mumbled hellos to some of the male apprentices by nodding in their direction. Then he picked up a pail and headed into the rows of vines.

We spread out into the vineyard, stooped in between the vines, and clipped bunches of grapes away from the branches, our straw hats bobbing up and down as we crouched and shuffled to the next plant. The morning sun warmed our backs, and from my row I saw Mateo's head bobbing as he worked.

Whenever I stretched to see his face among the branches, he looked calm, almost as if he was meditating. When he bent over the vines, he whistled. Four low beautiful notes. He held the first note for two beats, tripped over the second and third notes in half beats, then finished the tune back at the original note. Over and over again, he whistled his signature tune. The first note sounded clear, like he was blowing through a pipe. The third note was a little breathy.

Maybe Mateo had the kind of wisdom my mother had. She knew how to surround herself with what she needed to be happy. She was the happiest person I'd ever known, and I wanted to be like her. If I became close to Mateo, maybe I could learn from him.

When the midday sun hung directly over our heads, all the apprentices sat in a clearing, eating bocadillos and swilling bottles of water in between bites of ham and bread. Hanna and I watched Mateo as he ate silently at the edge of the group. Hanna said, "My heart is pumping for that man."

I looked at her. "Whatever for?"

Hanna's eyes glinted. "A fling in Argentina would be fun."

Jealousy rose in my chest. I sucked in a big breath and said, "Hey, Hanna. I'm interested in him too. You're going home after your apprenticeship, but I'm staying in Argentina. Could you leave him for me?" Hanna shrugged her shoulders and nodded.

Ah, she *wasn't* that interested after all. I felt pleased as I looked over at Mateo.

Once in a while, a brief smile flittered over his lips as he listened to the others talking. Not once did he look in my direction. Had I only imagined the flash of energy when our eyes had first met?

After lunch, we all lumbered back to work. The sun followed us back into the spaces between the rows of vines, and we stooped under the light green foliage to shade us from its blazing rays. As the afternoon hours passed and settled into an early dusk, we snipped the miniature purple globes from the branches and filled bucket after bucket.

After sunset, we ate dinner around a campfire. I stole glances at Mateo while I carried on a conversation with Hanna. He ate silently, his eyes directed only at the fire. Once in a while, the apprentice next to him would ask him a question and I heard him answer with just a few words, his voice like custard—soft, rich, and smooth.

Over the next few weeks, Mateo kept mostly to himself. He never spoke to me and never looked up when we were close to each other. I sensed that he avoided coming near me whenever he could, and our first encounter began to seem like a dream. Still, I felt a strong pull between us, a powerful energy I couldn't ignore.

To distract myself, I stayed busy harvesting the grapes and helping the other apprentices haul in the buckets to the crushing and pressing area behind the great barn. Bolade had explained,

"To make white wines, we're going to use the metal basket press to crush the grapes quickly into a must. Then, as swiftly as possible, we have to separate the skins, seeds, and solids from the juice so the skins don't color the liquid and the tannins don't dry or make the wine bitter." While Bolade supervised, we filtered the wine into stainless steel tanks, allowing the sediment to sink to the bottom. When the juice at the top of the tank was fairly clear, we siphoned it into new, clean barrels until it was free of residue. It was hard work, but rewarding to see what we had accomplished.

On Friday, at the end of Mateo's third week, when Hanna and I were helping Bolade add yeast to the white wine tanks, Mateo walked into the cellar with Carlos and Miguel, two other apprentices. Bolade called them over to observe the yeast process. Mateo came and stood next to Hanna, but didn't say a word.

Hanna said, "I'm Hanna, and this is my friend Leonie." She held out her hand toward Mateo, who slowly shook it.

Even in the dim light of the wine cellar, I saw his face redden as he said, "I'm Mateo." After introducing himself, he stepped back behind one of the other apprentices.

Bolade held a ladle of cloudy juice above a wine vat. "The yeast makes the sugar in the wine turn into alcohol, which creates that great concoction we call wine. Now, we let the wine ferment for a few weeks until the process is done."

We helped Bolade cover the vats loosely and then walked out into the fall daylight.

Hanna smiled slyly at me. "Let's go out tonight." She looked at the group, smiled brightly, and raised her voice. "I want to take a tango lesson. Anyone want to join us?"

Carlos said, "We do. Mateo, you should come too. It's a lot of fun."

Mateo shook his head and put his hands behind his back.

Miguel said, "Ah, come on, Mateo. Loosen up. It'll be fun."

With pursed lips, Mateo finally nodded.

THAT NIGHT, NINE OF us gathered at the dance hall in San Rafael, ten miles away from the vineyard. At 8:00 exactly, a dance instructor wearing a black dress with a single strap over her left shoulder strutted onto the dance floor. Her right shoulder was bare and the back of her dress dipped deeply, showing off toned shoulder blades. "The tango lesson will be starting in a few minutes. Please join me and my partner in a circle on the dance floor."

Mateo tried to sit down, but Hanna pulled him out to the floor and held his hand while waiting for the lesson to begin. I began to shake and muttered under my breath, "Really, Hanna? What a traitor you are."

A few minutes later, the instructor asked the dance students to choose partners. Within seconds, Hanna pushed Mateo's hand into mine. "You guys should be partners." Then she swooped across the floor and grabbed Franz's arm.

I glanced up into Mateo's face to see if he was pleased and felt that crackling energy like before. Our eyes locked, and his face lit up like a candle. "I'm Leonie."

His shyness melted away. "I know your name. Leon means 'lion.' Why did your parents name you like that?"

My face flushed. "A lion is a leader, and my mother said I'd be a trailblazer, that I needed a name worthy of a leader."

Mateo's eyebrows arched. "A trailblazer. That's an odd term for a woman."

I felt an uncomfortable prickling crawl up my neck, but I was distracted when the tango instructor walked to the center of the room. "My name is Belette, and tonight I will teach you the dance of love. I encourage you to think of the tango as a conversation between two lovers." That sounded *so romantic* and I was thrilled to have handsome Mateo as my partner. Belette continued, "Both partners are equally important. One cannot dance without the other, and both must participate to the fullest extent. To be a good tango dancer, you must commit to the tango conversation. Surrender to the music. Now, let's get started. The tango is a walking dance." Dramatically, she raised her right arm in the air and followed her hand with her gaze. "We'll learn how to walk, but first we must learn how to embrace."

Belette's partner, a man dressed all in black with a red scarf tied around the neck of his shirt, stood in front of her as she continued talking. "One type of embrace is when the partners stand apart from one another. I'm going to show you how to embrace with only your arms."

Soon Mateo and I were facing each other. His left hand held my right hand, and his right hand pressed against my left shoulder blade.

Belette embraced her tall handsome partner. "The Argentine tango originated from poor immigrants from Europe and the slaves from Africa who missed their homeland. In fact, the music and lyrics of tango echo with heartbreak and longing for lost friends and lovers. When Argentina banned slavery in the 1860s, free male slaves and poor European men gathered in the dance halls and brothels to commiserate their losses. They wore festive scarves around their necks and high-heeled boots. As they shared their misery, their cultures blended." Belette and her partner, embracing with their arms only, danced sensually around the dance floor and stopped in the center. "Next, I'm going to teach you how to embrace more seductively."

Mateo and I stood with our chests pressed lightly against each other. We clasped hands on my right, and Mateo's fingers touched the middle of my back. My hand pressed on his right shoulder blade.

The universe stood still.

Belette lifted her chin and turned her head slowly, inspecting the embraces around the room. "The tango is a blend of African *candombe*—drum music—and European waltzes and polkas. It is nostalgic. Although born in the poor barrios of Buenos

Aires, the tango didn't stay there. Now, it's famous all over the world." Belette's partner walked forward decisively and Belette followed him in his steps. They stopped in a dramatic pose, her head arching back. Then she let go of her partner and faced the students. "Now, let's learn how to do a basic walk."

When Mateo started to lead, I relaxed. He guided me lightly yet deliberately, and my feet moved effortlessly as I followed his steps. My arms relaxed onto his and we moved like a single unit. Like we had been together for years and instinctively knew each other's next move.

Suddenly, from across the room, Franz yelped, "Ow, my foot!"

Hanna replied, "I'm sorry, but your feet are as big as boats." The class erupted in laughter.

Belette had us practice the tango walk again and again. We practiced it while embracing with only our arms, then dancing in a closed embrace. Two hours later, beads of sweat dripped from our foreheads, our palms wet with perspiration. Mateo squeezed my hand.

As we walked back to the dormitory, Mateo said, "I like you very much."

I felt pins and needles. "I like you too."

He turned. "Would you take a walk with me tomorrow night?"

A surge of emotion flooded my stomach. Was he really asking me on a date? I could hardly believe it. "Yes, I'd love to."

WHEN I GOT BACK TO my dorm, I grabbed my laptop, sat on the bed, and video-called Elaine. My hair was still sweaty from the dancing and my face glowed. She answered quickly and I blurted, "I have non-winery news."

Elaine's eyes opened wide. "Oh, what?"

I shouted into the phone, and waved my hands. "I'm in love!"

Her eyes popped open. "What? With who?"

"A new apprentice came to the winery. His name is Mateo. We went to a tango lesson tonight and danced together the whole time, and he's asked me for a date." I sucked in a huge gulp of air.

Elaine's forehead pinched. "You're in love? Already?"

I set my mouth into a firm line. "He's been here for a while, and I've been watching him for weeks. Yep, I'm in love." Why wasn't she excited for me?

"Leonie, I'm happy for you, but it takes time to get to know a guy. Love doesn't happen in one night."

"I thought you'd be happy for me."

"I think I'd be happy if I didn't know what you've been going through. And if you weren't talking so intently about a guy you don't really know."

I changed the subject, and we made small talk for a few minutes, then I clicked off. Later, as I lay in bed, I brooded. She simply didn't understand. If she had met Mateo, she'd know how wonderful he was. No . . . what did I care. I was the one feeling love. I was the one whose life had just been touched by magic. If *I* knew it was real, I didn't need her approval. I didn't need anyone's approval.

CHAPTER 15

A week later, when I walked into the bottling room, Bolade was talking with Mateo, who was holding up his laptop to the light. "Here's an example," Mateo said. "This label includes a drawing of the wine-tasting room."

Bolade looked pensive. "You drew these labels using a program?"

Mateo nodded. "Yes, drawing is my hobby. I can create labels for all the new wines this season. It's no trouble at all."

Bolade leaned over the computer. "Hmm. We like the labels to reflect the varietal inside the bottle. For example, last year's viognier label consisted of a spray of flowers since the vintage possessed a strong floral bouquet. We want the labels to be distinct from each other and different than the year before."

"I can do that. Let me try."

I walked up behind Mateo and poked my head over his shoulder. "I'll help him. We can brainstorm together."

When Mateo turned to look at me, I caught a glimpse of irritation in his eyes, but he took a deep breath and smiled tightly, his face flushing pink. "Sure. Leonie can help me come up with ideas, and I'll present you with a gallery of options by the time we bottle the wine. What do you think?" He bit his lip while waiting for an answer.

Bolade stood back and planted his big hands on his hips. "Genius idea. I'll talk to Sara about it and see what she says."

Mateo's shoulders relaxed as he reached out to shake Bolade's hand.

In less than twenty-four hours, Bolade had talked to Sara, then told Mateo to start designing wine labels. For the next few days, as the apprentices harvested grapes, Mateo and I worked near each other in the vineyards.

Squatting near him, I said, "What about putting a drawing of the winery doors on the labels?"

"Mm. Not a bad idea," Mateo replied. He whistled his signature tune, and I was happy to see that the irritation I'd noted earlier had dissipated. As we continued our work, I daydreamed about future nights with him in the vineyard under the stars and our lips touching like flower petals.

LATER, AS WE WORKED in the winery decanting the new juices, we hovered over the transferring barrels, inhaling the scents and discussing the aromas in the room. The juices were strong and full of sugar. I leaned close to the barrel's wooden side and inhaled long and deeply. "I'm no expert, but I smell cherries coming from this barrel. Mm."

Mateo squatted next to another barrel, swirling his hand in front of him like an orchestra conductor. He laughed, his chuckle soft and low. "Over here it smells like blackberry."

I said, "If we practice enough, we'll get the hang of this aroma business."

Mateo laughed again, this time from deep within his belly. "The project depends on it."

Every night after that, Mateo and I met at the edge of the vineyard to go for a walk after dinner. As we strolled in the twilight, he held my hand. I tried hard to give him good suggestions for the wine label venture, and he seemed to listen to me eagerly, showing a deep passion that I found attractive. At the end of each night, he kissed me for a long time and said, "*Buenas noches, mi querida*," which made my heart skip a beat.

A few weeks later, Bolade asked the apprentices to help him

with the aging process. "First, use a small glass for tasting," he said, opening a spigot on a barrel and filling his glass half full of wine. He held the glass up to the light in the room and swirled it, his oversized hand dwarfing the tiny glass. "I'm looking at the wine's viscosity. Is it too thin or too full?" Then he sipped. "I'm tasting for spoilage. This wine is not spoiled." He smacked his lips. "The next taste test is to determine if the wine is too acidic or too flat. If it is too acidic, we can add malolactic acid to it, blend it with a less acidic batch, or change its container. If it's too flat, we can blend it with overly acidic wine."

By the end of the lecture, we all stood around in a circle, each with a glass in our hand, discussing what we tasted and what we would do to improve the aging. I was feeling confident in my winemaking ability, boosted by the success that Hanna and I had had with the appetizer menu.

Week after week, our training went on like this, the apprentices and Bolade looking for color changes in the wines. We swirled the wine high in our glasses to examine how it coated the insides of the glass for several seconds and then slowly fell back down in lingering rivers of color, signifying a luscious viscidity. Bolade's knowledge about wine amazed me. "We expect the whites to deepen in color and the reds to lose color. We also must appraise the wine's aroma to see whether it is developing a complex bouquet, creamy, or savory palate." I realized that I was in the presence of a master.

When Bolade determined a wine was ready for bottling, he gave us paper and pens and told us to write short paragraphs describing the taste. "Compare the vintage's flavor with other foods such as peaches for the viognier; cherries or raspberries for the malbec; pepper and blackberries for the cabernet sauvignon; and cloves, bell pepper, and vanilla for the merlot." We took turns reading aloud our descriptions to each other.

One day after we wrote descriptions, Bolade faced us with his hands on his hips. "Okay. Now I want you to combine all your best observations into a single paragraph for each varietal that we'll print on the back label of each bottle. One person must take the lead for each and, with help from others, develop the final description. Pour yourself another glass of your assigned varietal and get to work."

I was voted lead for the viognier, and Mateo worked under Franz to write the final description for the malbec varietal. For the rest of the afternoon, the groups of apprentices engaged in spirited discussions about the major aromas and palates of each new wine. We sipped. We swilled. We swirled the wine over our tongues, gums, teeth, and down our throats to savor its flavor over and over again. Soon, everyone was tipsy.

I savored the last sip of my wine. "Add the words 'notes of dried pineapple.'" We changed adjectives into nouns, listed good ideas at the bottom of the page to save until later, changed the structures and reversed the orders of sentences. By the time we had developed descriptions of each varietal, we were laughing and slapping each other on the back. Our palates were saturated, and our brains were sozzled. Finally, the meaty fragrance of *carbonada criolla*, a beef stew, wafted into the yard from the open windows of Sara's kitchen. We submitted our final paragraphs and wobbled to the restroom to wash up for dinner.

AFTER BOLADE AND SARA approved the descriptions, Mateo and I met in the tasting room to come up with the final drawings for each varietal's bottle. He drummed his fingers on the table while waiting for me to sit down, then cleared his throat several times, took a deep breath, and huffed it out. I sensed he was irritated.

I rubbed his arm. "Is something bothering you?"

"I usually work on projects like this alone."

"Now that we're a couple, isn't it nice for us to work together?"

He shook his head, and I felt a distance grow between us. Why wouldn't he want to work with me? That seemed sexist.

Despite our awkward conversation, we continued to work together, reading and rereading the paragraphs for each wine to find inspiration. We used the time of our nightly walks to gather more ideas, noticing the Virgin Mary watching over the land. I asked, "Should we focus on a particular flavor for each varietal, such as a peach for the viognier?"

Mateo patted my back like I was a toddler. "*I* think the illustrations should show something that symbolizes the special history of the winery, such as the picture of a pilgrim to signify the meaning of the winery's name, Romero."

He didn't seem to want my help, so to gain his favor, I suggested another idea. "Perhaps the bottle should include a sketch of something on the winery's property, such as the Virgin Mary statue?"

"No, I've decided."

Above us, as the stars lit up the Andes night sky, twinkle by twinkle, the bare vines decorated the earth like black lace, and the cold air turned the soil beneath into a silvery carpet. That night when Mateo bent down and kissed me gently with his warm lips, and when his lips touched mine, my heart melted, yet an unease had begun to settle inside me. He didn't seem to want me to have a voice in the project. I'd never been treated like that before—like someone whose opinion didn't matter.

WITHIN TWO WEEKS, MATEO finished his drawings for each varietal. To complete the labels, he added the location of the vineyard, the year of harvest, the winery's name, the alcohol content, and the required government warning—one label for the front of each bottle and one for the back. Each front label included a silhouette of the winery and the surrounding olive trees with a colorful drawing of each varietal's dominant flavor. The viognier's label was illustrated with a rosy, ripe peach. The malbec label had sprigs of cherries, the cabernet included blackberries, and the merlot had a drawing of a vanilla bean and cloves.

Sara peered down at the collection of labels displayed on the island counter in her kitchen. "Mateo, these labels are fabulous! They're creative and expertly drawn. You've really got some talent." Behind Sara, Bolade flashed a toothy smile.

Mateo stood tall beside me, his shoulders square, chest broad. "I'm happy you like my work." He didn't look at me or include me in the conversation. Didn't give me credit for any of the ideas. He alone took the credit. The unease that I had begun to feel grew larger.

AFTER THE WINERY CLOSED on Saturday afternoon, Mateo and I bicycled on the bottle-green routes at the foot of the shrub-dressed Andes Mountains. Mateo looked behind at me. "The name of the Andes comes from a Quechua word, *anti*, which means 'east.' These mountains created the border of the eastern region of the Inca Empire."

I smiled. "You know a lot about your country, don't you?"

Then he smiled. "I do. I learn what I can about things I love."

I was impressed with that.

Mateo continued. "The Incas settled in the Andes Mountains, generally in Peru. In the 1500s, the Spanish killed the Inca ruler and took over their capital city, now known as Cusco. The descendants of the Inca are the present-day Quechua-speaking peasants of the Andes, a large percentage of Peru's population."

My excitement about seeing Peru was growing day by day. "Wow, I can't wait to go there."

From the dusty roads, we saw condors flying like black generals from the valleys up the slopes of the startling steep mountainsides, their wide wings like sails across the searing sun. Sierra finches nestled in the deciduous trees and scrappy shrubs, building nests bit by bit from dry grasses, twigs, leaves, and flowers. Once in a while, we spied a wild llama or alpaca chewing its cud or romping with its young. My heart filled with excitement at exploring more of the country.

Mateo stopped his bike and lodged his feet on the ground. He waved for me to stop next to him. As he gazed up at the mountains, he straightened his back and his chest expanded. "In high school, I had to memorize the five largest peaks of the Andes Mountains in school. Aconcagua, Cerro Bonete, Galán, Mercedario, and Pissis. The Aconcagua was named for a Quechua word meaning 'Sentinel of Stone.' It is the highest point in the Western and Southern Hemispheres and has two peaks."

I tipped my head back to see as high as I could up to the tips of the mountains. They were breathtaking. I could see why Mateo was so proud of his country. Its geography was diverse, wildlife was exotic, and people were beautiful and friendly. His passion for his country and family was admirable.

The azure skies expanded in all directions and disappeared over the tips of the mountain range. The roads spread out like wide, creamy ribbons for miles in the distance, promising hidden treasures in every direction as they twisted to and away from the mountain range: burrows, wild potato bushes, birds dressed in nature-colored plumage, and geese who squawked like out-of-tune brass horns. I inhaled the ice-cold air, letting it flare my nostrils, awaken my lungs. It was exhilarating to feel the frigid air nip my skin.

A MONTH LATER, AFTER the work was done and the apprentices ate dinner together, Mateo and I joined hands and walked out into the night as usual. The moon lit Mateo's face. "Tell me about college."

I looked up into his dreamy eyes. "When I first applied to UC Davis, they rejected me. But I appealed, wrote a new essay telling them that I had admired the university ever since middle school."

"And then you got in?"

"I was accepted, thankfully. I made good friends who now have started their careers in San Francisco." I didn't want to explain to him that I was confused about what I wanted to do.

Mateo lifted his chin. With pride in his eyes, he said, "In Argentina, college is free for everyone."

"Whew, don't tell my dad that. Davis was expensive." At that moment, I remembered graduation day, that sad day without my mother. My smile faded.

Mateo stopped walking and pulled me to his chest. "What's gotten you sad all of a sudden?"

I leaned my head into him, feeling his heart pumping. "My mother was diagnosed with breast cancer during my sophomore year. She was once a vibrant and happy woman, but she struggled through the chemotherapy and radiation treatments. She lost weight, lost her hair, had no energy to get up and go to work. Finally, in my junior year, she died." My chest ached, and I could feel tears welling in my eyes. "Everything in San Francisco reminds me of her. That's why I'm down here, traveling around, trying to find a place where her death doesn't haunt me every day. I can't bear to go home."

Mateo's eyes grew troubled. "My father died from a heart attack when I was nineteen. I was devastated. My mother was too, but our whole family stayed together and helped each other heal. The pain of losing him is less now."

I took a long deep breath. We were now kindred spirits, linked by a heart-wrenching loss.

"When I was growing up," Mateo said, "my family lived in a suburb just outside of Buenos Aires. My mom still lives in our little house with my sister Yadira. My two brothers are married and have children. Our family spends lots of time together, eating barbecue and playing games late into the night. Family is important to me."

I thought about my broken family and pictured my father and brother sitting quietly at the dinner table, eating in silence.

Mateo cleared his throat. "I applied to work here to give

me time to think about my career. In my last job, I was a web designer for an online language company."

I squeezed his hand. "Impressive."

He squeezed back. "I was good at it, but it was time to grow. I thought working with my hands in nature would help me gain clarity about what I wanted to do next. I want a better job so I can support a family." He paused and looked up at the sky for a few seconds. "I've asked Sara if my mother can visit me at the winery, and Sara said yes. My mother wants to meet you."

I hadn't thought of any other person coming into our relationship. Certainly not this soon. "She does?"

"Yes. And I want her to meet you too, *mi querida*." Under the silver moon, he kissed me, wrapping his long arms around my back and shoulders so that I felt snug inside a cocoon.

Our whole world was silver that night: the Virgin Mary standing at the edge of the vineyard, the wires supporting the vines, the irrigation lines, Mateo's eyelashes, his hair, his face, the skin inside his open shirt. But while I was enjoying the beautiful scenery, my chest filled with apprehension. Mateo's mom was coming to visit?

Mateo smiled so wide, dimples appeared in his cheeks. "I want to show her everything. The winery, the kitchen, our dormitory, the vineyards, and especially the labels I made for this year's vintage."

He had taken all the credit *again*.

I decided to be a little more assertive with him because I didn't want him to think that I was a woman without an opinion and without talent. It was time that he knew what my dreams were. I changed the subject, but I stuttered with anxiety. "I . . . I . . . I want to go to Santiago and Cusco, and finally, to Machu Picchu. When my dad was in college, he climbed the trail to Machu Picchu, and found out that he wanted to be an architect. I promised my mother I would travel to find out what I wanted." My hands fluttered in front of my chest like moths around a light at night. Becoming self-conscious, I hid them behind my back.

Mateo looked into my face with a puzzled expression. He squeezed my hand and said, "But why would you want to do that? You went to college. Isn't that enough?"

I felt a little nauseous. "Traveling will distract me from losing my mom."

Mateo raised his eyebrows and leaned away from me. "Distract you? You can't avoid grief."

I opened and shut my mouth a few times before responding. "I'm not avoiding it. I'm trying to get over it."

Mateo furrowed his brow, but put one arm over my shoulders and led me further down a row of grapevines. When we walked past the Virgin Mary, I bent down to pick the wildflowers growing nearby and poked them into the little metal urn at Mary's feet. Remembering my mother's voice, I joined my hands together and recited the Hail Mary out loud, ending my prayer with a bow. Mateo placed his hands on my shoulders as I prayed. I remembered how my mother had placed her hands on my shoulders whenever she had something important to say.

As soon as I said *Amen*, a feeling of jealousy washed over me. I didn't want Mateo's mother to visit the winery. Mateo and I didn't have all that much time left before I left to travel. I wanted him to myself.

CHAPTER 16

A few weeks later, as I stooped at the edge of the vineyard pulling at the roots of weeds, Mateo's mother arrived. As I watched Mateo walk up to the taxi, open her door, and hug her, my chest tightened.

His mother was beautiful. Her olive skin glowed with good health, and her black hair flowed down her back in shining waves. She was shorter than her tall son, even shorter than me by an inch or two, but she had an hourglass figure and dressed impeccably in a deep pink blouse and complementary maroon skirt and jacket. A dark gray raincoat was draped over her arm and her kitten-heeled shoes matched it.

To empty my pail of weeds I had to pass by the front of the winery, and when Mateo saw me, he waved me over. "Leonie, I'd like you to meet my mother, Violane."

Violane spoke in a thick Argentine accent that vacillated like music. "*Mucho gusto.*"

I stood speechless for a long moment, comparing her immaculate outfit and manicured hands to my soiled T-shirt and jeans.

I tried to wipe the mud off my fingers, coughed, and bit my lip. "Welcome to . . . to Bodega Romero Winery, Violane. I'm sorry, my hands are dirty." Then I stood mute, rubbing my hands, pasting a smile on my lips while Violane and Mateo chatted about what the name of the winery meant.

I waited for a break in the conversation, then said, "Well, I'd . . . best . . . get back to work. Mucho gusto, Violane." I walked toward the barn and muttered under my breath. What a rotten first impression his mother must now have of me.

The next day, while I was sweating in the vineyard, Mateo spent a whole afternoon with his mother, touring the winery and property. They walked together, she holding onto his arm. He often looked down into her face as he spoke. As they strolled between the rows of grapevines and winery buildings, their hand gestures accentuated their conversations, and they chuckled. Later, I observed Mateo listening with respectful concentration as his mother talked. She listened to his every word. I bit my lip as I tried to pay more attention to my work.

At the end of the afternoon while I was leaving the vineyard and returning to the dorm for a shower, Mateo and Violane walked in my direction. I buried my face in the shade of my hat, tucked my chin down as if I was inspecting my shoes, and quickened my pace, disappearing through the door.

That Saturday morning, as Hanna, Franz, and I were preparing to make appetizers for the customers, Mateo and his mother walked up to Sara in the great hall where she was setting fresh flowers on the tables. I overheard Mateo say, "Sara, may my mother help make the appetizers today? She's a fabulous cook."

I cringed. Not only was Violane hogging all of Mateo's time away from me, but now he was letting her infringe on Hanna's and my appetizer success.

Mateo's voice sounded proud. "My mother makes fabulous family dinners."

I heard Sara answer, "How lovely. Violane, why don't you and Mateo visit the garden to see which plants can be harvested today?"

Half an hour later, Mateo and Violane came into the kitchen carrying a bucket of sweet potatoes, their earthy fragrance filling the room. Sara came in from the great hall at the same time, and

Violane pointed to the potatoes. "I know a recipe for making roasted sweet potato and goat cheese empanadas, Sara. We could make them for the customers today."

Mateo's eyes were bright in agreement.

I fidgeted with the spoons I was taking out of a drawer and coughed. "We've already set the menu for today."

Mateo scowled.

Sara took the bucket of potatoes from Mateo and held them up to her nose. "Mm, these smell like rich soil," she said, closing her eyes and lifting her face in pleasure. To me, she said, "Why not add another item for today's menu?"

Mateo puffed out his chest. "Mom, you can tell Leonie how to make the sweet potato goat cheese recipe. She likes to cook as much as you do."

I hunched my shoulders and sank my neck between them. What else was going to go wrong?

Violane got right to work. She blended flour and salt in a mixing bowl with dexterous hands, whisking in the egg, blending in the water, then pouring it into the flour to form a stiff dough. As I watched her, I clenched my jaw.

With floury hands, she lifted the dough out of the bowl and onto the cold granite counter. As she kneaded the dough, the muscles of her forearms rippled beneath her even olive skin, and the dough became smooth and elastic under the push and pull of her palms. She rolled the dough, turning the rolling pin from side to side to even out the circle she was making. All the while, in a clear confident voice, she gave instructions for making the sweet potato filling. Under her watch, I peeled the potatoes and put them to cook on the stove, feeling like all of my creativity had been robbed from me when Violane took over.

She took a break from her dough to test the doneness of the sweet potatoes with a fork. Next, she said, "When we drain the potatoes, we reserve some of the starchy liquid to make the mashed potatoes fluffier and more delicious."

I bent over the sink. Why not use milk as we always did? My mother used milk to make the potatoes creamier. I didn't say anything because Mateo was watching. As I mashed the potatoes, Violane leaned in close and told me when to add salt, white pepper, and goat cheese. She took the reserved cooking liquid and streamed it over the bowl I was using, adding it a little at a time. I could feel her breath over my shoulder; I felt tense with resentment.

When the sweet potato filling was done, Mateo's mother went back to preparing the empanada dough. As she used a biscuit cutter to make the rounds for individual empanadas, she whistled so quietly that I could barely hear the notes.

My mother whistled. Mateo whistled. And now Violane. It was as if they possessed an intuitive knowledge of how to be happy. But me, I couldn't even blow an even note. With a teaspoon, Violane placed the sweet potato filling into the center of each round, folded the dough into a crescent, and pleated the edges together into perfect braided edges.

I had nothing to do so I went over to stand by Mateo and reached to hold his hand, but he moved his hand away to clap at his mother's expertise. "*Bravo Mamá, bien hecho!*" Of course, she was a terrific cook. I clapped half-heartedly.

When the customers arrived, Violane helped us serve them. When she smiled and spoke to people, their faces lit up with joy, and they became even more social with her. But whenever she spoke to me, I became self-conscious and felt my face turn red. I'd been wearing old muddy jeans when she'd arrived in her stylish outfit. Now, I felt like a silly student, here in the very kitchen where Hanna and I had come up with the whole idea for the appetizer menu! Then there was Mateo. He seemed obsessed with her. Wasn't she here to get to know me?

What kind of impression was I making? Apparently, not a very good one since she was treating me like a child. Ugh. The visit wasn't going well. Did Mateo think it was?

After the customers had left for the day, Sara said, "Let's have a dinner in the great hall in honor of Violane."

Mateo sat next to his mother and told me to sit on her other side. I couldn't reach his hand under the table.

I made an effort to use polite and cordial language as I asked Violane about her children and her hobbies and listened as she described the big summer barbecues her family held: cooking steaks on the grill, playing board games on the picnic tables, and competing at bocce ball and cornhole. Her sons strung lights over the picnic area so they could stay up long after the sun set. One by one, her grandchildren fell asleep in a chair, on a blanket on the floor, or leaning over a table with his or her head resting on folded arms. Seeing how happy these dinners made her made me feel even more guilty about leaving Dad and Zach alone.

Violane asked me about my family, and I became tongue-tied as I explained that my mother had died while I was in college, and Violane reached out and touched my hand. I stuttered as I told her my father was an architect and that Zach was still in college at UC Santa Barbara.

Curiosity filled her eyes. "So, what are your plans now? I guess your time at the winery will soon be over, so what do you plan to do after that?"

I'd been dreaming about being with Mateo in the future, but we hadn't really talked about that. I didn't know what I was going to do except stay in South America. "I plan to travel to Chile and Peru for about three more months, and then get a job in Buenos Aires," I said, hoping she wouldn't pry any more. No such luck.

Her eyes grew large. "You're not going back to San Francisco? Your father and brother must want you near since your mother has passed."

My chest tightened. "Oh, no. I'm not going back there. I'm starting over down here." My voice wavered.

Mateo leaned over the table to look into my eyes after I spoke as if saying he had told me so. I caught my breath.

Violane was taking tiny bites of her crème brûlée, but she lifted her eyes away from the tiny round ramekin and looked at me. "Did Mateo tell you that his father died a few years ago?"

I squeezed my hands together in my lap under the table. My crème brûlée sat, untouched. "Yes, he told me."

"After Juan died, our family comforted each other. We can now move on with life, knowing we have each other to lean on. You can help your family relieve their grief, too, if you go home. You will heal too." Violane took another teeny bite of her dessert and placed it between her rosy lips, keeping her eyes on me.

A flood of grief filled my chest, tensing my shoulders and spreading like fire through my arms and legs. "Oh, I think we're all doing fine, and now I have Mateo. He's been a great comfort to me."

Mateo's face turned red, lines creasing his forehead.

The next day was the last day of Violane's visit. She would be leaving in the afternoon, so Mateo took the morning off to visit with her. As I was stooped among the vines pulling weeds, my hat shielding my face, I noticed them standing near my favorite spot on the property where the statue of the Virgin Mary stood. They were deep in conversation. I saw him look back at me once as he spoke, and his mother's eyes followed his gaze. Were they talking about me?

When it was time for Violane to leave, she, Mateo, Sara, and I stood near the front of the great hall talking about the vineyard. When a taxi arrived, Mateo bent down, picked up Violane's wrinkled leather suitcase, and placed it gently into the trunk. Then he pulled his mother's hand and led her to the car, opening the door. She paused, then turned around to face Sara and me.

"I am happy to have met both of you," she said, holding her arms open.

Sara grabbed me around the shoulders and pulled us into Violane's arms. "You're welcome here anytime. Please come back."

I pasted a smile on my lips. "I hope to see you again. Now I have a face to remember when Mateo talks about you." Violane blinked her long, dark eyelashes. Then without a word, she pecked me on the cheek, and turned to Mateo to hug him goodbye.

Watching the black taxi drive away, I silently inhaled and exhaled, long and deep.

CHAPTER 17

One day, Bolade asked us to follow him to the bottling room, where he placed us at different stations around the bottling rig. He sent Franz and Mateo out to get the wine from the aging room. Soon, we were running the bottling machine and filling empty bottles with new wine. Hanna and I topped the wine in the bottles with carbon dioxide to displace any oxygen that might be lingering above the fill line. Franz and Carlos capped the bottles with corks, and Mateo glued the labels on the front and back of the bottles. Cirilo and three other apprentices packed the bottles in boxes and transported them out to the storage room for shipping and sales.

Watching my fellow apprentices fill, cap, and label the bottles, I pictured my mother making fig jam over the stove. In a process that didn't seem much different from what we were doing in this bottling room, she stirred the thick sticky sweet fruit in a large pot, bottled it into four-ounce Mason jars, and steamed the jars in boiling water until the seals set. Sweat dripped from her brow like the water that now slid from my own forehead. Zach had waited in the kitchen doorway until she invited him in to lick the spoons. He loved her jam and spread thick layers of it on his toast every morning. As I stood among my peers in the bottling room, my heart felt warm with these memories. I was where I needed to be.

ONE SATURDAY, AS MATEO and I sat where the mountains touched the valley, he took my hands in his. I looked into his deep brown eyes and saw my life rolled out like a journey, a brand-new beginning. I yearned for his love.

Tears welled up in my eyes. "I love you. I don't want to return to the United States and never see you again."

Mateo caressed my arms with his fingertips. "After your travel, come to Buenos Aires and live with me then." He put his hands around my waist, pulled me toward his chest, and kissed me.

A tear trailed down my cheek. Mateo caught it with his finger and kissed it away with his lips. I ignored the flutter of apprehension filling my chest and said, "Yes, I'll do it."

His eyes lit up in the sun like topaz. "I'll finish my work here, and then I'll go back to Buenos Aires. When you get there, we can find an apartment."

My promise to Mom had brought me to Mateo. I was going to stay in Argentina. How was I going to tell Dad?

WHEN SPRING CAME, THE vineyards sang like Beethoven's Violin Concerto. The pruned-back branches stretched out along the wire supports like sinewy arms. Leaves wriggled out of them, and tiny clusters of green fruit pearls popped out to find the sun. The bees droned among the branches. Butterflies fluttered here and there looking for food, and ladybugs inspected the vines for pests and nectar. I breathed in the fresh air, filling my lungs, and the energy of spring infused me with optimism. When Mom died, I had split into pieces, but now I was stitching myself back together. I was less anxious, soothed by the consistent days of work in the vineyards and my successful project with Hanna. But most of all, I was excited about my upcoming travels and my future with Mateo.

Most mornings, the apprentices weeded between the rows of vines, poked through the branches for evidence of unwanted pests, set pheromone traps to deter infestations, and turned on the irrigation sprinklers. Every day when I passed the Virgin Mary, I sent love to my mother, wishing I could show her what I was doing and learning. I sent love to Dad and Zach, hoping they would like Mateo and wish me a happy life in Argentina. The Virgin Mary looked down upon me with her sweet face, the sun glistening in the raindrops around her shoulders where the rosaries hung like cascades of blessings.

In the afternoons we continued bottling the wines, and on the weekends we served wine and appetizers to visitors. Sara helped clean up the kitchen on Saturdays and Sundays after the visitors left, and one night she shooed away most of the apprentices and invited Hanna and me to drink wine with her.

When Hanna took out wine glasses for the three of us, she noticed that one of them had a chip on the rim. "I'll throw this away."

Sara put her hand on top of Hanna's. "Not at all, Hanna. That chip doesn't ruin the whole glass. It's still good enough for drinking to our friendship."

Could I live a happy life if I was scarred and chipped by sorrow?

I turned to Sara and Hanna. "As you know, I'm leaving in a few weeks."

Hanna stood up, took a few steps toward me, and embraced me in a giant hug. "We're friends forever, right?"

My eyes teared up as I hugged Hanna back. "Yes, friends forever. And when I'm finished figuring myself out, I'll be an even better friend."

I held Hanna at arm's length and said, "Two weeks ago, Mateo asked me to move in with him. After traveling, I'm flying to Buenos Aires."

Sara raised her wine glass. "I want to make a toast. Raise your glasses, you two. Leonie, may the love that you give to others find its way back to you in all its forms. I know you will find your purpose when you find out what you love the most." We clinked our glasses together.

"My mother told me that very same thing."

Sara's eyes looked soft in the afternoon light. "Women who find their peace know that the most important purpose in life is to love. Your mother understood this, of course."

I took another sip of wine and returned Sara's smile, then dropped my eyes as they began to tear again. "I came here to forget about the pain of losing her, but so many things remind me of her."

Sara set her wine glass on the counter. "My mother lived until she was seventy-five years old. I had a long time to be with her, and she taught me many things. Even so, when she died, I was overcome with grief. I knew that everyone eventually dies, but I didn't really expect my mother to pass away when she did, so I know how you feel. Losing her was like losing a part of myself."

I started to cry and tilted my head to compose myself. "My m-mother was my r-rock."

Sara placed her hand on my shoulder. "I found my mother again in my own life. I've discovered how I am like her and how my values originated in her. This makes me happy. Every day, I feel her with me as I love my family, work in the vineyard, and train the apprentices. I hope you find as much happiness as I have found here on this vineyard with my family."

Hanna raised her glass. "Yes, let's toast to that!"

LATER THAT NIGHT WHEN the moon shone outside my bedroom window, I thought about how wondrous it was that everyone on earth could see the same moon lighting up the sky each night, pushing and pulling the ocean currents at the edges of all the continents, like a mother guiding her children with a gentle nudge here and there.

No wonder I was so devastated by the death of my mother. She was my moon.

A WEEK BEFORE THE end of September, Luna video-called me. "I'm quitting my job and going back to school in Buenos Aires. I'm going to live with Clarisa."

"*What?*" was the only reply I could muster.

Luna laughed, a pealing of bells. "I'm going back to school to become a park ranger. That's one reason why I got this job in Iguazú Falls—to see how I'd like living in a national park. Well, I love it, and it's going to be my new career!"

I dropped my jaw. "That's exciting! When will you leave Iguazú Falls?"

Luna squirmed in her chair. "My last day is in two weeks. You're leaving the winery in a week, right?"

"Yes, so?"

She leaned toward the screen. "Can I meet you in Cusco and tour Peru with you? I'd like to hike to Machu Picchu. What do you think?"

I danced in my chair. "Oh my gosh! *Can* you? I'd love it! I'm going to Chile for four days, but then I'll fly to Cusco."

"Why Chile?"

"I figure if I can ride over some of the steepest mountains in the world, I'll develop some nerve. I need it."

Luna pressed her palms over her cheeks. "I'd be terrified."

I chuckled. "I might be."

"Are you sad about leaving the winery?"

"I am. Sara was a good mentor. I learned a lot: how to run a professional kitchen, create a menu, maintain the vines, harvest, and make wine. The work was therapy too."

Luna picked up a cup and sipped. "I'm glad you like my aunt."

"I made a new friend too, a woman named Hanna from Hungary. We worked in the kitchen together."

Luna snickered. "You're making friends everywhere, chica."

"I have other news. I fell in love with a man named Mateo. You'd like him. He's from Buenos Aires."

Luna clasped her hands together. "Wow, chica, you've been busy."

"He's asked me to move in with him. After Machu Picchu, I'm flying back to Buenos Aires and we're finding an apartment."

"Have you told your father?"

A glitch caught in my throat, and I coughed. "No."

Luna opened her eyes wide. "Why haven't you? What about Zach? Have you talked to him?"

I shook my head in frustration. "I've been talking to Dad and Zach every Sunday. I just haven't told them about this. They'll think it's a bad idea. They already think I should be home. Telling them I'm staying is going to devastate them."

Luna focused on the screen. "Are you sure about this?"

I took a deep breath. "Living with Mateo will make me happy." Yet why was I feeling nervous about this decision?

Luna smiled, but then looked to her left as if someone had come into the room. "I have to go soon, but I can't wait to hear about your plans. For now, what time should we meet at the Cusco airport?"

CHAPTER 18

I was about to discover whether I was brave or not.

I arrived in Mendoza early in the morning, and by 7:00 a.m. was sitting in the first seat on the second floor of a double-decker bus. While porters passed out breakfast sandwiches, the bus entered Highway 7 toward the steep triangular Andes Mountains. A sign announced the name of the pass—Paso Los Libertadores—and Mount Aconcagua rose like a sentinel on the right, looming like a guardian over neatly lined vineyards and charming wineries dotting the vast Mendoza Valley. With every minute that passed, the giant Andes range inched closer and loomed over the landscape like a crowd of ghostly figures.

We'd been on the road only twenty minutes when my ears started popping. Every mile brought surprising views. The famous Puente del Inca Bridge, a natural arch of rock, stretched over the Las Cuevas River, a tributary of the Mendoza River. Cacti spotted the foothills in haphazard polka dots. Snow capped the tips of the mountains, and deep gorges—carved by millions of years of river flow—cut into the valleys between the peaks. Herds of alpacas and llamas grazed in the valleys. Pristine mountain lakes punctuated valley crevices like mirrors for the clouds. Thick forests of pines blanketed the sides of the mountains with dark green foliage. Brilliant-colored birds—blue-and-black toucans, red-and-green quetzals, and orange-headed cocks-of-the-rock—flew in and out of the trees. A lone condor—a great black body, large white patches on its wings, a wattle on its neck, and a dark red comb on the crown of a bald head—sailed in front of the mountain range, scanning the land for carcasses.

The highway was so steep I tilted back in the comfy seat without using the recliner. In back of me, parents helped their children open their sandwiches, friends exclaimed as they sighted animals, and an old man buzzed his snores.

In three hours, the bus reached the Chilean border at 10,000 feet and joined a queue of dozens of other vehicles. The bus emptied, and we were herded like sheep into an immigration point where travelers handed over their passports. Then we reboarded the bus until it was time for our luggage to be checked for illegal goods.

After twenty minutes, we disembarked again, walked up to the conveyor belts to find our suitcases, then stood in line for inspection. Salsa music blared through tiny overhead speakers.

A border guard wearing a short-sleeve black shirt, camouflaged trousers, and a gun in a holster shouted, "Silence!"

My heart jumped.

Another guard pointed to my backpack. "Whose bag is this?"

I inched forward, raised my hand, and shivered next to him. He yanked open my backpack like a robber searching for jewelry and dug through my clothing, his hands disappearing within its folds. He said, "Got any fresh fruit in here?"

I shook. "No."

The guard dumped all my clothes and the statue of the Virgin Mary that Sara had given me out of the bag and rifled through a pile of jeans, T-shirts, underwear, bras, and socks in front of the crowd.

My face heated up as I stood by, helpless.

Then the guard shoved my clothes and the statue back into my backpack and shouted, "Cleared!"

I shuffled forward, pushed my clothes back into my bag, zipped it closed, then slunk back to the crowd of tourists.

The guard picked up the suitcase that had been next to mine, a green one with a pink ribbon tied on its handle. "Whose is this?"

A small woman crept forward and raised her hand. He flipped open the case, rummaged inside, and lifted out a bag of mangoes like a trophy, showing it off to the rest of the passengers. "Confiscated!" he bellowed, throwing it into a large garbage can. He slammed the bag shut and waved the woman out of his way. With hunched shoulders, she took her case and crept to the back of the group.

I tightened my fingers around the handle of my backpack as I watched the guards search several more pieces of luggage, each time impounding the offending contents and dismissing the guilty passengers like flies. What kind of country was Chile with all these harsh border patrol officers? Was I going to be safe traveling alone?

We reboarded the bus, and the bus driver pulled out of the border station toward Chile. The road was a series of switchbacks seesawing up the steep terrain toward a tunnel in the mountain. On the side of the road, a huge statue of Cristo Redentor de los Andes looked down upon the highway like a beacon of hospitality. The driver stopped the bus on the shoulder of the road so we could view the statue from the front and right windows. He spoke through the microphone. "This statue was erected here in 1904 when Chile and Argentina resolved their border dispute and pledged eternal peace between their two countries. The statue is seven meters high and made of bronze. Its sculptor was Mateo Alonso from Buenos Aires."

I whispered, "Mateo, a good name."

The driver continued. "On the statue's one-hundred-year anniversary, Argentina declared it a national historic monument. Engraved in Spanish at the feet is the following pledge: 'Sooner shall these mountains crumble into dust than Chileans and Argentinians break the peace which, at the feet of Christ, the Redeemer, they have sworn to maintain.'"

The bus eased back onto the road and lumbered up the rest of the switchbacks before the highway straightened out and entered the tunnel. I took a deep breath to relax myself. Except for dim overhead lights in the middle of the square chute, the tunnel was pitch black. The bus driver navigated the narrow shaft, still gaining altitude. After what seemed like hours but was only twenty minutes, the bus started to descend, lumbering down inside the dark heart of the mountain, its headlights revealing a sign welcoming us to Chile. With the darkness surrounding me like a blanket, I relaxed back into my chair and closed my eyes. No one on the bus spoke, and the only sound was the engine echoing in the cavern like a rhythmic hum.

I awoke to a bright light washing across my eyelids. Dazed, I opened my eyes and blinked. The sky, painted in a wash of white and blue streaks, extended far out into the distance until it disappeared into the horizon. Where was the land? I pulled my onyx necklace out of my shirt, clutched it in my fist, and wished for courage. Below, miles and miles of a serpentine road wound down the mountains like the bellows of an accordion. The grade was so steep that the road seesawed back and forth in countless folds, and ant-sized cars and beetle-sized buses crawled down the paved and potholed road. There were no barriers to prevent them from sliding off to a sure death.

My chest tightened, and I gripped the arm of my seat, squeezing my eyes shut. We'd never make it. The bus tires were going to slide on the gravel and pitch off the edge. I was never going to see Mateo again. Or Dad and Zach. *Why* didn't I go home? *Why* did I choose to take this ride over the Andes? I should have flown to Cusco. What was I trying to prove? That I had some kind of bravado? My onyx felt sweaty in my hand.

Wait, I said to myself. I tucked my onyx necklace back into my shirt. *Stop the negative thinking*, I thought. *I might never have this opportunity again.*

The scenery had been gorgeous: the Argentine side of the mountains—desert cacti, glaciers, precipitous peaks, rock formations, remote lakes, ravines, canyons, wild animals living in peace. And then the statue of Christ the Redeemer with its pledge of peace between Argentina and Chile. All the things I'd seen would inspire me long after the trip when I was miles and miles away.

If I was going to end this adventure on a positive note, I'd have to change how I was looking at the situation.

The miniature vehicles crawled slowly down the accordion road, and none of them caught their wheels on the precipitous edge. None of them pitched into oblivion. Our experienced bus driver had made the trip many times before.

I'd never take this trip again, never see this scenery—mountains taller than they are wide, like skinny isosceles triangles. Never again would I see how they sweep down into the Chilean flatlands. How the desert dust and glaciers feed the cacti and the forests grip the steep sides of the highlands. Behind me, I heard gasps and sighs.

My mom had wanted me to be a "trailblazer," to be adventurous, to be brave. This was my chance. I'd keep my eyes open all the way down the mountains so I could remember the serrated peaks, the serpentine road, the changing views of the sky as I traveled down to the Chilean valley.

I looked across the expansiveness of the sky to find the Pacific Ocean, but there was only a gray seam where the blue layer of sky met a leaden haze. In the wide blue, ospreys circled like haughty sentinels, dipping their heads in the western winds as if heralding the mountain peaks, Gothic spires of ancient cathedrals. The bus twisted and turned, and then the valley began to stretch west out from the foothills. Verdant pastures were dotted with grazing alpaca herds, looking like toy animals. Beyond the prairie, the city of Santiago rose like a platter of sparkling blue and glittering skyscrapers, gleaming stone buildings, colorful roofs of houses and tiendas. Swirling belts of freeways snaking around the city shone silver in the stark sunlight. My heart pumped loudly in my ears.

Eventually, the bus descended from the foothills onto the flat highway that turned west into the city. Neoclassical palaces and churches flanked the streets like old men wearing their best clothes. Plazas, green with lawns, shady from the shadows of palm and bay trees, colorful with borage flower bushes, and sheltered from the winds by the old buildings surrounding them, opened the city to the pale sky. The sun sank to the west and the city's shadows grew longer.

Men sat on wooden benches, their arms gesturing in passionate conversations. Along the streets, women walked together, carrying colorful baskets and bags, chatting, sometimes with small children a few steps behind them. Teenagers, wearing jeans and T-shirts, skateboarded down sidewalks, yelling to each other in slang. Students peeled out of school buildings, carrying backpacks and musical instruments. It was like the whole city came out to welcome us.

The bus pulled into a bus station, and the air filled with chatter from passengers, some weary with a fear of heights and others elated with the memory of a new venture. We all stepped down and grabbed our suitcases as the porter unloaded them from the bus's storage vault. One little boy who had sat a few seats behind me next to his father was whistling. Clasping his hands behind his back as he followed his father away from the bus station, the boy's lips were pursed into a perfect O. He flung back his head and laughed, then took up whistling again. I watched the father and son stroll down the street, and the boy's whistle faded into the city's sounds.

I'd been brave, and my courage began to make me stand taller. But I yearned to feel as carefree and happy as that boy. I pursed my lips and tried to whistle.

Air. Only air.

AS SOON AS I REACHED the lobby of my hostel near the Plaza de Armas, I opened my laptop and video-called Mateo. His face lit up the screen at once. A longing filled my chest and I regretted leaving him. I tried to smile. "I miss you already."

His wide grin lit up his face. "Miss you too. How was the bus ride over the Andes? Did you close your eyes?"

I squealed, shaking off the last of the fear from the trip. "At first I did, but then I told myself that it was the experience of a lifetime, and I was going to keep my eyes open and enjoy the view. So, I did." I gave Mateo a step-by-step description of my journey, including the little boy who whistled like he hadn't a care in the world. I said, "When I'm with you, I feel like that." We talked for almost an hour before my eyelids began closing.

Being brave was exhausting.

CHAPTER 19

A strange woman was about to teach me a lesson.

The next morning, I set out to see the city of Santiago. I took the metro to the central market. The Mercado Central was gigantic, its yellow building covering several blocks, its facade a series of arches covered with striped yellow awnings. In the center, a gigantic arch, decorated with iron filigree and topped by a yellow-and-white pediment, served as the palatial space's major entrance.

Once inside, the din of thousands of voices, footsteps, knives on steel, recorded music, acoustic guitars, and baritone singers shocked my senses. A pungent fish smell permeated the air, and I covered my nose with my hand, pausing to take a first view.

Light poured through window-sized openings in the cast-iron roof. A sign near the door explained that the gable had been shipped to Santiago from Glasgow, Scotland, in 1872. Air circulated the room from the breezes blowing in and out of the ceiling, and I wondered how much worse the fish smell would be without the ventilation.

Never in my life had I seen so much seafood. Trays of bodies, shells, legs, fins, and scales created mountains of offerings. Black, blue, silver, red, white, opaque, pink, and gold flesh covered slab after slab, stall after stall, aisle after aisle. Skinny, fat, long, round, and giant fish—sardines, sea bass, red snapper, crabs with short legs, crabs with long legs, corvina, pomfret, merluza, locos, camarones, salmon, mussels, and octopus. An aquatic splendor, the ocean's grandiose diversity and immeasurable plenitude were on full display.

Behind the counters, fishmongers, dressed in white coats and rubber boots, wielded knives like samurais, cutting fish into pieces. I watched one young man filleting fish for several minutes, his hands switching back and forth like a magician.

I shouted at him above the din. "How many fish do you fillet in a day?"

He grinned at me like an actor on stage waiting for applause. "One thousand, I think." When I thanked him for his response, he took his sharpening tongs and drummed them on the metal counter like Ringo Starr.

I chortled, waved, and moved down the aisle, turning and walking through the throngs of shoppers until I found the restaurants. Rows and rows of tables, less than two feet apart, were filled with people, plates of cooked fish in front of them.

A waiter, dressed in a starched white button-down shirt and black trousers, was passing among the tables with a platter holding a large crab. "*Toma una foto de la jaiba!*" A woman held up her cell phone. The man sitting opposite her at her table took hold of one of the crab's legs and bit on it. She clicked and the camera flashed.

After a few minutes of wandering around the tables, I found the host. He led me through the crowd to a tiny wooden table with two blue metal chairs. I plunked myself down onto the hard little chair. "Gracias."

I jumped when he slapped a menu down in front of me. "*Bienvenida, chica!*" Two musicians, playing acoustic guitars and singing in deep voices, skirted around the tables. I tried to concentrate on the menu despite the noise and bustle. When the middle-aged waiter came, I ordered *caldillo marino*—a broth with mussels, clams, fish, onions, and coriander.

I smiled and said, "A glass of water and another of white wine, *por favor*."

When the waiter came back with a glass of water a few minutes later, I drank it from top to bottom. When he brought the wine, he filled my water glass again. "Thirsty?"

I sipped the wine. "Yes." It was refreshing after a hot morning.

The stew came in a large bowl, steaming. The waiter set down tiny vessels of pepper, coriander, and lemon and told me to add them to the stew as I wished. He placed a plate of bread to the side. I blew at the steam and used a spoon to stir the concoction. The guitarists sauntered past my table blasting their instruments.

After paying for my lunch, I strolled over to the area where art vendors displayed their local products. Garish stalls showcased purses, shawls, T-shirts, dolls, Chilean flags, and other handmade wares. I walked up and down the aisles admiring this poncho or that purse, smiling at the vendors. Women held their babies in their arms as they waited for buyers. Male vendors shouted, "*Buenos precios!*" As I turned the corner at the end of an aisle, I spotted a thatched hut over to the side. A sign next to the open grass door said "*Psíquica.*"

Intrigued, I stopped, staring at the sign. What would a psychic say to me? Would she be able to tell my future? Maybe she could tell me about my new life in Buenos Aires with Mateo. Tentative at the open door, I peeked inside. A woman wearing a bright pink ruffled dress was seated at a table about six feet in front of me. Around the walls hung various pictures of the Virgin Mary: Mary with Jesus, Mary with an angel, Mary with her cousin Anne, Mary riding on a donkey with Joseph beside her. The woman was laying cards on the table. Each one had a picture with a caption on it. I stood there watching her until she looked up.

I raised my voice. "Are you available?"

Her voice was sweet and melodious, and although the cacophony outside the hut was deafening, I heard her. "Come in, come in."

I sat down in the comfortable purple chair in front of the table and scooted my feet underneath it. "Can you tell my fortune?"

The woman's smooth brown face was framed by black curly hair that fell past her collarbones and onto her breasts, where it hung in ringlets. Her pupils were like espresso coffee, dark and rich. When she smiled, her open lips displayed a set of perfectly spaced white teeth.

She looked into my eyes as if she was searching for a faraway place. "Hmm. Why do you want to know your future?"

I didn't expect to hear a question and wrung my hands in my lap, struggling to respond. "I want to prepare for anything that will be bad. I also want to become less confused about what I'm going to do in my life." I placed my palms on the edge of the table.

The woman stretched toward me and took my hands into her own. Hers were like gentle sunshine and cool like a slight summer breeze all at the same time. I relaxed my shoulders.

The woman's smile lit up her eyes. "If good things happen, they will be joyful events. You don't need to prepare for happy times. If bad things happen and you already knew they would come, you would have suffered long before they occurred. Let me tell you about the past and future."

She let go of my hands and sat back in her chair. "Anything on earth can reveal the past. The blooming of a crocus can manifest where a bulb was planted. The words in a book can illustrate the creativity of a writer's process. The movement of the clouds in the sky can reveal where rain has fallen. Even a hand or a face can reveal whether a person has lived a peaceful or a stressful life.

"The future? That's harder to predict. Why? Because the future is not formed until it happens. When the moon crests over the beach at night, we may predict that the crabs will crawl out of their hiding places and across the sand, but the crabs may decide not to do so for a myriad of reasons. Every cell, every breath, every burst of energy is connected to the whole universe, but all life-forms possess free will. They create their future through their actions." She leaned forward again and squeezed my hands. "This is the best advice I can give you. Pay attention to the present. When you work on the present, you are building your future, step by step, decision by decision, choice by choice. Building a future is like planting a seed. If you plant it in poor soil, forget to water it, and never let it get light, the seed will shrivel up and die. If you nestle it in rich soil, water it with love, and let the sun shine upon it, the seed will grow into a healthy plant. So, take care of your present and it will grow into a wonderful future."

I wasn't satisfied. "I want to know about the love I have for a man named Mateo. I'm going to live with him after I finish traveling around South America."

The woman looked into my eyes as if she could see my heart. "If you want great love, you must first love who you are."

"What do you mean? I'm trying to figure that out right now."

The woman's topaz eyes gleamed. "That's a wise decision. Explore yourself. This process will teach you who to love. A great love will love you for who you are."

Was the woman saying that Mateo didn't love me for who I was? That couldn't be right. He *said* he loved me. I loved him.

Her melodious voice softened. "You have relationships in your life that you have not nurtured. Unless you heal these relationships, you may damage other loves of your life."

My dad's face flashed through my mind. Zach's face came next. My mother's face appeared. I closed my eyes. "I'm doing fine," I said, trying to pull my hands out of the woman's grip. She held onto them, didn't let go. After a few seconds, I relaxed. "I'm traveling so I can find out who I am, what I want to do with my life."

"Your confusion about what you want to do has a purpose. In your search you will try many paths, and as you follow these various ways you will have opportunities to learn about yourself. If you were not confused, you would not search. If you don't search, you will never discover yourself. Your confusion is a gift from the divine, not an obstacle as it seems to be."

The woman released my hands, and I gripped them together, my fingers folding over each other. For a few moments, my mind went blank and I struggled to know what to say. Then a surge of hope washed through me. If I searched enough, I would find what I wanted to do. I lifted my chin and said, "Thank you for your encouragement." I stood up, placed her fee on the table, and waved as I exited her studio.

CHAPTER 19.5

In the fall semester of my freshman year in college, my friend Jasmine gets raped at a party. The first person I want to talk to is my mother, so I ask Jasmine if that's okay. She makes me promise not to tell anyone else.

"Mom, Jasmine got raped last night," I say over the phone.

"Oh no, honey. I'm so sorry."

"I want to help her, but I don't know what to do."

"Isn't there a women's counseling center on campus? Why don't you suggest that she go there for some support?"

"She did, Mom. But what can I do to help?"

For a few minutes, Mom doesn't respond. Then I hear her sigh. "Unfortunately, this is an experience that Jasmine must deal with. She might be afraid of being pregnant. She might be too scared to go out at night. She might feel ashamed. The best thing you can do is be ready to listen to her feelings. Show her that you love her and will support her even when she's confused and angry with life."

"But I want to do more!"

"Honey, I'm afraid you're finding out that life is not always happy and we can't erase the pain of some of our experiences. What we can do, however, is be there for one another. You could ask Jasmine whether she wants you to accompany her to her counseling appointments at the women's center. Does she want you to be with her when she tells her parents? Does she want you to keep it a secret? Do whatever she needs and change your support if she changes her mind."

CHAPTER 20

The next morning after showering, I dashed downstairs to the dining room, where a free breakfast was being served. I paused in the doorway to admire the view. The far wall was all windows, and the rooftops of Santiago spread below them like a colorful carpet. Tiled roofs, steeples, domes, and office building tops covered the city almost all the way to the ocean. Just before the distant sea, a strip of sand connected it to the Pacific. The twin steeples of the Catedral Metropolitana, Santiago's most famous neoclassical church, rose into the sky. Santiago had a whole collection of beautiful Catholic churches, similar to those in Argentina, but I wanted to visit something more unique. In my guidebook, I found the Baha'i Temple, a nondenominational worship space for people of all faiths.

Throughout the wood-paneled room, travelers sat alone or in groups of twos or threes on strong oak chairs at wooden tables. Sconces glowed on the paneled walls and wide-shaded lamps lit up the tables as if the room were a library instead of a dining room. The light from the windows and the lamps created a bright but cozy atmosphere.

Along the side wall, a counter offered breakfast fare: dulce de leche brownies, empanadas, small ham sandwiches, and a variety of fruits. I walked up to the drink buffet and poured myself a cup of strong black coffee, to which I added a heavy serving of cream. Grabbing a plate at the food counter, I scooped up a large helping of fruit and took a ham sandwich, wanting to be sure to eat a big enough meal to last all morning.

Scanning the room, I found an empty table by the window and sat down. I whispered words of gratitude for my safe trip to Santiago and chuckled when I remembered the precipitous winding road the bus had traveled down the Andes. I sipped coffee as I leaned over the metro map to find a stop that would get me close to the temple.

THE BAHA'I TEMPLE STOOD on a plateau surrounded by foothills. From the metro station, I walked out of the city toward an open, grassy plaza. In the center of the plaza rose a structure unlike anything I had ever seen. The temple was shaped like an onion. White walls like fan blades hung from the top and swirled down around the sides, leaving openings at the bottom. I climbed the long, stretched-out cement staircase leading up to the temple. The Andes rose like frozen goddesses behind it, and eddying pathways created open-air places. A variety of cacti dotted the landscape. When I reached the top of the stairs, I saw the reflection pool, extended out to the left of me, like the one in Washington, DC. Its glassy surface reflected fluffy clouds and a pale blue sky. Approaching the building, I changed my mind about its shape. Instead of an onion, the edifice was like a closed lotus flower with numerous swirls that complemented the undulating topography of the Andes behind it. The white fan blades were monumental glass wings, through which I could see inside to a marble interior. People milled in and out of the entrances.

I stepped inside a wide-open room. Seating, curved around the walls of the interior, created a nature-inspired environment. There were no religious statues or altars, just spaces for standing, sitting, viewing, and contemplating. Looking up, I gazed at the oculus in the apex of the dome. From there, sunlight spilled down into the great room like liquid gold, reflecting off the glass and polished marble floors. I wandered around the curves of the room enjoying the sensation of the moving light—mesmerizing. The glass, the walnut pews, the marble floors, the shadows of people, and the light reverberating in the room danced around me. My mind relaxed and cleared.

I sat down in a pew to people-watch. Against an exterior panel of the glass was a couple, both about sixty years old, holding hands and raising their other hands up to the ceiling. Their eyes were closed and their mouths moved in unison with words I couldn't hear. Sitting on a walnut pew about a quarter of the way around the room was a young man dressed in jeans, a T-shirt, hiking boots, and a backpack. His head was bent down and his hands were clasped in his lap. Beyond him, I saw a woman in her twenties dressed in a nun's habit—a black veil pinned to her curly black hair with bobby pins, a black gown with bell sleeves that flowed down to her ankles, and black leather shoes—sitting on the pew. One of her palms was cupped over her mouth and tears streamed down her face. She swatted her wet cheeks several times as she sat alone.

My heart ached for her. What was bothering her? Why was she sitting alone? Should I help? I clutched my daypack and crept past the praying man closer to her. After a few seconds, I tiptoed forward and sat down beside her. "Are you okay?" I peered into her face and extended one of my palms.

She gasped, looking up with red-rimmed eyes.

I offered her a tissue packet from my daypack. "I'm sorry that you feel bad. Please tell me what's wrong. Talking might help."

The nun blew her nose with the tissues for a few long minutes, then wiped her eyes. Deep furrows creased the skin between her brows. Anguish filled her eyes. "I don't know what to do, what to do."

I spoke in a gentle voice. "My name is Leonie. What is yours?"

Her eyes flickered to the floor. "I'm Sister Magdalena."

I nodded slowly. "Nice to meet you, Sister Magdalena."

She raised her face again, her eyes showing surprise. "You seem nice. Please call me Alma like my mother does."

I touched her arm. "Why are you sad?"

A flood of tears gushed down her cheeks. "I made a commitment to be the bride of Christ. Now I'm a traitor. I've broken my vows and have nothing to live for."

My heart jumped at her words. I felt her despondency and wanted to help her. "I can't imagine that you've done anything that bad."

She wiped off some tears that were hanging from her chin. "I'm a leper who is defiled."

Empathy filled my heart. "You're being hard on yourself. Surely you didn't do anything depraved enough to be judged so harshly."

A sob escaped from her mouth. She clasped both hands over it as tears rushed down her cheeks. I put an arm around her and squeezed her shoulders. She was stiff and resistant. "I must have done something to make him do it."

I rubbed her shoulder and bent over to look into her distressed face. We regarded one another for several seconds. "Who did what? I promise you can trust me. If you don't want me to tell anyone, I won't."

She choked up another sob. "Maybe."

Alma didn't know me enough to trust me, but I knew I could help her if given a chance. "You can. I think we're both about the same age. I'll understand how you feel."

She sniffed. "Father Peña."

Something serious had happened. "Father Peña? What about him?"

She twisted her hands in her lap. "He calls me to his apartment, and I have to go. I have to obey him."

I knew immediately she must have been molested or raped. Jasmine had felt anxious all the time: afraid she was pregnant, worried that her rapist would spread rumors about her throughout campus, riddled with shame.

I had accompanied Jasmine to the women's counseling center several times. Her fears came back again and again. I held her as she cried. She felt violated, and part of me did too.

I looked into Alma's face. "Why does he call you to his apartment? I'm pretty sure I already know."

She turned abruptly, looking shameful. "How could you know?"

My chest was tight with pain for her. "I think your experience is similar to one that a friend of mine had."

Alma blinked for several seconds, scanning my face. "Father Peña makes me undress and get into bed with him. He touches my private parts. Last time I was with him, he raped me. I don't know what I did to make him want to do this to me."

I gasped. "Did you tell your Mother Superior?"

She shook her head solemnly. "She's always talking about how wonderful Father Peña is and how lucky our convent is to have him. She would blame me."

I clenched my fists in my lap. "This is not your fault. You're the victim and Father Peña is a criminal. He has misused his authority." Maybe Jasmine's story would help.

I moved closer to Alma on the pew and took her hands in mine as I shared Jasmine's story. How ashamed and afraid she had been. The counselor had helped Jasmine understand that she couldn't defend herself and that she was the victim. She spent the rest of the year visiting the counselor until her shame lessened and she could walk around campus again, unafraid, wiser than before.

I lifted Alma's chin. "I'll go with you to talk to Mother Superior, if you want support."

"You don't even know me."

"I know that my care can help you heal." Jasmine had confided in me that the support of her friends was an essential part of her gaining back her self-esteem. My mother had been right. It was easier to fix problems with a friend's support.

I squeezed her hand. "Let me be your friend today." A strong urge to help her had overcome me, made me feel stronger somehow.

Alma took my hand and tugged it. "I'd like that. I can't live like this anymore, feeling like a mortal sinner, wishing I could escape, hating my own body. I came here to ask for God's forgiveness. Priests have no power here. It's just God and me. And a miracle happened. You came to help me."

We held hands, stood, and walked out of the temple together. I asked, "Are you from here?"

Alma's shoulders tensed. "I grew up in Santiago. Every Sunday, I went to church with my parents. I admired Jesus and wanted to spend my life doing the same good things that he did with his life. My mother and father were pleased when I chose to be a nun."

Together, we passed the inspiration pool, stepped down the long white staircase, and walked to the metro.

After getting off at the stop near the convent, I suggested that we get a bite to eat before talking to Mother Superior. "You want to feel comfortable so you can stay calm and clear. Food will help settle your stomach." I ordered hot tea and empanadas. While we nibbled on the savory pastries, we decided that I would accompany Alma during her meeting with Mother Superior, but Alma would do all the talking.

She looked frightened. "You'll stay with me the whole time?"

I nodded. "The whole time. I won't leave until you feel stronger. You'll see. Mother Superior will believe you and help protect you." I was proud that Alma had confided in me. I seemed to be good at this, helping people in distress. My mother had been a counselor, but Aunt Patty said before that she wanted to be a psychologist. That meant that she had wanted to help people like Alma. Maybe I could achieve what she hadn't.

MOTHER SUPERIOR WAS IN her office, sitting quietly at her desk, when we arrived. Alma knocked tentatively on the half-open door. “May I talk to you, Mother?”

Mother Superior looked up. Her gray hair was tucked inside a wimple and black veil. She wore a black gown with a belt around her waist and a white apron-shaped scapular. Her creamy skin glowed, and a pair of gold-rimmed glasses had fallen a little down her nose. “Come in, come in, Sister Magdalena. Oh, you’ve brought a friend. Hello?” She pushed her glasses back up with her pointer finger.

Alma stood in front of Mother Superior’s desk, trembling—her chin, her limbs, her body, her clothing fluttered. “This is my friend Leonie. I went to the temple to pray today about my problem. Leonie helped me understand that the best thing to do was to talk to you.”

Worry lines formed between Mother Superior’s eyebrows. She motioned to the chairs in front of her desk. “Sit down, both of you. Make yourselves comfortable and take some deep breaths. You’re quivering to death, Sister Magdalena.”

In a halting voice, Alma told Mother Superior about Father Peña’s appointments. About how he touched her and then raped her. She told Mother that she was sorry to be saying bad things about the priest, but I had helped her understand that Father Peña was wrong to do what he did.

Mother Superior’s face grew serious—the creases in her forehead deepened, her mouth set into a tight line, her jaw clenched. When Alma was finished, Mother said, “Wait here.” She went outside her office to find the logbook used for when nuns left the convent. Back at her desk again, she flipped through the pages and paused on one date and then another. From my chair, I could see that Sister Magdalena had signed her name out many times for the purpose of going to meet with Father Peña.

Mother stared at the open book, her hands holding it tightly. “Highly unusual.”

Alma looked at me.

Mother placed her elbows on her desk and clasped her hands together in front of her. "I don't think you would make up these stories, Sister Magdalena. I believe you. You are to never go to Father Peña's apartment again!"

Tears flooded Alma's face. I handed her some tissues, and she wiped her cheeks before speaking. For long seconds, the room was quiet. "No, I would never make up such horrid stories, Mother. Please help me."

Mother took a deep labored breath. "I will. You must be patient, but today I will report this to the bishop and follow the case so that you are protected. Your safety is my responsibility, and I'm determined that you feel safe here to lead a prayerful and peaceful life."

A sob escaped from Alma's throat as she clasped her hands together and bowed to Mother. "Thank you, Mother. Thank you for believing me." Tears fell onto Alma's cheeks, and when I handed her more tissues, she sponged her eyes, squeezing and drying them, sitting back in her chair, anxiety clouding her face.

Mother placed her hand on her desk and moved it toward me. "Thank you for supporting Sister Magdalena, Leonie. Please stay with her for a while. You've shown great compassion and have comforted her."

Alma gave me a tour of the convent's dining room, chapel, and garden. In the garden were several statues of angels in various poses. Near the statues were benches where the nuns often sat. Alma and I sat together on one of the benches. Without thinking, I created a prayer. "Please God, help Alma heal from this horrible event. Help her become a strong woman so that she can help others who experience violence and mistreatment."

Alma was still shaking, but turned to me. "Thank you for my miracle today, Leonie. I don't know what I would've done if you hadn't shown up."

CHAPTER 21

Back at the dormitory, I took my laptop into the breakfast room and video-called Elaine to tell her about Alma. "I felt so bad for her. I went back with her to the convent and helped her tell the Mother Superior about it."

"You did?"

I nodded. "Did I do the right thing?"

"Of course. A problem like that is difficult to deal with alone. I'm sure you helped her. Mother Superior can stop the abuse. I bet that priest gets transferred. I hope he gets convicted."

I leaned toward the screen as a wave of satisfaction ran through me. I had helped Alma. This was something that I was good at. Helping people in distress. "This event has inspired me to think about being a mental health counselor. Aunt Patty told me that my mother wanted to be a psychologist, but when she got married she became an academic counselor instead. I wonder what the education requirements are for something like that."

Elaine leaned back. "Wow, your travels *are* helping you explore what you want to do. I'm impressed. I think you're on the right path."

I beamed. "I think so too."

Elaine then became quiet, gazing at me through the screen. "But you could be more compassionate toward your dad and brother. You're not the only one grieving your mom's death. Your dad was her husband. I'm sure he feels torn in two. Zach is your younger brother. You've always stood by him, and he needs you now."

I shook my head with my eyes closed. These emotions were too overwhelming. I felt guilty about ignoring Dad and Zach, but I could hardly handle my own feelings. "Please, Elaine, don't."

She took a deep breath. "Okay, but think about this as you plan your life. Family is forever." Elaine adjusted in her seat. "I'm working at a temp agency now and applying for full-time jobs. One of the jobs I got was to create a marketing program for a charitable organization that preserves redwood forests in California. Another job was at the San Francisco Convention Center for animators for the film industry. I'm meeting interesting people." *She* sure sounded happy and content.

AFTER TALKING TO ELAINE, I called Mateo. He didn't connect right away, but after a few tense seconds on my part, his image appeared. I described meeting Alma inside the Baha'i Temple and what she told me about Father Peña.

His eyes filled with compassion. "How horrible. I'm proud of you for helping her. That's what I like about you. You're kind and compassionate."

Flickers of joy ignited in my chest. "Oh, Mateo. I wish you were here. I miss you so much."

He shrugged. "I miss you too, Leonie. Are you sure you want to continue traveling? When I'm done at the winery, why don't you just meet me in Buenos Aires?"

I felt like he had punched me. Didn't he understand that I intended to keep the promise I made to Mom? "I learned something about myself today."

He blinked and waited.

I leaned in, my chest fluttering with excitement. "I discovered that I'm good at helping people in trouble, people who need someone to encourage them to change their lives and sort out their problems. Maybe I should go back to school to become a psychologist."

Mateo's eyes turned cold and he turned his face away, his mouth tensed in a hard line. "Haven't you gone to school enough? Anyway, it's getting late, and Bolade wants us to get up early tomorrow morning."

A stab pierced my chest. He didn't want me to go back to school? That was my decision, not his. What *did* he want? At the end of the call, he said goodbye without telling me that he loved me.

I had to talk to someone reassuring. Like Aunt Patty. I clicked on her number. She logged on after two rings. "Leonie, what a surprise!"

I placed my hands over each other on my stomach to hold myself together. "Hi."

Her eyebrows shot up in surprise. "Are you okay?"

I shook my head. "I thought I was for a while, but now I'm not. I helped someone out of a difficult situation and discovered that I'm good at it. I'm thinking I'd be a good psychologist, to help people with serious issues."

Her eyes perked up. "That's great! I don't understand what the problem is."

My shoulders drooped. "Well, I just talked to Elaine, and she told me that I wasn't being considerate of Dad and Zach by staying in South America. And the guy I'm dating down here doesn't want me to go back to school. I'm going to move in with him after I climb up to Machu Picchu. He wants me to spend time with him, period."

Aunt Patty tapped her closed mouth with her fingers for several seconds, thinking. "Okay, let's take these one at a time. You know Elaine. She's a family girl. Of course she thinks you should come home. She'd never want to do what you're doing. Besides, I'm sure she misses you."

I nodded, agreeing with her.

"Besides, family relationships *are* important. It's okay if you want to travel, but don't ignore your dad and Zach. Even when you're far away, you can maintain good relationships with them."

That was something I hadn't thought about.

She continued. "Now, who's this guy that you're moving in with?" Her expression had gone serious.

I smiled, thinking of Mateo's handsome face. "His name is Mateo. I met him at the winey where I worked and fell in love. He comes from Buenos Aires. I met his mother when she visited us there. We have spent months together—walking, hiking, biking, and talking. One night, we even danced the tango."

Aunt Patty pursed her lips. "Well, let me just say this, he sounds wonderful, but your mother got married before she fulfilled all her dreams, and she regretted it. Think about whether you want to have the same thing happen to you."

THE NEXT DAY, I WENT back to the convent to visit Alma. When I arrived at 5:00 p.m., the gate was locked. I pulled the rope of the brass bell hanging to one side. Its chimes echoed through the garden. A young nun dressed in a black habit with a white wimple over her hair appeared from among the fruit trees. She brushed her hands and skirt before arriving on the other side of the gate. I stuck my face between two of the iron bars. "I'd like to see Sister Magdalena, please."

The nun tilted her head. "It's almost time for dinner, but I'll see if she's available." The nun bowed and walked through the garden, opened the wooden front door, and disappeared into the building.

A few minutes later, Alma walked slowly up to the gate. Her eyes were red, drooping with black circles. When she saw my face, a glimmer of hope crossed her face. "Leonie, you're back."

I pulled on the locked gate with my hands. "May I visit for a while?"

Alma sighed. "We're having dinner in about ten minutes. Let me ask Mother Superior if you can join us. Sometimes we have guests."

TEN MINUTES LATER, I WAS sitting at a long wooden table next to Alma. The dining room was a grand rectangle with four long tables, each one surrounded by eight nuns. A mural of Mary had been painted on one of the walls, her arms outstretched and welcoming. Young women brought each of the nuns a bowl of steaming soup. They placed plates of coarse bread in the center of the tables and poured them wine from large glass carafes.

Mother Superior stood up from across the table in front of me. "Let us say our evening prayer, Sisters." She pressed her hands together and led a prayer of gratitude for the food and each other. "Amen."

I picked up the soup spoon, dipped the tip of it into the hot soup, then tasted the thick broth, a fragrant blend of chicken, white beans, and vegetables. Mother Superior placed her hands on the table beside her own bowl. "You might be surprised at the food. We don't eat the delicious fish from the sea like most Chileans. We've taken a vow of poverty, so our food is simple. Nevertheless, Sister Sestina, our cook, is a wonderful chef. She can turn beans and potatoes into the most incredible concoctions. Sometimes I feel guilty eating her delicious meals."

All through dinner, Alma ate silently beside me. I arched my brows at Mother Superior across the table. She slyly waved her spoon in my direction. "After dinner, let's have a talk in my office."

Later, while Alma went to the chapel to pray, Mother and I walked to her office. "Sit down, Leonie."

I sat. "Alma is depressed. I thought you were going to help her."

Mother folded her smooth hands over her desk. "I reported the incident to the bishop, but what you don't understand is that the world can be a complicated place."

"What do you mean? Father Peña committed a crime. He should go to jail. It's simple."

Mother shook her head and frowned. "I agree. Father Peña did commit a crime, but he probably won't go to jail."

I raised my voice. "*He won't go to jail?*"

Mother raised her hand. "Calm down. Let me explain." She bit her lip. "In the Catholic Church, priests have power and it usually supersedes the wishes or welfare of everyone else."

My mouth dropped open. "But that's *wrong*! He *hurt* Alma. Probably for *life*!"

Mother tapped her hand on her desk. "Please lower your voice. I don't want the sisters to hear you." She sat a moment in silence, biting her lip. "I agree. When power is misused, as in this case, it's very wrong, yet unless the bishop expels Father Peña, there's nothing I can do except be vigilant in observing my sisters' activities."

I pressed my fists on Mother's desk. "I want to help. What can I do?"

Mother straightened her glasses. "You've already helped Alma. Without your support, she never would have had the courage to tell me about the abuse." Mother looked down at her hands on the desk and lowered her eyes. Then she raised her head and peered into my face. "But her healing will be difficult. Her life's dream has been shattered. She believed in the Catholic faith, but Father Peña's actions destroyed those. Now she's questioning her vows to be a nun. What are they worth? What do they represent? I'm going to enroll her in mental health counseling. Maybe she'll get back her faith one day."

I twisted my hands in my lap. I didn't have any idea how hard it would be for Alma after she *reported* the abuse, and I wasn't qualified to help her. I didn't know about trauma or mental health. But what I did know was I had an intense desire to help people like her. I *had* to go back to school to get the necessary training and skills.

After talking to Mother Superior, I took a walk with her and Alma around the garden. Alma had worked in the vegetable garden until noon. Her parents were farmers, so she had a green thumb. Mother said, "Sister Magdalena grows the most delicious tomatoes that I've ever tasted." The whisper of a smile crossed Alma's pale face.

After the sun trailed its orange skirts on the horizon, I closed the convent gate behind me and walked back to the hostel. The dormitory was quiet when I arrived. I dressed for bed in the bathroom and slipped under the covers as the gibbous moon lit up my corner of the room. The rest of the room was dark with shadows.

The world was cruel. I hated that. My hope was one day I could make it different.

CHAPTER 22

I picked up my luggage from the turnstile at the Alejandro Velasco Astete International Airport in Cusco, Peru, and joined the crowded line for customs, looking around for Luna ahead of the booth. Then it was my turn to approach the customs window. A dark-haired man wearing an olive-green button-down shirt with an official badge pinned to the front asked in a brusque voice, "What's the purpose of your visit?"

"Vacation."

He flipped open my passport to an empty page, inked it with a Peruvian stamp, then waved me on. I grabbed my large backpack, pushed the strap of my daypack higher on my shoulder, and walked out into the main part of the airport. Luna was supposed to arrive before me, so I had expected her to be waiting for me somewhere in the vicinity of customs. Where was she?

All around the cavernous room were shops and restaurants lit with bright spotlights and neon accents. One storefront window showcased Gucci and other high-end purses set up in rows like baskets of fruit on a market stand. Another window displayed the *New York Times* Best Sellers printed in Spanish.

People were everywhere. In a café, men dressed in jeans and button-down shirts stirred lattes. Teenage girls in running shoes and skirts sat at tiny tables eating pastries. A tavern next door blared a soccer game from several televisions while men sat at the bar holding martinis, scotch, and beers. A seafood restaurant offered ceviche and fish on a colorful menu beside the entrance. A few couples read the menu before wandering through the door.

All of a sudden, Luna's arms were around me. "Hello, Leonie, I'm thrilled to see you!" She squeezed me, lifting my feet off the floor.

I laughed and regained my balance, struggling to hold onto my luggage. "Where were you? Welcome to Cusco, Peru, both of us!"

Luna looked chic in a multi-blue silk blouse tucked into the front of her designer jeans. Her short leather boots and a leather moto jacket finished off her ensemble. "I got here forty-five minutes ago at Gate 10, just over there." She hoisted a large backpack behind her and grabbed a little suitcase from near her feet. "Hey, chica, let's go."

A Machu Picchu guide was waiting for us outside, holding a white sign with our names printed in beautiful cursive writing. The guide, somewhere in her early thirties, had long black hair and a glowing complexion. I had expected a tall, large-boned man, someone who had enough strength to carry a heavy backpack and camping gear. I couldn't believe this petite woman was a hiking guide. She was dressed in hiking pants, hiking boots, a T-shirt, and a hoodie, her rosy face brimming with positivity. "Welcome to Cusco, the gateway to Machu Picchu! My name is Vilma, and I'll take you to your hotel today, then give you advice about how to spend the next five days to prepare for your sacred journey to Machu Picchu."

Luna shook Vilma's outstretched hand. "We're eager for the hike."

My hands felt sweaty, so I wiped them on my pants before reaching for Vilma's.

In a white passenger van, Vilma drove us to the Saqray Hostel in the central historic district. "This is the tour van that will pick you up from your hostel in five days. You'll have to be ready early since the hike starts at nine o'clock from the trailhead."

Once we were checked in and our luggage stowed in our room, we met Vilma in the lobby sitting area, a room with a colorful collection of bright blue doors; red, pink, and blue futon chairs; pots of cedar trees; and vases of fresh flowers on the tables between the chairs.

Vilma guided us to three chairs on one side of the room. Three large glasses of lemon water sat on the coffee table. "I'm going to be your guide for the hike to Machu Picchu, but for the next five days, you're on your own to acclimate to the 11,000-foot altitude. If you have trouble, please call me. I'll be around town meeting with the other hikers of our group coming into Cusco." Vilma sat back in her chair. "You'll be expected to carry a personal backpack only. Our porters will carry your luggage and any food that we need for the excursion."

Thank God.

Vilma picked up her water glass and took a long, slow sip. "For the next five days, I recommend that you do everything you can to adjust to Cusco's 11,000-foot altitude. Drink twice as much water and rest for the first few days." Vilma moved her hands with expressive gestures.

Luna leaned toward the coffee table. "What do you mean by rest?"

Vilma smiled and the skin around her eyes crinkled like pleated cupcake liners. "You can go to the market, eat out, walk around town, but don't take off on an ATV excursion to see Inca ruins. Wait a few days. Your body needs to adjust to the decrease in the barometric pressure and lower oxygen levels in the air."

I cleared my throat. "But it's okay to do some of those excursions after the first two days, right?"

Her smile faded and a serious expression covered her face. "If you're feeling fine, you should be able to do some stronger physical activity by the third day. Now, listen to my next instruction. It's important. Cusco is renowned for a drink called the pisco sour, but I recommend that you avoid all alcohol until you return from Machu Picchu. Alcohol dehydrates the body."

Luna threw her head back and chuckled. "We'll have to save the pisco sour for our celebration after we get back then." She leaned over and nudged me in the ribs.

Vilma waved her hand at Luna, dismissing her comment with a grin. "And another thing. Eat carbohydrates, lots of them. They provide energy for the body and require less oxygen to digest. But don't eat too much the night before we start hiking. You don't want any mishaps in the first few hours of hiking." Vilma winked a long-lashed eye at both of us and smirked. "The tour will have altitude medication available for any problems, but the most successful hikers are the ones who follow these guidelines. Understand?"

We nodded in agreement. "Yes, yes."

Vilma held out two tickets. "Here's a Tourist Ticket that you can use to visit up to sixteen sites around the city this week. Many of the historical sites are within a ten-minute walk from here. I hope you have a great five days." She handed each of us a small folder with a photograph of a hiker on the front. "The van will pick you up at four thirty on Monday morning. In that folder is a list of what to pack and what not to pack." She got up, threw her personal pack over her left shoulder, and shook our hands. "See you soon." I watched Vilma open the bright blue front door of the hotel and walk out to the tour van.

Luna leaned back in her pink chair. "I'm going to finish this glass of water before I do anything else."

I picked up my glass and drank half of the liquid in several swallows. "Me too. Let's take a walk after this."

Luna put down her empty glass. "Sounds good. Where to?"

I pulled my phone out of my pocket and searched for Cusco highlights. "According to my phone, La Plaza de Armas is only a six-minute walk. The Archbishop's Palace also is nearby. We shouldn't miss that since it was built on an Incan foundation of stone."

Luna jumped up. "Let's go, chica." Together, we walked out into the early afternoon sunshine.

With the sun shining on her, Luna's hair looked like it had flecks of gold in it. "Every South American city seems to have a Plaza de Armas," I said. "Why's that?"

"The Spanish built the Plaza de Armas as the center of each city. The name means 'Place of Weapons,' where soldiers retrieved their arms. Now these plazas function as the central meeting places. They usually contain government and religious buildings as they did when the Spanish were in power."

We sauntered through the Plaza de Armas, exchanging ideas on what to do for the next five days. When we arrived, a great cast-iron fountain came into view, dominating the middle of the square. We crossed the plaza and stood in front of the fountain, watching the water cascade down its sides from a small spout at the top, onto the large bowl at the center and into the ground-level basin. I read a sign etched on an iron plate. "How beautiful. This fountain was made in New York as a gift to the city of Cusco. Originally, a Native American statue stood on the top, but that collapsed in an earthquake. In 2011, a new statue of an Incan emperor, Manco Capac, was erected." The iron had tarnished to a mossy green.

Luna waved her hand forward. "Come on. I want to find the famous twelve-angled stone that is part of the foundation of the Archbishop's Palace." We headed down Triunfo Street toward Hatun Rumiyoc Street, which we found to be a narrow alley between walls of blocks on either side. In a few spaces on the ground, vendors had rolled out blankets filled with handmade jewelry and other local crafts. They waved at us, trying to convince us to buy something.

Luna touched one of the tightly stacked granite walls. "Look at how sophisticated this Inca structure is. The blocks are cut so accurately and fitted so close together that I couldn't even push a paper clip between them. We think *we're* more advanced than older civilizations, but when I see architecture like this, I think the Incas were more advanced than we give them credit for."

I halted in front of a wall and shouted, "I found the twelve-angled stone!" Sure enough, one of the stones, inserted tightly in the middle of the building's foundation, had twelve sides and angles of different measurements.

Luna placed her hand flat on its side. "Can you imagine how the Incas built this?"

I flattened my palms against the stone, tracing its edge with my fingernail. Whoever had built this had left a permanent mark on the world. Would I? What would my life mean?

Luna massaged her stomach. "Let's eat some carbohydrates. According to Vilma, we *need* to eat in order to fortify ourselves for the hike. Besides, I'm starving."

In the Barrio de San Blas near our hostel, we read the menus of several tiny restaurants until we found one offering stews made with beef, pork, potatoes, and vegetables. The waiter gave us a table by the window and brought us Siete Raices, an herbal drink made from seven herbs, which he said would help us build up our energy for the Machu Picchu hike. "I serve this to hundreds of customers every year who come to Cusco before they hike up to Machu Picchu."

Swirling on his heel, he rushed to the kitchen for our stews.

The bowls came steaming hot, resting on large plates with three pieces of toasted bread on the rim. We ate, dipping the pieces of toast into the thick gravy and using it to wipe our bowls clean.

The waiter came back to our table with a menu. "Why don't you finish with some *picarones*?" He pointed to a photo of a small platter of golden doughnuts. We agreed and ordered coffee to wash them down.

Later, at the hostel, while Luna was taking a shower, I video-called Mateo to let him know that Luna and I were safely in Cusco. I was still upset about my conversation with Mother

Superior and wanted to discuss it with him. When his face popped up on the screen, my heart skipped a beat. "Mateo, I miss you!"

He smiled that seductive smile and I felt giddy when he said, "I miss our walks at night."

I let myself enjoy the little pumps of my heart for a few seconds and folded my hands in front of the keyboard. "Luna and I are in Cusco at 11,000-feet altitude. We're drinking water and eating hearty to prepare for the hike in almost five days."

He shook his head and made googly eyes. "You chicas are too much. You sure you want to do this hike? I hear it's pretty strenuous."

I leaned on the desk toward the screen. "That's precisely the point. We're testing our courage, and I'm trying to figure out more about myself." I placed a palm over the onyx under my shirt and smiled.

"You don't need courage. You have me. I'll take care of you."

But he was wrong. Apparently, I needed my own courage to get through life. No one could grieve over my mother's death for me. No one could decide for me when I could help a friend or keep my eyes open during a scary situation. Besides, his comment was chauvinistic.

I pressed two pointer fingers over my mouth. "Hey, I want to discuss something with you."

He looked intrigued. "I'm all ears."

I bit one of my knuckles before I started speaking. "Remember I told you about Alma who had been raped by a priest?"

He nodded. "*Sí.*"

I took a breath. "Well, last night I talked to her Mother Superior, and she told me that it was unlikely that the priest would go to jail."

Mateo rolled his eyes. "I'm not surprised, but why are you worried about that?"

I tensed my shoulders and straightened up like I had a stick along my spine. "I'm upset. Alma has been devastated. I want to help her, but she needs professional counseling, maybe for years and years. This means that if I want to help people with mental illness, I have to go back to school."

He turned his head away again so I couldn't see into his eyes. "Seriously, you have enough education. Don't go back to school. That'll take time away from us."

Mateo turned back to the screen. The softness of his eyes had vanished. I could see the ridges of his bones beneath his cheeks and the tightness of his jaw. He didn't look like the man with whom I'd fallen in love. He was harder, somehow. Then I remembered how he had taken all the credit for the wine label project. He didn't want me to go to school?

I didn't want to be his shadow. When we said goodbye, I felt relieved.

CHAPTER 22.5

When Zach is ten and I am twelve, Mom and Dad take us down to Ocean Beach where the city lights are dimmer and we can see the stars more clearly. Dad builds a campfire on the sand and we sit around it.

Gazing up, I see a star with a tail streaking across the sky. "Wow, what's that, Dad?"

Zach points up and yells, "I saw it too!"

Dad follows our gazes. "Oh, that's a comet." Together, the four of us stare at the pinprick of light sailing across the sky, trailing a tail of fire behind it. Then, suddenly, it is gone.

Dad says, "Some people believe that comets signify new beginnings. Others say they represent joyful relationships."

I easily accept this belief since we are a happy, close family.

CHAPTER 23

The next morning, Luna and I slept late, planning to spend the day relaxing so we could visit the Cusco Planetarium that night. I wanted to learn about Inca constellations before starting on our hike to Machu Picchu.

At 5:00 p.m., we walked to Plaza Regocijo to meet a guide for the planetarium tour. She led us and other tourists to a passenger van, parked a few blocks away. The van's driver drove us up to the Planetarium Cusco, located in the midst of an archaeological site known as Sacsayhuamán and the ecological reserve known as Llaullipata.

The main planetarium building was a modest wooden structure, more like a residence than a planetarium. With the other tourists, we gathered inside a large interpretation room where another guide introduced herself as Maria. Maria sported blue glasses, had long brown hair, and spoke with precise diction. She wore black hiking pants and a black sweatshirt with a constellation of glittery white stars on the front. She spread her hands out wide as if trying to sweep us into the room. "*Buenas noches. Bienvenido al planetario.*"

When the audience's chatter ceased, Maria continued. "The Inca culture was an agricultural society, so stars played an important role in Incan lives. They built pillars on the mountains and the hills around Cusco, so when the sun, moon, or stars rose or set between these pillars, they knew when to plant their crops at different altitudes. They associated the planets and stars with gods."

A few tourists shifted their position. Somebody sneezed.

Maria pointed up. "For example, the sun was the god Inti."

My parents had taken Zach and me to the Chabot Space and Science Center in Oakland, where we learned about Ursa Major and Ursa Minor, the Big and Little Dippers. I could easily find these two constellations in the San Francisco sky even when the city lights blocked out most of the other ones. The stars fascinated me. Sometimes I imagined they were millions of eyes looking down on the earth, holding secrets.

Maria used her hands to help her explain the Inca astrology. "The Inca named their creator god Viracocha. They believed that everything on heaven and earth was connected, that every animal had a corresponding star. They grouped stars into constellations to create pictures of animals, gods, and heroes, but the dark spots in the sky were also meaningful. In the Milky Way, which they thought was a river, they identified dark spots that they associated with animals who lived in rivers." She pointed out some of the more popular animal constellations—the serpent, the llama, the fox, and the condor—and explained that the Inca believed that the constellations and dark spots interacted, living in harmony. She encouraged us to hike up to Machu Picchu, which archaeologists believed was a sacred ceremonial site, an agricultural experimental center, and an astronomical observatory. Finally, she swept her hands up toward the observatory. "Now you will go into the observatory, where José will introduce you to the constellations of the Southern Sky."

We shuffled into a dark room filled with rows of seats formed into a semicircle. The concave ceiling was pitch-black, and a light from the back of the room shone a stream of light high above our heads. A masculine voice spoke over the microphone. "Welcome to the observatory, where I'll be showing you the constellations of the Southern Sky. My name is José. Find a seat and lean back to enjoy the show on the ceiling."

As soon as José lit up the dome above, my brain burned with questions. How did the Southern Sky differ from the sky of the Bay Area? Were there different constellations? Were there similarities? My family had spent countless nights outside, looking at the stars together. How I wished Dad and Zach were with me now. My chest ached with longing.

José continued. "I see some of you are from the United States, and you're probably wondering if the Southern Sky is the same as the Northern Sky. It's not. Down here in South America, we can see a few of the same constellations as you see in the Northern Sky, like Orion, but we don't have a bright North Star down here, and we can see constellations not visible at all in the Northern Sky." The darkness of the observatory looked real. I felt small compared to its vastness. With a laser light, José pointed out the Southern Cross and some of the other constellations unique to the Southern Hemisphere. "Has anyone ever seen a comet? Do you know what a comet is?"

José's laser light pointed to a streak in the observatory sky, and his voice interrupted my thoughts. "Comets are frozen leftovers from the formation of the solar system composed of dust, rock, and ice. Their nucleuses can range from a few miles to tens of miles wide, and as they orbit closer to the sun, they heat up and spew gases and dust into a glowing head that can be larger than a planet. This material forms a tail that can stretch millions of miles. Most comets revolve around the sun in an elliptical orbit."

I felt like a comet without an orbit. I had told Mateo that I'd live with him in Buenos Aires, but now I wasn't so sure. I was learning about myself by traveling, but I was also becoming aware of what Mateo wanted me to be, and that didn't match my own dreams. He didn't want me to continue my education. Hike to Machu Picchu. Or develop courage. Hidden by the darkness of the room, I placed my hands on the sides of my face and squeezed my eyes shut. Tears leaked out of my eyes and dribbled down my cheeks. I leaned back in my chair, took a deep breath, swatted the tears off my face, and forced myself to listen to José.

BACK AT THE HOSTEL, Luna and I retreated to our room, got into our pajamas, and sat on the beds facing each other. I felt pensive. "I learned tons of stuff tonight, but you've spent your whole life under the Southern Sky. Did you know it all?"

Luna rubbed her eyes with her fists and yawned. "I didn't know about what the Incas thought about the stars. That was new."

I pulled back the covers of my bed and got inside, propping my head up on a hand and bent elbow. "Just think what we're going to see when we're out camping on the hike to Machu Picchu. There will be no streetlights out there at all, just the glitter of thousands of stars above us. Thousands of animals and Incan gods watching over us." I rested on my pillow and imagined a sky vaster than the planetarium.

Luna crawled inside her sheets and turned off the lamp. "Mm. What a nice thought."

I imagined Mateo's face. "Luna?" I wanted to talk with her about him. Ask her what she thought he meant by what he said. Whether I was making the right decision by moving in with him. "Luna?"

She was fast asleep, a mini-snore escaping from her mouth with every exhale.

I lay back in bed, picturing Mateo's face and fell asleep.

I DREAMED THAT ZACH and I were both comets. Zach, his face sad, flew around the sun in a perfect elliptical trajectory, his fiery tail arcing like a crescent in the black sky. He looked back at me with sorrow and stretched out a fiery hand. He couldn't reach me. My nucleus had lost its way, veering in all directions, my tail switching back and forth, out of control. He shouted, and his voice echoed through the heavens. "If you come home, you'll find your orbit."

CHAPTER 24

When Luna woke up, I was already awake, sitting on the bed, showered, and dressed in clean hiking pants, a T-shirt, and a hoodie. My sun hat was beside me on the pillow. She climbed out of bed and pulled her bath towel off a hook behind the door. Luna said, "Hey, chica, we've been taking it easy so far. Why don't we do a little hiking today? Yesterday, a tourist told me that she had taken a bus to Pisac, about thirty-five kilometers northeast of here, where trails lead to Inca ruins. There's also a market where vendors sell Quechuan crafts."

I rubbed sunscreen on my face, looking in the mirror over the small dresser between the twin beds. "I'm ready for that, but first I want to eat a big breakfast. I also want to come back to Cusco early tonight to eat a big carbo dinner." I had to be prepared for the hike.

Luna laughed. "A great day—eat, hike, eat. Sounds fun to me." She walked into the bathroom and closed the door. A few minutes later, I heard the shower running.

I took out my laptop, set it on the desk, and video-called Dad. In less than a minute, his face appeared on the screen. He was sitting at the dining room table with a cup of coffee in his hand.

Before he could say hello, I said, "Morning, Dad!"

He looked relieved. "I've been worried about you! I miss my daughter. Where are you now?"

I took a sip from my water bottle and set it down. "I'm about to hike to Machu Picchu. I'm in Cusco with Luna getting acclimated to the altitude before the hike starts."

Dad's eyes lit up, his brown irises like chestnuts. "Ah, I had a great time hiking to Machu Picchu. But you're my little girl. I won't be okay again until you come home."

I clenched my jaw, rested my elbows on the desk, and cupped my chin with my hands. "Dad, I want to tell you something."

He set down his coffee cup, a furrow between his eyebrows.

I took a deep breath. "I met a great guy at the winery. He's asked me to move in with him in Buenos Aires."

Dad's face paled. He dropped his head, clawed his pillowy hands over his cheeks, and shook back and forth. "Oh, honey, I can't tell you who to love, but are you sure you want to do that?"

I adopted a sarcastic tone. "Do what, Dad?"

He adjusted in his chair. "Zach and I will fly down."

All of a sudden, my chest was filled with anxiety. For a minute, I couldn't breathe. "Dad, I'm trying to set up a new life down here, and if you come, I won't be able to think straight. I'm okay. Trust me. I'm old enough to make my own decisions."

He brought his hands down to his chest and folded them over each other, his eyes hurt and sorrowful. I looked away, feeling guilty. I heard him swallow hard. Twice. "You're going to have a fantastic time. Hiking to Machu Picchu was one of my favorite adventures. Take care, though. Drink lots of water. If you feel sick, tell your guides. They'll know how to help you. Please call me as soon as you finish the hike."

No one could make me feel as protected as he did with his long arms and big hands around my shoulders. I missed his great bear hugs. "Really, I'll be fine, Dad." Behind him, I could see the kitchen. A dirty omelet pan was sitting on the stove, and the toaster had been pulled away from its place by the wall. Even without Mom, life in San Francisco seemed to be moving along as normal.

His eyes watered. He blinked a few times and said, "I love you, darling. I'm glad you're having a good time. Let's talk soon." The screen went dark, and I sat on the bed for a few minutes, still seeing his face in my mind.

AFTER LUNA AND I finished big breakfasts of sausages, eggs, potatoes, and toast, we found the bus station and bought tickets to Pisac. A group of six young adults, somewhere in their twenties, was waiting on the bus platform, chatting and laughing.

It seemed to be a universal quest for people to search for meaning in their lives. What wasn't universal, though, was what people did to find it. Some people, like Aunt Patty, went to a particular church every Sunday. Other people traveled to faraway places where ancient civilizations had lived and worshipped their gods. I was traveling around South America like the people around me.

When the bus opened its doors, we followed the tourists inside. We found a double seat right behind the driver, slipped our daypacks under the seat, and slid the window open a crack. The bus whizzed out of the city.

After a short drive through a stark landscape, the Andes rising in the east like guardians, the town of Pisac inched into view between a muddy, meandering river on the left and a mass of houses, courtyards, steps, and stone streets on the right. The driver turned into the town and stopped on the side of the Plaza de Armas. The passengers disembarked like bees leaving a hive.

Engine running, the bus driver skipped down the steps, wiped the sweat off his forehead, and planted himself in front of the milling tourists. "I'll show you where the trail starts. See that path on the right side of the church? It leads up to the ruins, which are above the town on top of the mountain. Since the climb is straight up the mountain, it'll take about two hours to get there. Coming back down is faster, or you can take a taxi.

The bus back to Cusco leaves every fifteen minutes." The driver flipped his hat back on his head and reboarded.

Luna and I crossed the plaza to where a tiny kiosk held trail maps. We each took a map and wandered over to the front doors of the church to read them. I wiped my brow with a bandanna from a pocket in my pants. "Look, walking up the trail in this altitude may be pretty hard. Let's take a taxi up the trail, then walk down when we're finished. I don't want to get into trouble for Machu Picchu."

Luna fanned her map in front of her face. "Okay, chica. The site looks huge, so we'll still get a lot of exercise." She flagged down one of the taxis slowly circulating in the plaza, and the two of us got in.

When we stepped onto the mountain, the Cusco Valley stretched out below us, with Cusco, the ancient Inca capital, rising across the basin, child-sized from this viewpoint. I gasped at the enormity of the landscape and the mountaintop's strategic view. "This site served as a defensive base against a political invasion of the capital," I said, reading from the map.

For the next hour, we climbed stone steps anchored in the hillsides leading to lookout points. We explored sweeping terraces covering the sides of the mountains, poked our heads through the windows of stone houses, followed the curves of aqueducts, marveled at the precise stonework of a temple set high above the other ruins, and rested on the stone walls of crumbling buildings, their purpose lost in history.

I pulled my water bottle from my backpack, flipped open the top, and drank long drafts of the warm liquid. Luna inspected a pile of stones. Other tourists walked silently through the ruins as if the place was a giant cathedral, sacred, silent, and awe-inspiring. In the stillness, I felt connected to a spirituality that I couldn't define.

I was realizing, like the Incas, that everything in the universe was linked and sacred. I scanned the landscape of the Inca ruins.

The granite temple that rose like a phoenix, the stone block houses that clustered around each other, the aqueducts that once pulsed with water, the terraced farms, the outposts rising like brave soldiers. Each ruin, each space was a part of a whole. Each Inca citizen had had a particular function.

Life, too, was like that. Each event was a lesson and contributed to a person's life. I watched Luna bending over the stones and thought about how I had only met her a year ago, but she now felt like an integral part of my life. I had only met Mateo six months ago. The psychic was right. What I did in the present determined my future. The decisions that I made were important, so I should be thoughtful, not frivolous, when making them.

The sun baked the ruins like a hot oven, and after a few hours, we, parched and thirsty, headed down the trail toward the town of Pisac. We navigated hundreds of stone steps and avoided slipping down the sandy cliffs into thickets of fern and cacti. Our knees jarred on the steep downslopes, our hiking boots gripping the slippery dirt step by step. The heat swelled up our hands like pincushions, and we bowed our heads to keep the sun away from our faces. The whistling wind pushed at our backs, its sound whirling around our heads like an endless melody, whispering about history, deeds, and the secrets that experienced women knew and young women had yet to understand. Finally, after two hours of staggering down the mountainside, we reached the Plaza de Armas mid-afternoon.

In the plaza, we asked a woman for directions to the Pisac Market. After thanking her, we hobbled down the stone streets until we saw colorful stalls lined up against the sides of ancient buildings. El Grande Mercado was a massive collection of crafts. Rough wooden tables covered with white cloths displayed necklaces strung in pink opal, silver chains, sparkling earrings, and copper rings. Poles connected with heavy ropes served as hangers for wool blankets, skirts, capes, and trousers. Colorful wool hats hung on poles with hooks drilled into their sides. Makeshift wooden easels held framed and unframed charcoal drawings and paintings of figurines and landscapes. Vendors sat on stools beside their displays or stood in twos and threes talking to each other as they watched the crowd of milling tourists. Two little girls, about six years old, wearing brightly embroidered skirts and jackets with hoods, wandered among the stalls, one carrying a baby goat in a sling in front of her chest.

A cluster of carts in one corner offered produce and street food for sale. Corn, carrots, fruits, legumes, and onions were piled on blankets on the stone ground like miniature hills. Gunnysacks, filled with various sizes and colors of potatoes, offered up earthy smells, and raw meat and fish with bold aromas were spread out in rows over the tops of wooden counters. Vats of stew spewed aromatic steam into the air in front of ruddy-cheeked tradespeople dressed in white smocks. The sweet scent of candies rose from a pastel-colored stall, and the bitter smell of coca leaves emanated from large garbage cans lined with thick blue liners.

As I passed a vendor who sold dolls with yarn hair and woolen clothing, I heard a female bargaining with her. "How much for a doll?"

The vendor looked up at the woman from her seat on the ground with sad brown eyes. A little girl sat next to her, and on her other side dolls made with yarn hair and embroidered clothing were piled on a square of fabric. "*Dos soles.*"

The tourist held out a single coin in front of the woman's face. "I'll give you *un sol* for a doll."

The vendor held a doll in her hands, and caressed its head like it was a baby. For a few seconds, her eyes became lost like a movie was playing in front of her face. She glanced down at the little girl sitting beside her with her empty bowl and spoon and sighed. "Okay, *un sol*."

The tourist tossed the sol into the vendor's lap, reached for the doll greedily, then turned to her friend beside her and said in English, "What a great souvenir! And I got it for almost nothing."

Quickly, without looking back at the vendor, the two women bustled away.

A tear fell from the vendor's eye as she put an arm around her daughter and squeezed her shoulder. "Wait just a little longer, *mi cariña*. We don't have enough money for food yet."

Empathy for the woman and her child filled my heart. I touched Luna's elbow, silently gesturing for her to wait, walked slowly up to the vendor's blanket, and squatted in front of her, saying in Spanish, "I'd like to buy one of your dolls."

The woman blinked her dark brown eyes and the tear fell down her cheek and off the edge of her jaw as she looked up into my face. She held two dolls up for me in front of her chest. One was dressed in a pink embroidered skirt and jacket, and the other wore a blue dress and a matching hat.

I took the pink doll from her to look at it more closely. Obviously, the woman had spent hours stuffing the body and limbs of the doll and hand-stitching them together. The doll's hair was teal, mustard-yellow, and dark-pink yarn, braided across the crown of her head, and hanging in tresses over her shoulders and down her back. Black felt eyes and a red felt nose and mouth were sewn onto the doll's muslin face. Its bright pink jacket and skirt were embroidered with green thread in a diamond pattern, and tiers of lace decorated the skirt, reaching the doll's toes. I took a twenty-soles banknote out of a pocket in my backpack and handed it to the woman. "I don't want any change. This doll is a work of art. Beautiful. I admire your talent and hard work."

The woman smiled, and her crooked teeth gleamed in the afternoon sun. Her voice was like a gentle whisper. "Gracias, gracias."

I reached down and took one of the woman's rough hands into mine. "Thank you for the beautiful doll. When I look at it, I'll remember how hard you worked to make her."

She pressed my hand with her gratitude. "Muchas gracias." When I let go, she placed her palms over each other across her heart and nodded slightly.

I waved to the woman's little girl, said goodbye again to her mother, tucked the doll under the crook of my arm, and walked back to where Luna was standing at the end of the aisle.

Luna gathered me in an embrace. "You're amazing. I'm sure you erased the bad memory of the other tourist with your appreciation for her work."

I held my doll up for Luna to admire. "That woman was heartless. She paid almost nothing for a doll that took hours and hours to make. I'm glad I showed the craftswoman how much I value her time and talent."

Luna hugged me again. "What I saw, chica, is that you have discernment and a great heart. I'm proud to be your friend."

Warmth filled my chest.

Feeling happy that night, I video-called Zach. I had been thinking about him a lot. He was sitting at his desk, an open biology book in front of him. "Leonie, I shouldn't even answer your calls. You've been selfish. Only thinking about yourself. Not me. Not Dad."

I bit my lip and nodded my head. "Zach, you're right. I've acted badly. I've been anxious. I'm sorry I've ignored you. Please forgive me." My cheerfulness dissipated.

Zach crossed his arms in front of his chest and frowned. "Where are you now?" The tone of his voice was chilling.

I hugged myself and trembled. "I'm . . . in Cusco with Luna, a friend. We're . . . getting ready to hike Machu Picchu in a few days."

He tightened his arms across his chest and stuck his chin up to the screen in defiance. "Sounds fun, but Dad told me that you're planning on staying in Argentina to live with a guy."

My face heated up. I shivered. "He did? Well, that's true. I'm trying to be happy down here."

He blew out a huff of air, his eyes like daggers. "You can't run away from grief, Leonie. You're going to have to face it one day or another."

I took a few seconds to collect myself. "Zach, I want us to have a good relationship. Can't you support my decisions? I'm an adult now."

He rested his chin on one of his hands and leaned so close to the screen that his facial features looked enormous and frightening. "Well, you're acting like a confused five-year-old. Call me when you grow up." The screen went blank.

CHAPTER 25

I woke up the next morning with a headache. All night, I had clenched my jaw, and I had nightmares that I couldn't remember. It took Luna half an hour to get me out of bed.

Finally, by 9:00 a.m., Luna and I sat at a table in the breakfast room with cups of strong coffee and breakfast pastries. Luna was holding a ChocoMuseo brochure. "Let's go on a tour of a chocolate plantation today. Research says that chocolate was first cultivated in the Amazon Rainforest more than three thousand years ago." She looked up at me. "This means that the civilizations before the Incas grew cacao trees and made a brew out of the chocolate beans."

Chocolate. Zach loved it. He first discovered it when he was three years old. My parents took him to a birthday party for his friend Kevin. During the party, they couldn't find him. Finally, they discovered him behind a door, stuffing his mouth with chocolate. Each week, he bought himself a chocolate bar, trying new brands to taste: Hershey's, Cadbury, Lindt, Ghirardelli, Ferrero Rocher, Toblerone. One time, during summer break, he even bought ingredients to try making chocolate himself. When I'd asked him how it turned out, he said it was awful. My mother made double-chocolate brownies every Christmas. She gave us chocolate eggs for Easter. Zach loved them all.

Aunt Patty craved chocolate too. Whenever you asked her what she wanted for her birthday or for Christmas, she said, "See's Candies." In fact, Mom's parents both worked for See's

Candies. Grandpa built and renovated their stores, and Grandma wore a white dress and black name tag and sold candy. Apparently, the love of chocolate was in our genes.

I yawned and looked up from my pastry at Luna. "Let's go. Who doesn't love chocolate?"

Luna looked up from the brochure. "The ChocoMuseo has a tour that leaves for a plantation in the Valle de la Convención at 10:00 a.m. The tour includes a walk in the plantation's orchard, a tour of the processing area, lunch, and a chocolate-making workshop. Eat up. Let's go."

By 10:00 a.m., we stood in the lobby of the ChocoMuseo with a group of other tourists, waiting for the bus that would take us to a chocolate plantation owned by the Sierra family. I heard excited conversations in Spanish, English, and Portuguese. Chocolate was a universal attraction.

After about an hour, the bus turned off the highway onto a rough-paved road leading up to a group of buildings surrounded by a forest of cacao trees. The trees, with white and dark mottled bark, rose loftily toward the sky, fanning their spindly branches around their trunks. Large red pods, like pointed oval garnets, hung from the trunk and branches.

A middle-aged man walked up to the bus as we disembarked. He wore dirty brown sandals, espresso-colored canvas trousers with pockets in front and back, a sweatshirt with frayed edges that was the same shade as the cacao bark, and a straw hat. His clothes, face, and hands were so brown that I imagined he would disappear if he wandered among the cacao trees. Even though he wasn't any more than five foot nine, he stood up straight, his bulky shoulders back, his large chest open with confidence. "A warm buenos días to you all. Me llamo Carlos." His voice reminded me of the purring of a car engine.

The group responded with enthusiasm. "Buenos días, Carlos."

Carlos waved a stocky arm toward the trees. "My family has owned and run this chocolate plantation since 2002. That's when the Peruvian government eradicated the coca farms that used to produce cocaine. The area sadly contributed to drug trafficking back then, but what were once scores of coca farms are now family-owned cacao plantations. The cacao tree produces a fruit from which chocolate is made. Follow me and I'll tell you the story of chocolate."

Oh, Zach would love this. My heart sank as I remembered our fight.

We followed Carlos around the group of buildings via a dirt path that led into the middle of the cacao trees. Carlos placed a hand on the trunk of a nearby tree and looked through the forest as he started speaking. "Many plantation owners bought land and planted trees, but their crops resulted in yields too low to earn a living. My family experimented with the growing of the trees in order to increase production. Now, we carefully fertilize the forest and prune the trees to increase the fruit yield—a year-round endeavor. We've shared our methods with our plantation neighbors so that the production of our whole region helps the income of all our farmers. Our region's chocolate is known for its quality and high nutritional value." No wonder he looked so confident. His family had done something extraordinary, helping their neighbors thrive as well as themselves.

Luna interrupted my thoughts. "I always thought chocolate was unhealthy."

Carlos grunted. "Chocolate itself is a beneficial addition to your diet. It's the added sugar that's unhealthy. The chocolate, though, contains antioxidants and anti-inflammatory properties."

Luna brought her fingers to her lips and smacked them. "It certainly makes me feel good."

Carlos cut a cacao fruit off of the trunk of one of the trees. "We eat the fruit right off the tree when it is ripe without any further processing. For lunch, we'll serve it to you. It's extremely nutritious. First, it's full of fiber and protein—good for digestion and muscle. It also contains potassium and magnesium, good for nerves and body cell production. However, most people love it because the fruit boosts your mood and instantly increases energy levels." Carlos held the cacao pod against the trunk of the tree and cut it in half with a large pocketknife, pulling the halves of the pod apart with his muscular hands to reveal the fruit inside—a white soft mass of pulp, dotted with dark-brown seeds. He passed the fruit to me to share with the others. Around us, trunks rose like muscular arms out of the forest floor and divided into multiple upward branches, reaching into a mass of leaves that crowded out most of the blue sky. Between the long skinny trunks, the Andes Mountains rose in the distant haze like blue triangles.

Carlos led us out of the forest toward the buildings. "I'm going to show you what we do to process the fruit once we pick it." He opened a large wooden door. Inside were several long tables in the center and stainless-steel machines along one wall. The ceiling was arched, like an airplane hangar. "This is where we extract the seeds from the pulp," said Carlos, using his big hands to point to the center of the building. "We save the pulp for our own consumption, and this is what you'll be eating for your lunch." He smiled, showing a top row of pearly white, twisted teeth. "Once the beans are extracted, we load them into these baskets and take them to the fermenting building. Come on." He waved us forward.

We followed him through the long building, out the door on the other side of the hangar, across a dirt expanse into the wooden door of the next building. On rectangular wooden tables—twenty-something yards long—were shallow pans filled with brown cocoa beans. The walls of the building only reached three-quarters of the way up to the curved ceiling, leaving the room open to the outside. "Here we ferment the cocoa beans. This process is somewhat like the fermentation of wine. Does anyone know anything about winemaking?"

I raised my hand. "I worked in a winery for a year," I said, hunching my shoulders.

"So, you know that fermentation involves yeast, sugar, and carbon dioxide. Yes?"

I nodded in agreement, hoping Carlos wouldn't ask me any questions. I was a novice, not an expert. One of the guys in our group brought his hand up to his face, and for a split second, I thought he was Zach. I got a glitch in my throat and coughed several times. Luna looked at me like I was an alien.

Carlos strode along the sides of one of the long tables. "The beans begin to germinate as soon as they are removed from the pods, as soon as the air touches them. Natural yeast settles on the sugary beans and the sugar splits into alcohol and carbon dioxide. Another by-product is acetic acid, which is vinegar."

Luna wrinkled her nose. "Is vinegar what I smell?"

Carlos chuckled. "Yep, the smelly by-product of fermenting." He continued to walk down the length of the table, as self-assured as a general. "As fermentation occurs, the temperature of the beans rises, causing the germ to die. We transfer the beans from one sweatbox to another so they get just enough oxygen and exposure to yeast." Carlos pointed to the shallow pans on the tables, indicating they were the sweatboxes.

Luna stepped forward to the front of the group. "How do you know when the beans are finished fermenting?"

Carlos turned around, lifted his foot behind his back, reached a hand down to his sandal, and refastened the frayed Velcro strap. "We test them for chemical compounds and inspect them for color and insect damage. Basically, though, they are done fermenting when the beans change from light brown to purple to a rich brown. The vinegar smell transforms into a chocolate brownie aroma. Come on, you'll enjoy the next building."

The next building was a structure of thick posts holding up a roof. Under the curved ceiling, rows of long tables filled the dirt floor. Large fans, positioned at either end of the structure, propelled air across the surface of the beans. "We dry the beans to reduce the water content. This reduces the roasting time and improves the roasting process." A warm, earthy aroma wafted through the room.

Finally, Carlos took us inside the last building, where stainless-steel ovens backed up against the walls. He opened the door to one of the ovens to show us the cylindrical baskets used to hold and turn the beans as they roasted. "The roasting sterilizes the beans, removes unpleasant acids generated during fermentation, and develops the complex flavors for chocolate that we all love."

Automatically, we lifted our noses to smell the toasty brownie scent that still lingered in the room from the last roasting process. I breathed in through my nostrils. "The temptation is irresistible."

Carlos opened the exit door of the roasting room and turned around. "Guys, I'm not going to show you the grinding and conching processes because you're going to experiment with those after lunch. Now I'll take you to the dining hall."

He walked out the door and strode back to the forest where he took a dirt path through the trees. We followed him and soon came to a small stone building surrounded by the forest. Inside were round tables set with cutlery and paper napkins and a buffet table covered with bowls and platters of food.

A middle-aged woman and two teenage girls waited behind the buffet table. Carlos stood in front of the buffet and smiled. "This is my wife, Ava, and two daughters, Sofia and Mara. They made the food that you will eat today, and they'll serve you as well."

Ava had wavy black tresses that she had pulled up behind her head into a thick ponytail. Her face glowed with health: a smooth forehead, deep brown irises, and clear skin. She wore a long multicolored tiered skirt under a white cotton blouse embroidered with flowers around the split neck. Her daughters had long black hair pulled back into braids. They wore white cotton blouses and long skirts similar to that of their mother. All of them were smiling.

My stomach grumbled. I hadn't had enough for breakfast, and the walk through the forest and processing plant had raised my appetite even more. "I'm famished, Luna. How 'bout you?"

"Me too, chica. *Tengo mucho hambre!*"

Carlos rubbed his hands in front of his trim stomach. "Before lunch, guys, you're going to taste the cocoa fruit before your palate is overwhelmed by other food. We're bringing each of you a small bowl of the pulp and seeds from the cocoa plant. It has a consistency of pudding, so you'll want to use a spoon."

We waited, watching Carlos and his family pass out miniature bowls filled with a white pudding. When Ava handed one to me, I took my spoon, scooped a small morsel of the pulp, and placed it onto my tongue.

Luna picked up her spoon. "What does it taste like?"

I mashed the pulp around my tongue and gums. "Mm. Honeydew melon? Lychee? Passion fruit? All of those combined?"

I put another spoonful into my mouth. "Mm, mm, mm, I could eat this all the time. Didn't he say it was healthy?" I didn't know that Carlos had walked up behind me and was watching our reactions.

His voice was husky. "Yes, very healthy. Remember, it includes protein and lots of minerals, the health food of the Amazon forest."

I wanted to tell Zach about the plantation. But when would we ever talk again? My chest throbbed. Tears welled up in my eyes. I blinked them back before anyone noticed.

Carlos invited us to line up at the buffet. The table, draped in a mustard-yellow tablecloth, displayed freshwater fish from the Amazon River, a creamy shredded chicken dish called *ají de gallina*, stir-fried beef known as *lomo saltado*, and *juane*—a steamed rice and chicken concoction cooked in banana leaves and flavored with spices, fried plantains, and mango salad. The meal was accompanied by fruit juices.

When we were all served, Carlos and his family filled plates of food for themselves and sat down to eat lunch with us, pulling one more chair at each of the four tables so every table included a family member. Ava joined our table.

Luna raised her glass of juice. "Hey, chicas, here's to great adventures." We clinked glasses.

I turned to Ava. "Your family is closely connected to nature. In my country, I know a lot of people who never have left the city, never seen a farm, don't know how their food is raised, and have never seen a night sky unpolluted by the city's lights."

Ava put down her fork. "That's probably true of people in Peru as well. I grew up in Lima, and had never lived in the country until Carlos and I bought this plantation. I'm happier living here, more relaxed. I learn new things every day since nature dominates our life with its weather and biodiversity: how to enrich the soil, how to protect the crops, what to wear when the winter winds chill my bones and the summer heat sears my skin. We live in rhythm with nature, and I feel more alive."

I nodded in agreement. "When I hike I feel more alive too, more in tune with the earth. My mother once said that nature was her church."

Ava laughed, her voice like the trickling of a tiny waterfall. "Nature *is* my church. The plants, the insects, the air, everything is interdependent. It's the best example of living in harmony." She picked up her fork again and started to eat.

Thirty minutes later, Carlos announced that each person would be making their own dessert in the chocolate-making workshop. "Listen carefully to Ava's instructions," he quipped with a smile. "The quality of your dessert depends on your confectionary skills."

Oh, Zach. You could learn how to make chocolate if you were here.

The workshop room was near the front of the property by the processing buildings. At each person's station was a bowl of cocoa beans, brown sugar, cream, and a small collection of cooking equipment. Ava stood at the front of the room behind a table. "Using your blender, grind the beans until they are the consistency of coffee grounds," she said, pouring cocoa beans into the blender pitcher on her table. She secured the lid and pushed a button. We followed her instructions. Soon, whirring sounds filled the room. She held a mortar and pestle in her hands. "Then, use a mortar and pestle to smooth the brown sugar into a fine powder. After that's done, add the crushed sugar to the ground cocoa and blend them into a powder."

I poured my sugar into the mortar bowl and pounded it with the wooden pestle until the soft sugar was an even consistency. Then I poured the sugar into the blender with the cocoa and turned it on.

Ava raised her hand. "Stop for a minute. We're going to continue blending our mixture to heat it up. When the mixture heats, the cocoa butter will be released from the beans, which will allow the mixture to moisten into a muddy consistency, a process called 'conching.' More blending creates a paste and, finally, the mixture transforms into a silky liquor."

For the next twenty minutes, the room was filled with the clicking of buttons, the grinding of machines, questions, comments, and laughter.

Ava raised her hands to get everyone's attention. "When your mixture is a silky liquor consistency, take the lid off your machine to release any condensation and acidic compounds that make the flavor bitter." More whirs, and as lids were lifted, bursts of air and swirls of louder churning filled the room.

Ava waited for a few minutes and then continued her instruction. "The next part of the process is called tempering. You want to cool your chocolate in stages. This encourages the most stable crystals to form, which creates good gloss, texture, mouthfeel, and snap."

Luna licked her lips.

I envisioned Zach licking the spatula when Mom made brownies.

Ava pointed to our tables. "At your station, you have two bowls. Pour warm water into the first bowl and let the bowl warm up. Meanwhile, the chocolate is cooling in the blender." My blender showed a cloud of steam inside. I looked back at Ava to hear the rest of her instructions.

The room became a clatter of pottery and spatulas as we started the tempering process. By the time we had poured all the chocolate into the cooled bowls, many people wore splashes of chocolate on their T-shirts and drips of chocolate down their forearms. Luna used her tongue to lick chocolate off her wrist. "Mm. Good already." She smacked her lips.

I licked my spatula. "Creamy."

Ava waved her hands, and the students paused. "When you're ready, pour your chocolate into the little custard cup and the rest into the chocolate mold on your right. We'll put the molds in the refrigerator, and before you leave today, you'll have chocolate bars to take home with you. Meanwhile, eat the chocolate in the custard cup for your dessert. There are spoons on the tables where you can sit."

We sat down, picked up a spoon, and started eating. Carlos walked between the tables as everyone ate. "Feeling happier yet? More energetic?"

We cheered as we licked the luscious brown cream.

THAT NIGHT, WE HAD to pack for the Machu Picchu hike since the tour shuttle would be picking us up at 4:30 the next morning. The bus had to get us to the start of the trail, Piscacucho—commonly referred to as km 82—by 7:30 a.m. After I was packed, I took my computer out to the breakfast room to call Mateo.

When he clicked on, he was standing in his dorm room. A suitcase was open on his bed, and clothes were draped all over the furniture. "Hey. I'm packing to go home to Buenos Aires."

My heart skipped a beat as he sat down by his computer to talk to me. "Luna and I went to a chocolate plantation today. All I could think about was my brother, Zach, who loves chocolate."

"Never mind Zach. I wish I was there."

That comment didn't feel right to me, but I shrugged my shoulders and reached for the chocolate bars I'd bought at the plantation and held them up for Mateo to see. "Luna and I bought plenty of bars to take on the hike."

An irritated expression came over Mateo's face. "Why is it so important for you to do this hike?"

I sank back in my chair and felt uneasiness grow inside me again. "I promised my mom that I'd travel while I was single. My dad hiked to Machu Picchu and it helped him find out that he loved architecture. Hiking the trail is a challenge, and if I finish it, it'll be something I'm proud of. Why aren't you excited for me?"

Mateo looked surprised and turned his head, staring at the screen from the side of his face, his expression changing from summer to winter. "This goal of yours is getting in the way of us. I'm going home now, and you could be meeting me instead of trying to become a hero on a mountain."

I shuddered in my chair. "Hey. Be happy for me. I can't wait to see the stars out there, far from the city lights."

Mateo looked pensive as he spoke. "Well, while you're hiking, I'll be helping my mother renovate her house. I'll also start interviewing for graphic design jobs." After we ended our video call, my stomach tightened as I slipped my computer back into its case.

CHAPTER 25.5

When I am seventeen my mother takes me to England, and as part of our trip we join a pilgrimage in the town of Walsingham, a rural village in Norfolk County. On an early summer morning, we walk with other pilgrims on a dirt road between dew-kissed meadows. The creamy sunshine lights up the land like a dim lamp, and flowers decorate the meadows like a patchwork of embroidery: yellow-and-pink mugwort, purple teasel, and blue fleabane. A beautiful and peaceful setting for a spiritual voyage.

My mother explains that a pilgrimage is a journey, where, through the experience, people go in search of a new or expanded meaning about themselves, others, nature, or a higher good. Such a sacred journey can lead to a personal transformation that people use to improve their daily lives.

As we walk with the other pilgrims, we sing songs about the Virgin Mary and pray. My mother holds a rosary in her hands. I appreciate the prayers but like the singing most of all. The sound of the music stirs my heart as I enjoy the pretty fields of flowers. I feel light, like I am floating over the road, my feet not quite touching the ground.

We end the pilgrimage at the Slipper Chapel, a petite stone chapel built in 1325 as a shrine to Mary. The church has a large wooden door enclosed inside a pointed arch and a huge Gothic stained glass window. My mother and I enter the chapel and sit on one of the walnut pews. The tabernacle is trimmed with gold, and a giant statue of Mary stands to the left of the altar. As dozens of pilgrims whisper inside the tall and elegant nave, I feel happy to be with them, like I have made new friends.

CHAPTER 26

The next morning, I woke up in a sweat. We showered and dressed in layers: sun-protection tank tops and sweatshirts, hiking pants, two pairs of socks, hiking shoes, and hats. Luna slung her heavy pack over one shoulder and opened the door. "Let's go." I zipped up my pack and closed the door behind me.

Our guide Vilma, dressed in a blue tank top, hoodie, and hiking pants, was waiting outside the idling shuttle in front of the hostel. She said, "Get in, and we'll pick up the other eight trekkers." The shuttle crawled around the Plaza de Armas, then turned down a cobblestone street to the next pickup site. Finally, ten people, daypacks on our chests and large backpacks on the floor, were crowded in the shuttle. The vehicle rumbled out of the cobblestone streets of Cusco and up the highway toward the Inca Trail.

Vilma stood at the front of the bus and spoke with a confident voice and expressive hands. "Our ride is going to take about three hours, so I'm going to use this time to share some Inca history with you." She lodged her long legs and boots against the edges of the aisle and held onto the backs of two chairs. "The Incas started living in the Cusco region beginning in about 1230 CE. They made Cusco their capital, which is why the city has so many cobblestone streets and stone foundations. Even though the Spanish soldiers destroyed many Inca buildings in the 1500s, they built their new city on top of the Inca foundations, built with such skill that they are able to withstand earthquakes."

Luna shook her head. "And we think we're so intelligent."

Vilma displayed a diagram of the Inca Empire on the video screen at the front of the bus while holding a picture of a man dressed in ancient clothing. "The ninth Inca ruler, Pachacutec, built Machu Picchu. The trail we will take was an original Inca trail, and because it contains many places to enjoy the views of the Inca Empire, archaeologists believe that it was built to serve as a pilgrimage to Machu Picchu." Vilma gestured with her hands. "You've been acclimating to the high altitude in Cusco for at least four days, so you should be able to finish this hike without too much hardship. But I want to caution you. Even though the trail is only twenty-six miles long, you'll be walking in difficult terrain at high altitude."

Pressing my hand against my onyx necklace under my shirt, I whispered to Luna, "You think we're ready?"

Luna nodded.

Vilma gripped the rails on top of two bus seats. "Use discipline. Pay attention to your feet at all times. If you looked at the trail on a map, from the south, it would resemble a backward check mark. The first day, we'll be walking down the short end and we'll camp at the bottom of the check mark. Tomorrow, we start up the long end of the check mark until we reach the Sun Gate at Machu Picchu."

A shiver snaked up my spine. I didn't feel ready.

Vilma's hands floated in front of her. "You'll be trekking beside cliffs, on slippery trails, over pebble-sized rocks, in hot sun or cold wind. Don't rush off at the beginning like a gazelle. You'll be the first to overexert yourself and might not be able to finish after all."

Jeez, I'd better stay alert. I was notorious for tripping over my feet, falling down the stairs at home at least three times, one time breaking my big toe. I looked down at my hiking boots, willing them to keep me safe.

Our bus arrived at Piscacucho, km 82, at approximately 7:30 a.m. Vilma introduced us to the porters who would carry our large backpacks on the trail. In less than fifteen minutes, our group—Vilma, ten hikers, and eleven porters—started trekking the trail. She raised her voice. "By the end of the day, we will have traveled eight miles to Huayllabamba, where we'll camp for the first night."

A haze clung to the hills. Fluffy white clouds dangled in the light blue sky like mobiles of cotton balls. The wet air washed our faces and caressed our torsos, but by the time we had walked an hour, the mist had dried up and the sun baked both the air and our heads, even though we wore hats.

Vilma trekked back to us. "Did you apply sunscreen? Are you drinking enough water? You can't drink the water from the streams since the animals defecate in them. Refill your water bottles with the water supply carried by the porters."

The trail was well marked, and every so often we passed mini-stalls set up to sell nuts, granola bars, and bottled water. There wasn't much elevation gain, but the path was strewn with marble-sized rocks. Several times, I skidded despite the traction of my hiking boots, catching myself by balancing with my arms. Rivers of sweat streamed down my front and back. My face swelled with heat. We passed all the mini-stalls and were soon on our way into complete wilderness.

After two hours, Vilma stopped in a patch of shade and passed out protein bars and nuts. "You need to eat something every two hours."

Parched, I drank all the water in my flask, then lay prostrate on the ground, fanning my overheated face. Luna dragged me to my feet and took me to a porter to refill my water bottle. Before long, we were following Vilma again and the rocky trail. We hiked, silent, for another hour. I felt my onyx necklace bounce against my chest inside my T-shirt and took comfort in knowing it would give me courage.

At lunchtime, we found shade under a grove of trees, and the porters passed out sandwiches, fruit, and coca leaves. I bit the coca, chewed it, associating its aroma with freshly cut grass. The crackly, dry pieces softened on my tongue, producing a bitter, herbal flavor, not unpleasant, with a lingering smoothness. After swallowing the fragments, my throat numbed as if a dentist had injected anesthesia into my mouth. About ten minutes later, my energy rejuvenated. I was ready to start hiking again.

By early afternoon, we came upon a ridge that overlooked the ruins of Patallacta. Vilma pointed down to a large round plateau with a small village built on top of it. A river flowed around the plateau's front like the moats around castles in England. Except this moat was natural. *Zach would've loved seeing these ruins*, I thought.

Vilma said, "These ruins are now believed to have been a satellite of Machu Picchu, a place where hundreds of laborers lived and grew food for the residents of Machu Picchu."

We scaled the ridge down to the ruins where Vilma showed us a sun temple. Underneath it was a cave, charred from the fires of offerings by local mountain people. Inside the temple were two windows. She pointed to the window on the left. "On the June solstice, you can see the Corona constellation through this window. It's a U-shaped constellation of seven stars that points northeast." Next, she pointed to the window on her right. "On the December solstice, you see Corona through *this* window." Luna and I gawked at each other, amazed at how the Incas built structures that followed the stars so accurately. They seemed more advanced than contemporary scientists. And I wasn't surprised that the Incas had inspired my father to become an architect.

After climbing back up to the Inca Trail, we followed Vilma until we reached Huayllabamba, just as the sun was setting over the western mountains. In the midst of a clearing, a semi-permanent campground, consisting of a cook tent and numerous sleeping tents, welcomed us. Gratefully, feeling new blisters and cramping muscles, I dropped to the ground, waiting for our tent assignment. Luna sat down beside me.

The daylight dimmed, the air chilled, and the velvety sky burst open with millions of dazzling stars, their brilliance deepening as dusk progressed into darkness. Under the stars and the dining tent, camp cooks served us a chicken dinner with four different kinds of potatoes. They poured *chicha*, a fermented corn beer, which relaxed us, our conversations becoming easy. For dessert, we ate a Peruvian apple pie made with a hearty crust, sliced apples, and cinnamon. I ate like a starved coyote.

After dinner, Vilma gathered us around a semicircle of stone seats. "Time for a bedtime story," she said, standing in front of the stones and spreading her outstretched hands up to the sky. "You won't understand the Incas unless you understand how their belief systems were integrated with their views of the cosmos." She waited while we all found a seat. "They observed the motions of the Milky Way and the solar system as seen from their capital, Cusco, and connected the movements of constellations and planets to their agricultural seasons."

I leaned over toward Luna and whispered, "So the stars were like their calendar?"

Luna nodded.

Vilma pointed out the Southern Cross, a constellation of five stars. "This constellation was important to them because they believed it was the center of the universe." She picked up a bag from the ground in front of her, unlaced the tie, and pulled out a cross-shaped object, with four equilateral arms and a hole in the center. "The Incas called this a *chakana*, which to them symbolized the dynamic between the universe and the life it contained. Each quarter of the cross represented the different worlds, revered animals, Inca commandments, and human principles."

A slender man dressed in a fleece vest and sweatshirt raised his hand. "What were the Inca commandments?"

Vilma raised the chakana and pointed to the third quarter. "It's Freddy, right?" The hiker nodded. Vilma nodded too and continued, "Don't steal. Don't lie. Don't be lazy. Labor was an important value for them. In fact, every year, Incas had to dedicate a certain amount of time laboring for the benefit of their community."

I raised my hand, waving it a little. When Vilma stopped talking, she turned to me. I asked, "What were the Incas' human principles?"

Vilma pointed to the fourth quarter of the chakana. "They were love and well-doing, knowledge, and work." *Ah,* I thought, *we have the same principles.* Our group erupted into a chatter of conversations, some focusing on the Southern Cross. Others took turns holding the chakana and pointing to its quarters, arms, ends, and the hole in the middle, which Vilma told us represented the Inca capital, Cusco.

When Luna and I retired to our tent, we crawled into our sleeping bags and peered through the open window flap at the pitch-black sky pricked with millions of flickering stars. I propped myself up on my elbow to face Luna. "Something's been bothering me."

Luna's shadow turned in my direction. "What?"

I could hear the low voices coming from the other tents and clatter in the cook tent. "Mateo isn't being supportive of me taking this hike."

Luna's sleeping bag rustled in the dark. She said, "Chica, a red flag for sure."

"Yeah, he'd rather I go to Buenos Aires to be with him instead. I told him that I'd promised my mother I would explore on my own, but he doesn't get it."

Luna wiggled out of her sleeping bag and sat up near the top opening, her feet still hidden inside. "He's being selfish."

I lay back down. "Or, does he just love me so much that he can't wait until we're together?"

I could see Luna's eyes in the light from the stars. They gleamed. "How do you feel when you're with him?"

Inside my sleeping bag, I folded my arms across my chest in a hug. "When I see his face, my heart beats like a hummingbird. But at the same time, he does things that make me feel like I'm invisible."

I heard Luna shiver. She scooted back into her sleeping bag on her back. "Invisible? What do you mean?"

I inhaled, trying to relax every cell in my body, then exhaled as slowly as I could. "Oh, never mind. I'm tired. Let's get some sleep." While the noises of the campground disappeared into the mysterious nocturnal sounds of the jungle, I closed my eyes, happy that Luna was near.

CHAPTER 27

The second day, we woke and ate before the sun came up. Soon, we started hiking up the steep path to Dead Woman's Pass. The trail was treacherous, made up of broken steps, and as the altitude climbed, my breathing became more difficult. I tried to regulate breaths by counting to four while inhaling and exhaling.

A few hours into the morning, we met a crowd of other hikers, seated off to the side of the trail on a sloping embankment, chewing on granola bars and swigging gulps of water. Their hiking clothing clashed with the muted green terrain and their rank body odors wafted toward us. I held my bandanna up to my nose to fend off the stench. What did I smell like? I pulled up the front of my sweatshirt to check it. I sniffed and tasted dust.

We left the hikers behind and trudged higher, climbing hundreds of steps as the elevation rose thousands of feet. My fingers swelled like sausages. Clammy sweat soaked the layers of my clothing. I slipped several times as I became lightheaded. My head throbbed. I wanted to bend over the side of the trail to vomit. As I pursed my lips closed, I wished for Mom.

Finally, Vilma stopped the hike. Her forehead showed beads of sweat, her cheeks were flushed with exertion, but she looked perfectly comfortable. "Everybody okay? The porters have canisters of oxygen if you're lightheaded. Don't be shy. It is better to be safe than sorry. Today's hike is the highest altitude of this trail."

I plopped down in the dirt, holding my head. "I need oxygen." I was too dizzy to see past my feet. Any minute, I was going to puke.

Luna lowered herself down in the dirt next to me like a ninety-year-old woman. Her face was pale. She groaned. "Me too."

A porter handed a canister to me, which I grabbed with both hands. I held it to my mouth, sucking in the air with gulps. Then I stuck my head down between my knees.

Beside me, Luna was holding an oxygen canister to her mouth, inhaling noisily. From between my knees, I watched her breathe as I waited for my dizziness to clear. Finally, I could see the people around me milling about, eating protein bars and guzzling water. Luna continued to inhale from her canister, then bent down, dropping her head between her knees. When she sat back up after a few minutes, color had returned to her face.

Vilma passed us two protein bars each. "Feel better? Eat." She then passed out coca leaves for us to chew on as we continued our ascent. "Coca will help relieve your altitude sickness."

I stuck the leaf into my mouth and chewed.

She backed away and grinned, triumphant. "The Inca Trail is a fantastic adventure. Along the way, we endure highs and lows, growth and boredom. We experience sublimity when we witness the ancient ruins and the vastness of nature. We encounter fear and relief when we avoid the treacherous drops and dangerous altitudes. A journey of heartbreak and soul-searching. Who are you? What can you do? How will you do it?" She had oodles of energy, boundless enthusiasm. Mom had been like that. My dizziness subsided. I stood up, and pulled Luna to her feet.

Before long, we were back hiking the trail. Just before we got to the top of Dead Woman's Pass, all I could see was a bowl of blue sky. We clawed our way up the last steps to the summit and stood at the top of the pass, our figures poking into the blue like candles on a huge birthday cake. A sea of mountains undulated around us, wave after wave of peaks—craggy, green, and white.

Luna and I stood next to each other in silence, staring at the endless splendor.

After pausing at the top of the pass, Vilma led us down the steps on the north side of the mountain where the shade cooled the trail, then she pointed back to the crest behind her. "Now you can see the woman. Her face, her breast, her belly." We followed her fingers. Sure enough, the woman was lying on her back on the summit, her profile and torso outlined against the blue sky.

Vilma cleared her throat, and we turned back to listen. "Cresting the pass is a significant psychological and physical milestone. You've manifested your inner strength and mental toughness just to get to this point. We're now at an altitude of over 13,000 feet, the highest point on the trail, higher than Machu Picchu. Only lower altitudes lie ahead, so you can rest in the knowledge that altitude will not defeat you. After today, you'll have two more days of tough trekking, but you'll get to Machu Picchu, with continued focus and discipline."

Vilma's words encouraged me. I pulled at Luna's hoodie. "Luna, we're going to make it."

Luna turned to look at me. "I had my doubts about an hour ago."

My muscles ached and my breathing was labored, and the next few hours passed by in a blur. I took each step with caution, near steep cliffs, on a slippery surface of dust and pebbles. Mom had stressed the importance of focusing on the present, and I had struggled with that, focusing on the next day, week, month, semester. The hike was teaching me why focusing on the present was so important. I had to watch each step so I wouldn't slip down a cliff or break a leg during a fall, regulate my breathing so I wouldn't become oxygen deficient, eat more calories to create energy, apply plenty of sunscreen, and wear a hat to prevent sun exposure. Without focusing on the present, I wouldn't get to Machu Picchu. With sheer determination, I kept up with Vilma, our superhuman guide, sometimes clutching my onyx necklace for more courage. Late in the afternoon, we scaled down to the next camp at Pacaymayo at 11,800 feet. The sun baked the rock-outlined steps on the way down, and we peeled off our sweatshirts and vests to cool off.

I didn't know how badly I smelled, simply hoping that I wasn't as rank as the male hikers I'd passed whose body odor reminded me of dirty dorm bathrooms. I longed to take a shower and asked a camp worker where the showers were. "No showers," he said in Spanish. "Night three. Wait." He gave me a basin of warm water to take a sponge bath. I took the basin, undressed in the tent assigned to Luna and me, and washed up before dinner. Searching my backpack, I found clean clothes.

Dinner was set up under a canopy. The camp chefs served quinoa soup for the first course and grilled trout and vegetables for the second. Afterward, we drank chicha while we showed each other our pictures of Dead Woman's Pass and the treacherous steps that we had climbed. We were giddy with accomplishment. Vilma sat at the head of the table. "You did well today. Pat yourselves on the back. Tomorrow's hike will be another day of surprises."

After dinner, around another stone circle, Vilma told us more stories. We heard clamor from the cook tent—pans clanging, dishes being rinsed, clipped conversations in Spanish. A gentle aroma of frying bacon wafted through our circle. An hour later, the lights of the tent were extinguished and the cooks retreated to their group tent for the night. Their conversations continued in a mixture of Spanish and Quechan. They dragged chairs over dirt, clinked tin cups, and laughed boisterously, feeling right at home in the wilderness.

When Luna and I retired to our tent, we were wide-awake. Again, we left the flap of the window open so we could see the magnificent diamond-studded night sky. I sighed. "We proved our endurance today, even though we both hugged oxygen tanks and felt like puking." I hooted, then became quiet again. "I have so many wishes. I want my life to matter."

Luna turned her face toward me. "Chica, your life matters now. You're contributing something important now."

"No, look at that vast sky and the millions of stars. I feel insignificant compared to that."

"You're like one of those incredible stars out there. Without you, the sky wouldn't be as bright. The view wouldn't be as vast and amazing. Every star is important, Leonie. I am. You are. We need to believe in our individual significance."

My chest twinged with disappointment. "Then why do I feel invisible next to Mateo?"

Luna combed her hair with her fingers. "You know, chica, if anyone made me feel like that, I'd break up with him."

I gasped. "But I love him. How could I?"

Luna stopped combing her hair and clasped her hands behind her head. "You'll have to find out what kind of love you want, I guess. I'd want a love that made me feel good about myself."

CHAPTER 28

I groaned and grabbed at the spasm in my left shin. Wriggling out of my sleeping bag, I hopped onto my right leg, and firmly stomped my left foot on the ground. Luna looked at me with a question on her face. "What?"

I kept stomping. "I've got a cramp." After a couple minutes, the spasm subsided. I sat down on top of my sleeping bag and, hoping to increase the circulation, rubbed my legs.

Luna squirmed out of her sleeping bag and took off her sock. "I've got a blister on my right heel and sore quads from climbing all those steps yesterday."

I rubbed lotion on my legs. "Yeah, my quads are sore too. In fact, my hips, shins, and feet all hurt. I'm going to drink tons of water this morning to see if that helps."

A little later, as we sat under the dining canopy with the other hikers, we listened to the happy chatter of the cooks. They gave us coca tea to drink while we waited for breakfast. I wrapped my cold hands around the cup, watching the steam rise into the chilly morning air. Soon, the cooks brought out platters of food. We piled the food onto our plates and ate like elephants. They poured us more cups of coca tea to wash it down.

Less than an hour later, Vilma led us onto the trail again for a long day's hike to Phuyupatamarca, the next campsite. A cloud forest thickened over the trail—moisture as thick as San Francisco fog. The air cooled, and the twitters, caws, flitters, wooshes, and warbling of birds grew from a soft melody into a cacophony. We watched hummingbirds, whose colorful plumage speckled the forest like gems, flitting in and among the branches of the dripping trees. Tiny lavender flowers grew amid gigantic fern leaves. Ferns, moss, and fungus crowded the landscape, layering the ground like a rich green salad. Delicate yellow-and-purple orchids and bushes of scarlet rhododendrons dotted the foliage with color.

My parents knew the names of flowers. At Easter, lilies bloomed in the backyard. In the summer, the azaleas and hydrangeas burst into pink petal profusions under the shade of the oak tree. My mother pruned her roses year-round, and my father planted daffodil, tulip, and iris bulbs that popped out of the ground in early spring. It was natural, then, for me to want to know the names of all the technicolored hummingbirds and orchid varieties, and when Vilma started pointing out the different species, I paid attention. Her knowledge was like an encyclopedia. I asked, "How did you learn about all the different plants and animals in the Amazon?"

She turned around and waved her hand toward the jungle. "I've been a trail guide for seven years and hiked this trail over twenty times, so I've seen the cloud forests and their inhabitants enough to be able to remember the different species. Also, my father was a biology teacher, so I grew up with someone who talked about plants and animals all the time. When I'm not hiking, I study them. I have learned that the secret to becoming good at something is to practice."

By the time we dragged our sore muscles into Camp Phuyupatamarca, the sky had turned navy blue and the sun was trailing its yellow tail behind the Andes Mountains. Vilma strode into the camp. "Phuyupatamarca means 'of the clouds.' Generally, the camp is surrounded by thick clouds since it is near the low Andean jungle where rainfall is plentiful and condensation provides continuous moisture, but not this evening. Come on, I have something incredible to show you." She trotted up a narrow path through the rocks and waved at us to follow her. In single file, we marched up the steep trail lined with trees, bushes, and hidden boulders. At the edge of a cliff, she stopped and pointed across a massive ravine of valleys and mountains. I looked up and caught my breath. In front of me was a colossal mountain, blanketed in a thick layer of snow and mist, its craggy peaks cutting into the navy-blue sky like serrated blades. One by one, the other hikers gathered behind me and stood silently as if witnessing a miracle. Vilma inched her way through the group and led us to a higher platform for a better look. Her voice was breathy, excited. "The mountain's name is Salcantay, meaning 'savage mountain.' It is the highest peak of the Willkapampa Mountain Range and was one of the most important mountains of the Inca culture. This is one of the best views in the whole world. You can see a vast part of the Inca Empire from here. Over there behind that mountain is Choquequirao, ruins that resemble Machu Picchu. Over there is Llactapata, which means 'high city.' Beyond that is Espíritu Pampa, the last capital of the Incas before they fled the Spanish by disappearing into the forest. Tomorrow, you're going to see the Sun Gate at Machu Picchu, but this here is better than the Sun Gate. It's a perspective of the Inca Empire that you can't get anywhere else on the planet." I forgot my tired muscles, gazing at the astonishing display of Inca complexes, built on the precipices of some of the largest mountains in the world, surrounded by nature's vast spirituality.

Vilma pointed to a velvet green mountain to the north. "See that small green sharp peak down there? That's Mount Machu Picchu." She then trailed her finger along a ridge where a barely visible trail was fast disappearing in the darkening landscape. "That's the Inca Trail that goes to the Sun Gate. We'll be walking that early tomorrow morning." We admired Mount Machu Picchu, but, one by one, our heads turned back to gaze at the massive mountain that Vilma had first pointed out. It dominated the western landscape like a god. We stood silently like a congregation in front of Salcantay, the great Inca deity, cloaked in the savage snows of nature. I could see why this incredible landscape made the Incas believe that they were protected and their culture was ordered by the reliability of the stars and seasons.

That night, everyone took turns taking showers in the bath tents. I washed my hair and lathered my skin with soap, peeling off the sweat and dirt of three days. In the shower, I also rinsed my dirty clothes and, later, hung them up to dry on the clothesline outside my tent.

After a dinner of chicken smothered in a paste of garlic, spices, vinegar, and soy sauce and a warm salad of colorful potatoes, we took our dessert, bowls of *crema volteada*—a caramel, custard-like concoction—to eat under the stars while sitting on flattish stones. The night air had cooled, and the black sky was bursting with billions of stars, the bright Milky Way swirling across the heavens like a glittery river.

Vilma sat on a stone in the middle of us. She had showered too, and her hair was still wet and tied back in a ponytail. She wore a clean pair of dark sweatpants and a fleece navy-blue hoodie. "Any questions?"

Hands went up fast.

As I tasted the brown sweetness of the custard, I half listened to the conversation, but also retraced my journey from Buenos Aires to Iguazú Falls to Bodega Romero to Santiago to Cusco.

I remembered the faces of the people I had met.

Clarisa had inspired my courage to travel.

The mystic I had met at the Block of Enlightenment had given me the onyx necklace to protect me and help me grow strong. She also advised me to not dwell on the past, but work on creating my own future.

I placed my hand over my necklace. Flora, the florist, taught me that a person could find something that made them deeply content. She loved working with flowers.

Martina, the woman I met on the bus to Iguazú Falls, taught me how comforting it is to have friends for life.

Next to me, Luna had finished her custard and was lying back against a rock, her eyes closed. When I told Luna that my mother had died, she had comforted me with her kindness. She was always ready to talk with me about anything, happy or sad.

At Bodega Romero, I learned *and* fell in love.

Sara was like a wise aunt who allowed me to experiment enough in order to succeed. I was proud that Hanna and I had helped Sara increase her earnings.

And then I fell in love with Mateo.

In Chile, when I met Alma, I learned that I wanted to help people overcome their pain and improve their lives, but Mother Superior taught me that I needed more education and experience to be that person.

The last year and a half had been a journey.

No, wait. My whole life had been a journey. That's what life was, a journey of experiences and opportunities to grow. If life *was* a journey, then all of life was equally important: each year, each month, each day, each hour, each minute. The present was the most important moment that led to the next most important one. What determined success was whether a person decided to use their life to grow or to stay stuck in the past. Each moment, I had to nurture what I valued in order to create the life I wanted.

I noticed the shadows of the trees and heard the wild creatures combine their voices into a night symphony. I peered at the faces of the other hikers, wondering what *they* were thinking.

Suddenly, I understood why *hiking* to Machu Picchu was so important. Without hiking the treacherous Inca Trail, I wouldn't have been able to appreciate Machu Picchu. I needed to see how the stars blaze in the night sky, to learn how they once acted as guides for the Inca—where to live, when to plant, what to believe. I had to witness the Inca ruins where ancient travelers rested, ate, and replenished their supplies. Feel the way my body craved oxygen, climbing the steep altitudes, and how my muscles ached after trekking on stones, slippery pebbles, and dirt. To be surrounded by the immenseness of the mountains and the wet abundance of the cloud forests. To become overwhelmed by nature's magnificence, the god that managed life and provided the nourishment for it.

I tilted my head up to the brilliant night sky, searching for a comet. Was anyone else striving to get back on track, like a comet searching for its orbit? Sitting quietly in the middle of the Amazon forest on my flat stone with sweet pudding in my mouth, my journey felt profoundly personal.

CHAPTER 29

At four thirty the next morning, everyone was awake, dressed, and sitting in the dining tent. The freezing air bit our faces and turned our breath into puffs of fog. Shivering, we curled our hands around steaming hot cups of coca tea.

After breakfast, we descended the mountain range toward the ruins of Phuyupatamarca. Observing the steep and wet steps winding down the mountainside, I groaned, “Oh, no. My shins already ache.”

Under the shade of thick growth, I turned sideways to maneuver down, securing one foot and then the other. We scrambled through the thick growth and ever-changing cloud forest for three and a half hours before stopping to rest.

Vilma passed out protein bars. “Drink water and eat.”

One by one, we sank onto the dirt in the shade, our legs shaking with overexertion. Too soon, we were back on our feet.

Several yards down the trail, Vilma stretched her torso and poked her head inside a dark opening. “Ah, the Inca tunnel. This tunnel was excavated by the Incas more than five hundred years ago.” We gathered around her to see for ourselves, the shaft wet and dark, its walls as sturdy and safe as when it first had been built. She waved us forward. “I want to reach Machu Picchu as early in the morning as possible to witness the sunrise lighting up the magnificent Machu Picchu ruins,” she said. “Let’s go. You won’t regret it.”

I took a deep breath and watched my feet sludge forward. They were numb. Feeling shaky and lightheaded, I plunged down the descending trail for another hour and a half, using ancient stairways that barely clung to the steep mountainsides. Rain leaked from the sky, a weeping goddess, and clouds wrapped around me. My muscles sore and cramping, finally we arrived at the control booth and entered the Machu Picchu Historic Sanctuary. The last stretch of the stone trail zigzagged up a mountain and then undulated up and down to a stretched set of white stairs extending toward the sky. "See those tall stone pillars at the summit?" asked Vilma, raising her arm almost to the side of her head and pointing up. "That's the Sun Gate, known as the Intipunku in Quechua."

We ascended in twos. I used every ounce of energy I had to hoist myself up each steep step. When we reached the final stairs to the sacred and ancient gateway, the steps became even more vertical. "I can't navigate that," I said, sinking into my chest.

Luna placed her hands on the stone. "Use all fours, chica. We're almost there!"

I stretched my hands out and grabbed the edges of an upper stone. Like a tired monkey, I clambered, heaving myself up one vertical step at a time. My breathing was labored. I grabbed my onyx necklace out of my shirt and clung to it like a tiny life raft. Letting it go, I reached for the next stone and groveled up, scraping my hands on the sharp edges of the rock. I searched for Luna and found her legs sprawled over a stone high above me. I heaved and pulled. My breath turned into short shallow puffs, a dog pant. I climbed one more stone, then another, my legs overextended like rubber bands. Finally, above me, Luna stood up at the crest of the ridge. She held a hand out. I grabbed it, pushed my weight off a stone with the other hand, and reached the top.

Together, we surveyed the scene on the other side of the ridge. Upon the horizontal top of a highland, surrounded by a necklace of jagged green-and-white Andes Mountains, was the long-awaited Machu Picchu—an oval collection of stone structures clustered around an elongated, grassy plaza. The sun had just risen above the Andes peaks in the east and cloaked the site in a honeyed glaze of radiant light, the stones glowing like topaz. I wiped away a tear from my cheek and reached for Luna's hand, squeezing it. Forgetting my aching muscles and heaving chest, I said, "We're here. We made it." Those ancient people had created heaven on earth on the perch of a mountain. A paradise surrounded by majestic mountains and unspoiled forests. Nature had preserved their sacred site for centuries. For Luna and me.

The golden granite, brilliant in the morning light, made me feel like a sun god. My fingers rifled over my shirt, feeling only my collarbone and the sweat on my neck. Where was my onyx necklace? With both hands, I hunted for it, opening my jacket to look inside, peering at the ground below me. It was nowhere. I examined every pocket, took off my coat and looked inside. Oh my God! Had I lost it while climbing those steep stairs? Had it snagged on a branch on my way up? I kneeled down at the edge of the ridge and scanned the steep stairs that I had just climbed. The sun shone on the surface of the stones, revealing their smooth surfaces. My necklace was nowhere in sight.

Luna knelt down beside me. "What are you doing here?" She leaned down to peer at my face. "What's wrong?"

My voice came out hoarse. "I . . . lost my necklace, the . . . the one that the mystic gave me at the Block of Enlightenment. She said it would . . . would protect me and give me strength. I think it fell off my neck when I was climbing the steps." I wiped my face with the end of my T-shirt, smearing my tears with the dust on my skin. I raised my head and turned to Luna.

Luna's eyes were full of compassion. "I'm sorry, Leonie, but it's unlikely you'll find it now."

I gazed down the cliff. "I know."

Luna took my hand. "You know what? Your necklace probably fell off somewhere on the way up, but you made it all the way. Without it." She wiped the sweat off her face, creating a dirty streak across her cheek.

I concentrated on the streak.

Luna grabbed one of my hands. "Maybe you don't need the necklace anymore. Maybe it fell off because you've proven that you are strong enough to go on without it."

The streak on Luna's face was blending in with beads of sweat. Little threads of her brown hair were trailing across her forehead and around her cheeks. I considered what she had said. Finally, I pushed myself up from the ground and stuck out my hand to pull her up. I hoped she was right.

"PICTURE TIME!" YELLED Vilma, motioning for us to gather between the pillars of the Sun Gate. She held her camera up to her eye, and *click*, she recorded the moment. Below us, on the terraced hillside between the Sun Gate and the ruins, llamas munched on wet grass. Within the ruins, a dozen hikers wandered, their heads down as if in prayer. We descended into the village in twos and threes. Vilma strode ahead of us and turned around when we reached the bottom of the terrace. "Many people come to Machu Picchu and wander around the ruins without a guide. They're disappointed because they don't know what they're seeing. They don't learn about the Incas or the purpose of the ruins. I've been up here over twenty times and I've researched Machu Picchu's history, so today is your lucky day. I'll be your Machu Picchu guide." She twirled around on the granite floor like a drunk ballerina in hiking shoes.

We applauded in unison.

After a slight bow, Vilma continued talking. "Behind us is Machu Picchu Mountain, which means 'old peak.' I want us to loop around the ruins toward that other big mountain at the north end, Huayna Picchu, which means 'young peak.' We're not going to climb either of these mountains since you'd all be worn out and wouldn't have enough energy to get back to Cusco tonight. We are, however, going to climb the shorter mountain, Huchuy Picchu, meaning 'small mountain,' from where we'll get a magnificent view of the whole site without the disadvantage of being too high or blinded by clouds. But first, let's turn left to the Machu Picchu City Gate. I have something remarkable to show you."

Together, we strode across the valley floor of the citadel and up to a huge rock with three stairs carved into one side and a flat top. Vilma stood in front of it and pointed back at it with a grand gesture. "This is Funerary Rock. Experts gave it this name because they think the rock was used for preparing bodies for burial. Over there," she said, pointing farther, "excavators found graves with human remains, so that area is called the Cemetery. Let's walk down the terraces. The Main Gate is just ahead."

When we reached the Main Gate, Vilma led us outside the portal and then had us turn around to look back through it. "The first thing an Inca saw coming through this gate is Huayna Picchu, or its English name, 'Young Peak.' This was not an accident. Mountains were sacred to the Inca. They associated them with *apus*, spirit guides. Since the name of this mountain means 'young,' perhaps its apu provided protection for young Inca. We don't know really, but we do know that the Inca were expert builders. They *intended* for pilgrims coming through this gate to see this mountain through the portal."

Next, Vilma led us to a curved stone structure built upon a natural rock jutting up from the floor of the site. "This building is an example of fine architecture since, even though it is curved, the stones fit tightly together, showing off the precision of the Inca stonework." Vilma waved to us to follow her into a cave under the building. "They used meticulous cuts to fit their stones together. These ruins have endured harsh weather and earthquakes for five hundred years."

Luna looked at me with astonishment. "We saw examples of this in Cusco."

Inside the curved structure, Vilma continued her explanation. "This is called the Sun Temple, or El Torreón." Three windows had been created high up in the walls. Two were rhomboid-shaped and faced east and south. The third one was larger, and below it, holes had been bored into the rocks below.

I turned toward Vilma. "Strange that the temple only has three windows."

Vilma nodded. "Some experts believe that this temple was a rudimentary reproduction of the Koricancha in Cusco, the Sun Temple of the Incas."

Luna groaned. "We didn't see that when we were in Cusco."

Vilma chuckled. "You wouldn't have. The Spanish dismantled it and built the Catholic Church of Santo Domingo on top of its foundation. During Inca times, however, the Koricancha was a sacred place. It was the place for all major religious activities."

I rubbed my forehead, my voice weary. "I can't remember all this."

Vilma chuckled. "Don't try. Just remember that the Inca created intimate connections between their lives, the earth, and the universe. They understood that they were part of the universe's vast complex, and they understood that their lives would be governed by it. The window that looks out to the east is aligned with the sunrise on the day of the June solstice. The sunlight shines through the window and casts a rhomboid of light onto the big rock in the center. That suggests that they considered their lives an integral part of the universe."

We followed Vilma up to the highest point of Machu Picchu. An irregular-shaped four-sided stone with many steps and a tall stone projectile on top stood several feet away from a precipitous cliff where the edge of Machu Picchu dropped into oblivion.

Vilma raised her voice. "This rock is called Intihuatana, meaning 'a place to tie up the sun.' Experts believe that the purpose of the rock was astronomical, to help the Inca plant and harvest crops. The sun sits directly above the stone on March 21 and September 21, when it creates no shadow at all. The spring and fall equinoxes are still important agricultural milestones, especially for people living in high altitudes."

Luna touched the granite. "Like an ancient sundial calendar."

Vilma looked over at some tourists standing closer to the rock. "Yes. The Incas had no books, so they created monuments to help them know when to plant. See those people holding out their hands? Pilgrims come from all over the world to feel the cosmic energy emanating from this rock. They believe it is sacred. Take about twenty minutes to try it out for yourselves or take pictures. Then we'll find a place for lunch before we climb Huchuy Picchu."

Luna and I walked all around the rock, observing its irregular stair cuts and watching tourists hold out their hands to feel the energy.

A male tourist, with black curls sticking out of a wool hat with a fur trim, shouted, "I felt it, did you?"

His girlfriend pulled her hand away from the stone and rubbed it on her parka. "My hand got hot!"

I held my right hand close to the rock, hoping that I would feel a little magic. When I waved at Luna to join me, she moved up to the rock and stuck out her hand too. We waited.

CHAPTER 30

As Luna and I stood over the sacred rock, a woman walked up and stood beside us. From her pockets, she pulled two crystals that she held over the stone, one in each hand. The woman's hands were wrinkled and blemished with sun spots, but her face was free of lines, her eyes clear. She smiled at me when she felt me watching her. "Where do you live, my dear?"

My face flushed with embarrassment. "I'm Leonie, from San Francisco. This is my friend Luna."

The woman's black eyes rested on my face. "I'm Sofia. I live in Puno on the shore of Lake Titicaca. Every year, I come to Machu Picchu to honor the gods of my people."

I smiled at her. "Your people? Who are your people?"

"My people come from the forests of the Andes. We are the heirs of the Inca Empire, and we follow many of the traditions that the Incas did."

Luna leaned forward toward the woman. "Most Peruvians are Catholic, but you're not?"

The sun was high in the sky, and I felt small beads of sweat moisten my forehead, thankful I was wearing a hat that shielded my face. Sofia's face, on the other hand, was fully exposed to the sun; her scarf covered only her hair. But her skin had a healthy glow and she didn't seem to be bothered by the sun's brightness. She looked down at the crystals in her hands. "I go to church when the spirit calls me, but I am here to honor the apus of the mountains that have protected my people for centuries and guided us through the seasons."

Luna repositioned her hand over the rock. "So, you believe in both Catholicism and your native beliefs?"

Sofia drew her crystals away from the rock, held them close to her torso, and observed them as if they were beloved children. After a few seconds, she closed her fingers over them and inserted one in each of her skirt pockets. "Of course, my dear. Religion, beliefs, they all help people to find their origin. I embrace any practice that brings me peace and helps me feel closer to my creator."

Luna quickly pulled her hand away from the rock, looked down at it, and rubbed her forearm. "Do you believe this rock possesses a magic energy? Is that why you held your crystals over it?"

The woman took out the crystals and held them up toward Luna and me. Each of them was an oval piece of clear quartz etched with leaf and blossom patterns. Under the sun, circles of rainbows radiated out from their vortexes, spreading a kaleidoscope across Sofia's face. "Look how the sun takes energy from the crystal and spreads it around to all of us," she said, peering at our faces.

I touched my cheeks.

Sofia smiled, her full lips parting to show a set of crooked yellow teeth. "Crystals are vessels of energy. They amplify energy through the facets of their shapes. I use them to improve my life—healing, thinking more clearly, enhancing my focus, stimulating my immune system, balancing the functions of my body, and connecting to my higher self."

Luna peered at the crystals. "They can do all that?"

Sofia bounced the crystals in her hands. "Not by themselves. My intention is the most important. When I focus on their energy, they become magical. When I concentrate hard enough, my intentions come to pass. With these crystals, I strengthen my body and my spirit."

Sofia handed one of the crystals to Luna and the other to me. "They're beautiful, no?"

I turned the crystal over in my hand. "Why come all the way to Machu Picchu to get energy from this sacred rock?" I wanted to believe her.

"The rock is not what's important. My pilgrimage to the rock is the most vital. During my journey from Puno, from Lake Titicaca to Machu Picchu, I clear away all my worries that get in the way of what I wish to accomplish spiritually. I walk away from my daily concerns in order to concentrate on my higher self."

Luna handed the crystal back to Sofia. "Wasn't Lake Titicaca a sacred place for the Inca people? Couldn't you have found a place closer to home to renew the energy of your crystals?"

Sofia took the crystal from Luna, and held her hand out to me for the other one. "Yes, it was. The Inca thought that the sun god was born on an island in the lake, Isla del Sol. But Lake Titicaca was revered by other people long before the Inca came, the Tiwanaku being the most well-known. The reason I come here, though, is because I must travel to get here, making a pilgrimage with the intention of renewing my spirit. Without the journey, my intention and the renewing of my higher self wouldn't happen. A pilgrimage gives me time to reflect. I meet new people who bring me new experiences. I have space to move my body in healthy ways."

A flood of happiness surged through me. "Our hike to Machu Picchu was a pilgrimage too. I was so absorbed in watching my step, conserving energy, and breathing regularly that I rarely thought about anything else."

Luna grabbed my hand. "Yes, that's what it was like for me. I feel like I've taken a long, spiritual shower, except I sorely need a bath." She laughed.

Sofia put her crystals into her pockets once again, then sat down on a stone ledge nearby. "I want to give something to you, my new friends. Something that I hope will help you to remember to renew your spirits so that you can reach your highest potential in this life." She opened the drawstring of a blue pouch hanging from her belt, stuck her right hand inside, then took out two tiny pink pouches with drawstrings. She held out the sacks to Luna and me. "These are my gifts to you, dear friends. Open them."

Luna and I untied the drawstrings and dropped the contents into the palms of our hands. Crystals. Clear, ovoid crystals. Luna released a soft whistle through her teeth, but I stood still, staring at the beautiful stone.

Sofia covered our hands, holding the gemstones. "Maybe you will never come back here, but since you are here today, hold your new crystals over the Incan stone so that they absorb the sacred intentions of the Inca people. If you wish to absorb their good energy, you will receive good energy." Luna and I smiled at each other, approached the Inca stone, and held the crystals over the lowest step, the sun casting a shadow of our arms and hands onto the stone.

Sofia came up behind us. "When you look at your crystal, I hope you will remember the old woman that you met at Machu Picchu, who traveled miles and miles on her own spiritual journey. Maybe that will inspire you to create your own personal pilgrimage on a regular basis so your spirit can stay strong and healthy. You don't need to come to Machu Picchu for your pilgrimage. Energy is everywhere. Just find a place where the energy of love is strong, and you will find what you need."

AFTER HUGGING SOFIA AND wishing her a safe trip home, we joined the rest of the hikers with Vilma to have lunch. Our group sat at the edge of the citadel. The porters took sandwiches and drinks out of their heavy satchels and passed them around. They cut up guavas, lucumas, and melons and placed them in a large bowl that we passed from one to another, taking pieces of fruit until they were gone. The porters cut up more fruit, and we ate that too.

After lunch, Vilma led us to the base of the Huayna Picchu Trail near the north end of the citadel. After five minutes, she took the left fork of the trail, which a sign indicated was the trail to Huchuy Picchu.

My buttocks tightened again as I climbed. "Ugh," I grunted.

Soon, we came to a ridge next to some terraces. There, the trail circled around the peak of the mountain. In some places, ropes had been attached to the sides of the mountain for hikers to use as leverage. The mountain was dense with life. Canary-yellow hooded siskins crooned lullabies. Green jays with blue heads, green backs, and yellow bellies called loudly, and enormous hummingbirds whirred over our heads with bat-like wings. Silent butterflies settled onto orchids and nestled in the branches. I held a finger up beside a brown speckled creature resting on a yellow orchid, and the butterfly stepped onto my hand, pulling her wings up behind her. My heart quickened as the fragile creature twitched her antennae and finally lowered her face to kiss my finger.

In about thirty minutes, we reached the summit. One by one, we sat on the ridge just below the peak in a twisted line and looked down at the archaeological wonder of Machu Picchu. The view was clear, the sun lighting every inch of the fortress. The terraces where the Incas grew crops. Clusters of noble residences to the east. Ancient factories and small stone houses for the workers. And most wonderful of all, an aerial view of the temples and the Sacred Stone.

I sat as still as a statue. Maybe I would never see it again, the carefully constructed place of enchantment in the midst of the Amazon Rainforest and the Andes Mountains, but it would live forever in me. My heart grew larger as I gazed upon the sun-drenched paradise, a place that required a pilgrimage to reach, that was built to honor the infinite connection of humanity to the universe and its parts.

The wind whistled through the trees behind us, its sound crisp and clear. A breeze caressed my neck and shoulders, and I thought of my mother and how she had showered me with love. I knew that every moment she had shared with me was an integral part of who I was. She would always be close. All I had to do was reach deep inside myself to find her.

Just like the Incas were linked to the stars, I was connected to my mother and always would be.

CHAPTER 31

"Mateo's not meeting me at the airport," I told Luna, swatting a wisp of my hair out of my face.

Luna turned her head. "That's odd. I would've thought he'd be anxiously waiting for you, chica."

I pursed my lips and shrugged my shoulders. "I know. I was disappointed. He said he had to finish his mother's roof project today." Finishing a roof wasn't an important enough reason to miss meeting your girlfriend whom you hadn't seen for a few months.

Outside the airport, we caught the metro to Clarisa's apartment. Luna would be living with Clarisa in Buenos Aires while she attended the university, and Clarisa said I could stay with her until I moved in with Mateo.

I threw my backpack on one of the beds in the second bedroom of Clarisa's apartment. "Mateo wants to go out for a walk in the Costanera Sur Ecological Reserve."

Luna grabbed a wad of dirty clothes out of her backpack and threw them in a corner on the floor. "Well, chica, that sounds romantic. I'll bet you can't wait to see him."

The old unease filled my chest again as I imagined Mateo's face. With a sarcastic tone, I said, "I'm all butterflies."

Luna raised an eyebrow. "Have you been there yet? It's a huge preserve on the River Plate with hundreds of species of wildlife. But why the attitude?"

I sighed, blowing the air out of my mouth in frustration. "Once again, I feel unimportant. I can't count the number of times Mateo has made me feel this way."

Luna sat in the middle of her bed, crossed her legs, and folded her hands behind her head. "Yes, you mentioned that on the hike. The feeling sure isn't getting any better. What are you going to do?"

I raised my fists and shook them. "I'm been thinking about it. I don't want to be unhappy, that's for sure. He didn't like that I went on the hike. He doesn't want me to go back to school. Everything that's important to me is what bothers him. This, here, is the last straw. I'm not going to move in with him. Tomorrow, I'll let him know."

Luna said, "It's about time you took some positive action, chica." She smiled and got off the bed. "Clarisa will be home soon, and she wants to have dinner with us."

When I had last seen her, Clarisa was finishing her classes at the university and applying for teaching jobs. She now was teaching Spanish to high school students at Escuela de Educación Técnica 2. "Great. I can't wait to see her. I'm interested in hearing about her job."

Clarisa dashed through the door, her rich brown hair cascading down her back. She wore navy trousers, a matching blazer, a white silk blouse, and navy slingback shoes. On her ears, pearl post earrings completed the outfit. She paused in the doorway, her signature orange fingernail polish curved around the doorknob. Luna uncrossed her legs and rushed over to her. "Hey, chica! It's been a long time." They hugged as I walked up behind them.

Clarisa's swanlike neck turned to greet me. "Leonie, how've you been?"

I reached for a hug. "You look so professional in your suit. Teaching seems to agree with you."

"Thank you," said Clarisa, releasing me. "Get your sweaters. Let's go out for dinner." She pushed her purse strap back onto her shoulder.

On Avenida Corrientes, we found a place called Los Inmortales, dedicated to the artists of Buenos Aires. The tables, covered in white tablecloths, were lined up in rows. The chairs had dark wooden backs and beige cushioned seats. Framed black-and-white photographs of various artists covered the walls alongside shelves of wine bottles.

The host greeted us at the door. He led us to a table by the wall with the photographs. When he pulled out my chair for me, I sat down as tired as an old woman. He folded his right arm across his torso, bowed slightly, and returned to his post at the door of the restaurant.

Before we could start chatting, a waiter in black trousers, starched white shirt, and black apron approached our table. He paused before speaking. “Would you like to order something to drink, ladies?”

Clarisa answered in a confident voice. “A bottle of malbec wine from the Mendoza region.” Our waiter paced up to the bar at the other side of the restaurant and spoke in clipped speech to the bartender. Before long, he returned with the wine and three glasses.

Soon, we were surrounded by people. A guitar player sat in a corner of the room playing the blues, and we listened to his music as we sipped our wine. The menu included a long list of international entrées, but the star of the menu was pizza. I counted forty-four different types: pizza with olive oil, mozzarella, Roquefort, provolone, Parmesan, mushrooms, ham, bacon, pineapple, and dozens more ingredients. So hard to choose.

I saw one with olives. Zach and I loved them. I imagined him digging into a pizza piled high with olives of every kind. An ache rose in my chest. “Let’s get one with olives.”

Luna pointed to her menu. “And another with mushrooms.” Finally, we ordered two pizzas to share: one with cheeses and mushrooms, and the other with ham, cheese, and olives. After about fifteen minutes, the waiter brought our order on pizza stones, which he set on trivets in the middle of the table. He poured us more wine from the bottle and left us to enjoy the food.

Clarisa had never been to Cusco or Machu Picchu. I waved toward the ceiling. "Oh, the sky at night. Billions of stars. The Milky Way. It was stunning." I took a bite of the olive pizza.

Luna sipped her wine. "Every night, our guide lectured us about the Inca culture."

I swallowed. "I should have been an Inca woman. I *do believe* we are intricately connected to everything in the universe."

Luna ate a bite of pizza and wiped her hands on her napkin. "We met this older woman from Lake Titicaca who gave us crystals to encourage us to go on more pilgrimages. She travels to Machu Picchu every year to clear her mind and renew her spirit."

Clarisa licked her lips and picked up her wine glass. "Wow, *she* sounds intriguing. I want to be like *that* when I get older."

I jumped in my chair. "I want to be that right now. The last year and a half *has* been a pilgrimage for me. I've built up courage and developed confidence by working at Sara's winery, traveling, and climbing to Machu Picchu. And I did some of that without my magical onyx necklace."

Clarisa stopped chewing, and spoke with food in her mouth. "Why? What happened to the necklace?"

I glanced at Luna before answering. "I lost it on the hike. It's buried under ferns and orchids, probably for thousands of years."

Luna cleared her throat. "I think the necklace fell off because Leonie didn't need it anymore."

Clarisa looked at me out of the corner of her eye, waiting for me to say something.

I had just put the last piece of my pizza in my mouth, so I chewed it for a minute or two. I looked first at Clarisa, then switched to Luna. "Oh, I don't know. It was comforting to have it. I wish I still did."

Luna grabbed my hand. "But you finished the hike without it. And you've decided to go to school again. See, you're doing fine without it."

I nodded. "I am doing fine, I guess. I love the idea of going back to school to become a psychologist."

Clarisa flickered her long eyelashes. "A psychologist? How'd you decide that?" She swept her hair back with both hands, then grabbed the edge of the table as she turned to me. She seemed excited.

I clasped my hands and put them up to my face, hiding a smile. "When I was in Santiago, I helped a nun who had been raped to report the crime to her superior. I wanted to help her more, but her Mother Superior explained that she needed professional help to overcome her trauma. That's when I learned I needed more education if I wanted to help people with severe mental health issues."

Luna waved her hand above the table, signaling that she wanted to talk. "Leonie also helped a vendor in Pisac who had been taken advantage of by a tourist. She bought one of the vendor's dolls and paid her a higher price than she was asking. Leonie told the woman how much she appreciated her artwork. You should've seen the gratitude on that woman's face."

Clarisa became contemplative. "Luna told me that you met a man named Mateo at Sara's winery. So, you're moving in with him?"

Suddenly, a weight dropped onto my heart. I sighed. "I've been thinking about that a lot. I've decided to tell Mateo that I'm not going to move in with him until we know each other better. I think I made a hasty decision."

Luna was biting her lip. "You'll be seeing him tomorrow. *Buena suerte*."

BACK AT CLARISA'S APARTMENT, I went into the bedroom to put away my sweater. Hearing a video call come in on my laptop, I flipped open the screen. It was Zach.

"Leonie! How are you?" he asked, surprise in his voice. He wasn't angry at me anymore. Thank God.

"Hey, Zach. I'm doing great. I finished my hike to Machu Picchu and now I'm in Buenos Aires."

"Are you coming home for Christmas?"

I pasted a smile on my lips and turned away from the screen. "No. I'm staying here."

His voice sounded like a sob. "I'm hurt. Dad is too."

I swallowed my guilt, blinked, and looked up into the corner of the room as if I was examining the quality of the paint on the wall. "Look, I don't want to hurt you guys, but I need to find a way to be happy now that Mom is gone."

His eyelashes were wet, a single tear dangling like a rock climber from a ledge. "I lost Mom too, Leonie. You're not the only one. Dad too. We can all heal together. Christmas will be unbearable without you here." He wiped away a loose tear from his cheek. His shoulders sank toward the screen and I could see one side of his bedroom behind him: the wrinkled blue bedspread, posters of whales and porpoises on the wall above it, a lamp on the walnut nightstand without a shade, a stack of books on the bed.

Feeling like I was there with him, I panicked.

I whispered, "Zach, I'm not ready to go home. I don't know if I'll ever be ready."

His eyes bored into me like he was about to transport me home with sheer resolve. "I'm not sure you can heal without coming home. Running away won't work."

I grabbed the edge of the screen. "Look, Zach, let's talk again soon. I gotta go. Love you. Luna and Clarisa are waiting for me. Tell Dad hello."

I clicked off before he had a chance to say goodbye. Immediately, he and his room were gone. As I shut the laptop, I lowered my head onto the cover and squeezed the images of home out of my head.

CHAPTER 32

The next morning, Luna took off to sign up for her new classes at the university, and Clarisa went to work. I was left sitting at the table drinking my second cup of coffee and finishing up a medialuna that Clarisa had picked up the day before. Mateo had called to let me know how to get to the Costanera Sur Ecological Reserve via the metro. He wanted to meet at 10:00 a.m. so we could walk before the weather got too hot and humid.

The reserve was on the east side of Buenos Aires. At its entrance, a large map illustrated the walking paths of the 864-acre park. Photographs of birds, mammals, reptiles, and amphibians, such as the rufescent tiger heron and white-faced whistling duck, covered the map's border. I chose the Camino del Medio to reach our meeting point along the River Plate. The path was a compact dirt road, wide enough for bicycles, walkers, and strollers to pass each other. Along the trail, grassy clearings were surrounded by trees and bushes around cement benches and tables. Marshes were crowded with pampas grass, floating rosy-billed pochard ducks, and half-submerged trees. On one muddy bank, I spotted a dozen cereal-bowl-sized turtles crawling in and out of the brown mineral-rich water. Farther along, alder trees bordered the trail, and a chorus of birds sang a symphony. A guira cuckoo repeated its sarcastic coo like a spoiled child.

Finally, I reached the spot where Camino del Medio intersected with Camino de los Alisos, the trail that bordered the River Plate. A cement border and fence of concrete posts and steel wires lined the river. The golden sun hung like an ornament over Uruguay on the opposite bank, its buttery tail twisting on the surface of the heaving latte-colored current. I sat on a green wooden park bench near the water. Soon, Mateo's lanky frame appeared and his figure pitched a short, bobbing shadow toward me from the west.

My heart quickened. The river roiled on my left like the confusion in my head. I stood up and walked slowly toward him. When we reached each other, I wrapped my arms around his waist and pulled him to me. He felt stiff, but put his arms around me and hugged me back. I lifted my face up and reached for his lips, but he took my shoulders in his hands and pushed me backward gently. We stood at arm's length. He said quietly, "I have something to tell you."

I wriggled out of his grip. "I have much to tell you." I felt my face turn red and my brain grew fuzzy.

Mateo reached for my hands, took them in his, and pulled me down the path toward the green bench where I had waited. For a while, we walked in silence, feeling the increasing heat of the sun. He said, "Let's find a shady path. The sun is too hot here." We turned left onto the Camino del Medio. Soon, the trees bordering the path blocked out the sun from across the river, and we were sheltered by shade. He listened patiently while I told him about the ruins on the Machu Picchu trail, the constellations in the night sky, the brightness of the Milky Way. He laughed about the breakfasts of coca tea. He opened his eyes wide when I described the treacherous climb near Dead Woman's Pass. I talked about energetic Vilma, the jolly camp cooks, the oxygen I used for one day's hike, the multicolored orchids and birds in the forests, the Sun Gate and Sofia from Lake Titicaca. My heart pumped as I felt his closeness, and I felt conflicted about my decision not to move in with him.

The alder trees gave way to a marshy area where a brood of lake ducks splashed their wings and used their bills to clean their bellies. Mateo pointed to a wooden bench half hidden behind a clump of pampas grass and young alder trees growing in the marsh. "Let's sit down for a while." The trees and pampas grass shaded the bench so we were submerged in their shadows.

I sat down, thinking about how I was going to tell him that I wanted to wait before moving in together. I shivered. He reached for my hand and held it tightly in his. "Leonie, I've decided we should break up."

I sat like a statue, struggling to take in his words, then leaned away from him in surprise. A sharp pain jabbed me inside. "Wh—what do you mean?" I asked, my voice cracking. "What happened?"

He scooted away from me. "You're too independent for me. I don't want someone who goes off hiking on her own and wants to go back to school for more education. I want a companion, someone who wants to dedicate her time to me."

I couldn't believe what I was hearing. What he was saying was that he didn't even like the person I was trying to become. Someone who was strong, who could make a difference in the world. I reached for his hand and he put it behind his back. I said, "We don't know each other enough yet. Let's keep trying."

His voice was a soft baritone. "I'm sorry, Leonie. I've made up my mind."

I wrapped my palms around my torso and bent over. The pain in my chest throbbed. My breath came in great gulps. Tears lathered my face. "I l-like the person I'm becoming. I like that I finished the hike to Machu Picchu d-despite how hard it was. It makes me feel stronger than I've ever been!"

Mateo lifted me from the bench and guided me toward the entrance of the park with his arm around my back. As we trudged down the path, rosy-billed pochard ducks honked; swallows and *doraditos* camouflaged by miniature clumps of trees twittered and warbled. Lizards sunned on rocks. A few walkers passed us going the opposite way, staring at my tear-stained face, then looking away.

"Mateo, I can't believe what you're saying!" I said, clinging to his arm, not caring who was listening.

"Leonie," he said, his voice falling away. "I know who I am, and I think that you're finding out who you are. You're a brilliant, caring, strong woman, just not for me."

At the exit, he hugged me. "I wish you happiness and peace, Leonie. The time I spent with you was wonderful."

How could he do this? He turned and walked away from me down España Avenue. I clutched my torso, holding myself together. As clouds darkened the sky and blocked out the hot sun, I staggered toward the metro. Raindrops fell onto my forehead, mingling with the tears on my cheeks. Soon, sticky drops of rain drenched my shoulders and hair. I let them. A low rumble of thunder echoed across the sky, and as I started to run, the rain beat down so hard that puddles collected in the pot-holes and the water in the gutters churned like a boiling kettle.

When I arrived at Clarisa's doorstep, I shook off as much water from my clothes as I could, squeezing the edge of my tank top like a dishcloth, clawed off my shoes and socks, threw them against the wall inside the door, slammed open the bedroom door, and peeled off my wet clothes. Groping through a blur of tears, I turned on the shower and let the warm water flow over my face and body. The water washed away the tears and rain. After toweling off, I pulled on a clean T-shirt and shorts and looked in the mirror over the dresser. My eyes were bloodshot, my nose red and swollen. My wet hair hung around my neck and shoulders like strings.

Hiding my face behind my hands, I flopped down onto the bed. The tears started again, and I cried hard, the way a person can only cry when no one's watching, a deluge of tears and barks escaping from my mouth, heaving deep, rasping breaths, my mind so wrapped up in anguish that it went numb. Agony, the desperate suffering of feeling out of control and hopeless.

What would I tell everyone? My big plan to start a new life with Mateo had vanished. I was on my own again.

When Clarisa and Luna came home, they invited me to have dinner. Through the closed door, I said, holding a tissue up to my nose, "Go without me. I don't feel well." At one point in the evening, I crawled off the bed to wash my face, staring at my sorry self in the mirror: my auburn hair tangled in knots, the whites of my eyes crossed with red veins, my face streaked with dried, sticky tears. I took several deep breaths. Then, wetting a facecloth, I washed my face with cold water until it was clean of tears and a little less swollen.

What would Mom do?

CHAPTER 32.5

I am seven years old and Zach is five. We are sitting at the dining room table with Mom and Dad, eating one of Zach's favorite meals, chicken and dumplings. Dad is telling a story about when he had to walk to school every day in the snow, even in the summer. Everyone is laughing except my mother. She is smiling, her eyes like jewels.

Next, the four of us are sharing stories about our friends. Dad talks about his best friend Scott, in first grade, who was short, but grew up to play basketball in college. Mom shares a story about Dottie, her friend from down the street, who gives the same Valentine's Day card to her husband every year, and he never notices. We erupt in laughter.

Zach describes a new friend Sean he has just met in kindergarten, who likes to play marbles like he does. When Zach visited Sean's house, he saw his giant marble collection. They played outside on the patio, and Sean's mother gave them fresh strawberries to eat.

When it is my turn to share, I can't decide which friend to talk about. There is Ann with the long straight brown hair and clear skin, Becky with a mop of curly hair and ready smile, and Daisy who loves to jump rope. Finally, I tell stories about all three of them and my family listens with rapt attention.

"Remember, having true friends is one of the most precious parts of life," Mom says. I look up into her face and know it's true.

CHAPTER 33

The next morning, I pretended I was sleeping until Luna left the room. I heard her and Clarisa making coffee, taking plates out of the cupboard, and scraping chairs across the floor. A little later, I heard Clarisa wash her cup and plate, say goodbye, and close the front door. It sounded like Luna was turning the pages of a book at the table. Maybe she was looking at the class schedule or a textbook. Finally, I heard her zip up her backpack, open the outside door, and lock it.

Beside my bed, the clock ticked the seconds away and I buried my face in my pillow to block out the light coming through the blinds. As I listened to the clock's rhythm, I rocked back and forth, wishing for my mother's arms to cradle me. That day, Hanna was arriving in Buenos Aires to stay with her friend who lived close by. I had promised to meet her plane in the afternoon. Somehow, I had to get myself together before then and come up with a new plan.

What would Mom do?

I imagined my mother whistling as she worked in her flower garden. Mom had tried to teach me to whistle, because she said that if you could whistle, you could find happiness wherever you went.

But mine came out all air, not like the clear flute tones of my mother's. I tried again. And again. It was no use. The sound that came out of my mouth was tuneless and wheezy, the eerie sound of wind in the night. I didn't feel like whistling anyway. I felt like hiding my face in my pillow and blocking out the throbbing in my chest.

Mom would get out of bed. Or rise out of her recliner and stride into the kitchen to make lunch even if she felt nauseous. I hauled my feet to the floor and sat up, combing my hair out of my face with my fingers. For a minute, the room spun around me—the clock, the dresser, the bathroom door—whirling as if they were part of a storm. Round and round and round, until gradually the spinning stopped and objects became clear. I blinked and rubbed my face with my hands, sitting still for several long minutes.

Mom had said that a shower was a great refresher. She even recommended alternating between hot and cold water to energize the skin and invigorate the spirit. I followed her advice. I undressed, turned on the shower, and waited for the water to warm up. Once in, I lifted my face, allowing the pleasant stream to massage my forehead, face, and neck. I let it run down my back and front and swirl around my legs like a waterfall. With the loofah, I rubbed my chest, my arms, my legs, my feet. I turned the knob for cooler water, and goosebumps covered my body as I let the new temperature—as cold as melted snow that had traveled for miles downstream—envelop me. I turned around so that the chilliness could refresh every inch of me. I turned off the water, grabbed the towel hanging outside the door, and stepped out.

Mom would try to look her best, and I would too. I braided my hair into one long strand down my back to keep it off my neck and brushed my eyelids with light blue eyeshadow. It was going to be another hot and humid day, so I dressed in a blue knee-length cotton skirt, a white T-shirt that had short ruffled sleeves, and navy canvas sandals. I grabbed my jean jacket.

Clarisa and Luna had left me coffee so I added milk to the steamer, turned it on, poured the coffee, and ladled the steamy milk over the surface. *Mmm, comforting.* What was it that my mother made for breakfast when we didn't feel well? Oatmeal? No, scrambled eggs and toast with butter. I made some, spreading the butter on the toast so that it reached all the way to the edges, like Mom did. After eating, I felt better: My stomach was settled and I was reenergized.

HANNA'S PLANE ARRIVED ON time, and I met her at the luggage turnstile. She dropped her suitcase, opened her arms, and wrapped them around my shoulders. "How are you, Leonie?"

I mumbled into her shoulder. "Happy to see you. So happy."

She knew me too well. "Something's wrong," she said, leaning back to peer into my face better.

I nodded. "Yes, something *is* wrong, but let's get out of this airport first and I'll tell you all about it."

Mom had always said that friends were the best therapy. With her friends, she talked about raising children, cooking for a family, troubles at work, and coping with illnesses. I had always admired her supportive relationships.

After taking the metro across the city, Hanna and I stopped at Café Tortoni. A sign near the door noted that it was the oldest café in Buenos Aires, founded in 1858 by the Frenchman Jean Touan and named after the famous Tortoni café in Paris, an artist hangout. Inside the classical walnut doors and windows, the café stretched into a long rectangle, interspersed with evenly spaced polished brown columns that opened up to side bays. Walnut paneling and richly painted chestnut-colored walls decorated the alcoves. Pictures of artists who had visited throughout the decades hung on the walls. We sat at an elegant marble table in dark brown wooden armchairs under a golden chandelier. The menu offered coffee and other brewed drinks, sandwiches, light breakfasts, and desserts. We ordered thin ham and cheese sandwiches made with flatbread and freshly brewed lemonade.

Hanna leaned back in her chair, arching her back over the sturdy wood. "Now, tell me what happened."

I couldn't look at her right away, so I twisted my hands together. "Mateo broke up with me."

"He did what?"

Heartbreak pierced my chest. "He doesn't like how independent I am."

Hanna pulled at her ear with her right hand, looking away from me for a minute, thinking. "What will you do now?"

I shook my head. "You know, I was going to tell him that I didn't want to move in with him just yet. Some of the things he did bothered me."

Hanna reached across the table and brushed my arm gently. "Like what?"

I blinked as I remembered. "Remember when I helped him create the labels for the wines?"

"Yes."

"He took all the credit for that."

Hanna scrunched up her mouth and a worry line appeared between her eyebrows. "Oh yes, I noticed that. I didn't like it at the time. You don't need someone who takes your glory. You're talented. Remember what we accomplished with the menu and the food. We made Sara a lot of money."

I looked down at my coffee. "I'm proud of what I've done. But being me made *him* uncomfortable. The fact that he broke up with me before I said anything to him about not moving in together—hurts." I pressed a hand over my heart. "Did I tell you that I'm going back to school to become a psychologist?" I looked up to see her reaction.

Hanna whistled like a trucker. "Wow. That's great. So, you've figured out what you want to do!"

I was stunned. "How'd you do that?"

Hanna opened her hands over the table. "Do what?"

"You whistled."

She blinked. "Everybody can. Can't you?"

"Nope. I've tried."

She flapped a hand toward me. "Ah, so what? Why don't we take this week to have fun?"

THAT NIGHT AT CLARISA'S apartment, Hanna helped me tell Clarisa and Luna about Mateo. Clarisa gave me a big hug, then hopped out of her chair, opened a cupboard, and grabbed a bottle of malbec. "This requires some vino-therapy." Luna grabbed four wine glasses from another cabinet and set them on the table. Clarisa poured wine into them. She raised her glass and donned her beguiling smile. "Salud!"

Luna raised hers. "Salud! Chica, you're going to be fine. Given a little more time, you would've broken up with Mateo. You don't want someone who doesn't love you for what you are, which is strong, gifted, educated, and friendly. You've accomplished a lot in the last year."

I *had* grown, and I *was* thinking about pulling away from Mateo. Besides, I had friends to support me in what I wanted to do. I raised my glass. "Salud. To my new life."

We talked late into the night and ate empanadas that Clarisa had bought on her way home from school. When they were all gone, we nibbled on alfajores and opened a second bottle of wine. Hanna poured more wine into her glass and raised it over the table. "To friendship."

Mom, you were right. The best way to heal is to talk to a friend.

CHAPTER 34

Hanna left late to return to her friend's apartment, so we decided to sleep in and meet in the early afternoon. I slept well until about 7:00 a.m. but then tossed and turned, thinking about Mateo. My insecurities came back. I was a boat floating down a fast-moving river with no rudder. What was I supposed to do? After hours of poor sleep, I finally got out of bed about 11:00 a.m. and took a shower. I drank some cold coffee and ate three pieces of toast before heading out to catch the metro.

"Let's go to the flower district. I want to visit a florist who I met here a year ago."

Hanna's face lit up.

"The florist's name is Flora. She knew she would always want to sell flowers because she loved being around beauty." I pictured Flora in her green apron showing me around her tiny shop.

Hanna sighed. "She sounds lovely."

I remembered the flower that Flora had given me that day. "She gave me a yellow rose to signify that we'd always be friends."

Hanna's eyes grew animated. "Let's go! To her flower shop."

We exited the metro on Calle Sarmiento and walked past several flower stalls and shops filled with bouquets. When we arrived at Flora's shop, we stood in the shade under the willow tree. Underneath the shop window were dozens of white and green buckets filled with roses of every color, lilies, carnations, chrysanthemums, tulips, orchids, and jasmine. Their perfume was intoxicating.

Flora appeared in the open doorway, holding a bouquet of colorful Gerber daisies. She wore her shoulder-length raven hair pulled back with a scarlet scrunchie. Her face was free of wrinkles except for the dimples that punctuated the ends of her smile. Under her green apron, she wore a pink T-shirt and capri blue jeans. The apron was stained with soil and watermarks. The creases of her hands were dark with crusted dirt, and her hands were as chapped as before. "I know you. You're the young woman to whom I gave a yellow rose about a year ago. You're my friend." She tucked the bouquet of Gerber daisies into one of the buckets on the pavement, then held out her arms, asking for a hug.

I was astonished. "You remember me?" I sniffed and blinked away the happy well of tears behind my eyes, went to her, put my arms around her shoulders, and kissed her cheek. She hugged me back. I turned and reached out a hand toward Hanna. "This is my friend Hanna. We met when we worked at a winery in Mendoza this last year."

Flora's eyes brightened. "Oh, my goodness. It's so nice to meet you. Come in, come in. Please have some lemonade with me to cool down. It's hot and humid today."

Grateful, we followed her into the shop, over the gray cement floor, past the displays of vases filled with flowers of every color, and beyond the fresh floral and greenery wreaths hanging on the pink-tinted walls. In the back was a colorful circular tiled table surrounded by four basket-weave chairs. Beside the table, pushed up against one wall was an eight-foot stainless steel counter and sink and old scratched beige cabinets and mismatched knobs. Flora opened one of the cabinet doors and pulled out a clean rag, which she rinsed under the faucet at the sink. She bent over the table, swept bits of greenery into her left hand, then used the cloth to wipe the table. "Sorry for the mess, but I had many orders this morning and used every surface around to get them ready. Please sit down, but you may have to sweep some plant clippings off your chair first."

While Hanna and I brushed our chairs, Flora disappeared into a back room. We heard water splashing into a sink and a soap bar being plunked back down into a soap dish, the clattering of glasses, and the opening of a refrigerator door. In a few minutes, she came back carrying a blue melamine tray with a pitcher of lemonade and three glasses. I took one of the glasses off the tray. "This is generous of you, Flora. Thank you."

After pouring the lemonade and serving us, Flora sat down, her green apron ballooning over her torso. She smoothed it with one of her soil-lined hands.

I surveyed the flower displays and buckets of flowers lined up against the back wall. "We were planning on spending the day looking at flower gardens all over the city, but being in the midst of a flower shop is even better."

Suddenly, we heard footsteps coming into the shop. Flora rose out of her chair and Hanna and I turned around to see who it was. A woman with her hair held back in a net, bushy eyebrows, wide lips, and uneven yellow teeth had entered. She wore a blue gathered skirt with a tight waistband around her plump middle, and a white colorfully embroidered blouse. Her hands were wrinkled with sun spots, and her left ring finger wore a thin metal wedding band. On her feet, she sported a pair of brown flip-flops that slapped against the cement floor. I knew her, but from where?

Flora held out her hands and embraced the woman. "Martina, what a nice surprise."

Martina? Wasn't she the woman I met on the bus going to Iguazú Falls who had a blue suitcase under her seat and a basket of cookies on her lap? She was going to visit her grandchildren.

The woman turned to the displays of flowers. "I want to buy a bouquet of flowers for my friend Triana who just lost her mother." When she looked in the direction of where Hanna and I were sitting, she pulled back her head and peered at me with her eyelids half closed. "You're Leonie. I met you on a bus over a year ago." When she spread her wide lips into a smile, I could see that one of her front teeth was pushed back more than the other one. It *was* her, the woman with the blue suitcase and basket of cookies.

Flora stuck her hands in the pockets of her apron. "Well, this is a day of reunions. I met Leonie over a year ago, and today she showed up in my shop with her friend Hanna. Martina, why don't you join us for a glass of lemonade. It's hot, isn't it?"

"I would love to. It *is* hot, no?"

I brushed plant clippings off the fourth chair as Martina joined us, and Flora fetched another glass. Martina sat down between Hanna and me, and Flora poured her a glass of lemonade.

I put my hand over Martina's. "I'm sorry that Triana lost her mother."

She took a long swallow of her lemonade and wiped the sweat off her forehead. "On the bus, you mentioned that you lost your mother too. You were heartbroken, I remember. How are you feeling now?"

I tensed up. Without warning, a flood of tears cascaded down my cheeks. I covered my face to prevent the moans from escaping my mouth. Soon, a warm arm stretched across my back and long fingers squeezed my arm. I recognized Hanna's cottony scent. I removed my hands from my face and, through bleary eyes, blinked at the faces around me. "To tell you the truth, I'm a mess. My boyfriend broke up with me saying that he didn't like who I was. That was hard to take because I should've broken up with him! If Mom was alive, I'd never have stayed with him this long. I miss her." I sat motionless as I realized what I had just said. Knowing that I had a valid reason for breaking up with Mateo was empowering. My feelings were just as important as anyone else's. It was up to me to make sure they were protected.

Flora reached for my hand. "I was twenty years old when my mother died. I still miss her hugs and soft voice. She taught me how to make the beautiful floral wreaths hanging in the shop."

Hanna squeezed my shoulders again with her long fingers, then sat back in her seat. "My mother died when I was twelve. Of course I miss her, but I feel her all the time so the pain of losing her is less now."

Martina patted her hairnet. "So, we've all lost our mothers. My mother died two years ago when she was ninety-two years old." Martina took one of my hands into her large plump warm palms and placed my hand on the surface of the cool tiled table. "Losing a mother at first feels like losing part of yourself. You feel disoriented and lost, but someday you'll find your footing and be able to find her in your life in a different way." Thinking back, I *had* become better at finding Mom in my own life. Talking about her was one way. Maybe Dad and Zach were right.

Hanna reached over and placed one of her long-fingered hands over Martina's. "I was bitterly heartbroken when my mother died, but my father helped me recover from her loss. He showed me how much he loved her and how he always would love her. When we talked about our memories, my grief lessened, and I felt good that I had such a wonderful mother to love."

Her father helped her?

Flora stretched a hand across the table and pressed it on top of the others. "My mother was my mentor. I learned from her, and I'm like her. Everyone recognizes that I'm her daughter, which makes me happy. She loved flowers too. She said that whenever something dies, living things grow out of it. 'Flowers, for example,' she said. 'While they bloom, they let the bees take their pollen and use it to grow new flowers and life for bees and other creatures.' Since she died, I've come to understand that while she lived, she shared herself with me. Now that she's gone, I have parts of her inside me."

We were all broken, like a chipped glass that can still hold wine. I was a raft in the ocean, and these women were helping me steer through the froth and waves, to avoid drowning. We all had to survive the ocean of life. Even me.

CHAPTER 35

That night, I couldn't eat or drink even though I was dehydrated from being in the sun all day. I developed cramps in my stomach, so I went to bed without dinner. In bed, I folded my body into a fetal position to try to alleviate the sharp pains, but they persisted. I trembled, shivered in pain, tried to distract myself with happy thoughts, but only felt knives stabbing at my insides. Suddenly, my throat filled with fluid. I tottered to the toilet, clumsily flipped up the lid, and bent over the rim. My core shook; the fluid in my throat churned. Finally, a foul-smelling gruel shot out into the bowl like a torrent of lava, congealing on the sides and clotting in the water. After using a towel to mop my face, I crawled back to bed. Drool leaked from my mouth onto the pillow, and my forehead felt hot, feverish.

By the time Luna came in, I had visited the bathroom four more times, each time resulting in another explosion of vitriol into the toilet. My eyes felt like sandpaper and my skin was pasty.

Luna took one look at me and ran out of the room to get her sister. A pajama-clad Clarisa raced back into the room with Luna.

"She looks terrible," Luna said.

I was so weak, I couldn't talk and merely lay on the bed like a broken puppet, my arms and legs bent in awkward positions.

Clarisa took her cell phone out of her pocket. "I'm calling an ambulance."

Suddenly, I blacked out.

I REMEMBERED BEING lifted onto a gurney, watching the ceiling float above me as I was wheeled out the door under the yellow streetlight and lifted like a long sandbag on a board through the double doors of an ambulance. Inside, two faces hung over me, their mouths moving without sounds. A sharp needle jabbed my right arm. A thick wetness spread under my buttocks. I winced and blacked out.

When I came to, I was lying on a bed in a room full of machines, whirring and beeping. A long tube traveled from a needle in my right arm to a bag of clear fluid hanging on a metal hook. A nurse stood at a computer, clacking on the keys, while another tore off the packaging of a needle, dabbed the back of my left hand with a wet piece of cotton, and inserted the needle into a vein.

Voices talked over me back and forth like the drone of a television on low volume. A stick was placed under my tongue, a puffy Velcro pad was wrapped around my left upper arm, and a rubber thimble was plugged onto my right index finger. Men and women in scrubs peered over at me and then read the mysterious numbers blinking on the machines. I let my head fall to one side, my arms listless, my body heavy on the mattress.

Sometime later, an official-looking woman wearing a white coat with an embroidered name on the pocket leaned over me. "She's not going home today. She's dehydrated and probably has E. coli. Send that blood sample to the lab as soon as possible. When this IV is finished, put on another one. She needs electrolytes and fluid, a lot of both."

Suddenly, I wretched and jerked up in the bed, clapping a hand over my mouth. A nurse swung around, grabbed a kidney-shaped bowl from behind her, and stuck it under my chin. Over and over again, I heaved yellow liquid into the dish, my stomach juddering like a wrecked percolator. The nurse took away the bowl and wiped my mouth with a tissue. I was dog-tired, didn't care how many needles they wanted to stick into me. I collapsed and slept.

There was no window in the room, so I couldn't tell whether it was light or dark outside, but hours must've gone by as the medics drifted around me, poking my arms and hands, adjusting the tubes, and checking the machines. A robust man came into the room. He stood as a nurse unclamped bags and tubes from metal stands and laid them beside me on the bed. She pulled up the squealing metal bars on both sides of the bed and glanced over at the robust man. "Take her up to the fourth floor, room 456. The nurse will take care of her from there."

More floating ceilings, more faces, lights, voices, the whishing doors of an elevator opening and closing, ceilings with edges, glaring lights, a doorway, pastel pink walls, and a window with sunlight. The robust man disappeared, and a nurse wearing a purple top and matching pants rolled a metal stand with a computer into the room behind the bed. "What did you eat? You have E. coli, a serious infection. You need a platelet transfusion."

I couldn't answer her. My eyelids felt heavy. I turned my head toward the window. Outside, the sun was rising over some trees and buildings in the distance. It was morning, but I closed my eyes and fell asleep. Throughout the day, I slept while the nurse hooked and unhooked more bags to the IV needle in my arm. Each time, she explained what she was doing, but I couldn't concentrate. The words went in and out of my brain like an express train passing through a station.

Hanna and Luna came. They stood on either side of my bed and each took one of my hands into their own. In my imagination, I took hold of their friendship and slipped it under the cover, close to my heart. Hanna spoke to the nurse who shook her head from side to side, worry lines wrinkling her forehead. Staring at Luna, Hanna said, "Oh, no." I couldn't hear the conversation after that. Instead, I heard the beeps of the machine counting the remaining seconds of my life like a metronome.

The nurse seemed to be in my room all the time. She held a plastic cup with a straw up to my mouth and told me to drink.

The liquid was sweet and fizzy, but my stomach was so sore from retching, I could barely sip. Finally, I stopped vomiting, fell asleep again, and dreamed.

THE NEXT MORNING WHEN I woke up, my stomach felt calm. The nurse at the computer turned and smiled, but her voice was clipped and businesslike. "You're not so pale today. You must be feeling better. You're still getting fluids and a plasma transfusion, though. You'll be staying in the hospital for at least a few more days." She handed a plastic cup for me to hold and I sipped from its straw. "We're going to give you some light food this morning. Try to eat as much as you can, but don't force it." She finished her work on the computer and left the room, the door swinging closed behind her.

A few minutes later, a female orderly wearing blue scrubs came into the room carrying a tray, which she set on a table and swung over the bed in front of me. She removed the metal cover over the plate, and I found scrambled eggs and two pieces of buttered toast beneath it. The food reminded me of Mom. A pot of tea stood behind the plate, and she poured the tea into a teacup, then left the room. Alone again, I nibbled on the eggs and toast and sipped the hot tea, which felt soothing to my throat. I studied the machines with blinking lights, dripping tubes, changing numbers, and squiggly lines. I realized something terrible had happened to me. How severe was it?

The rest of the morning, I stared at the silent pictures flashing on the television. News programs, talk shows, soap operas. I wasn't interested in listening, but the pictures helped me feel less alone. For lunch, I ate a little bit of soup and saltine crackers. While the orderly was taking away the lunch tray, Luna and Hanna walked into the room.

"I'm happy to see you guys."

Luna's voice sounded relieved. "Wow, chica, you look better. Yesterday, you were in bad shape."

I scooted myself back in the raised bed so I could see them better. "I thought I saw you yesterday, but I was pretty groggy."

Hanna placed her long fingers over my forehead. I could smell her cottony scent as she bent near me. "I'm glad you're feeling better."

I pulled up the blanket to cover my hospital gown. "My mother said that friendships are one of the most wonderful parts of life."

Luna came to stand next to me. "Your mother was a wise woman, chica."

I reached out to Luna, but my hand fell back on the blanket. "Thanks for coming to see me. It's boring watching television all day, and I don't have anything to read."

Luna pressed her hands in front of her chest and folded her fingers over one another. "Chica, I have something important to tell you."

I was eager to turn the conversation over to something besides me. "Really? Is it about you attending university?"

She straightened her fingers, bent them backward. She looked serious. "No, it's nothing like that."

I struggled to guess what it was, but couldn't think of anything important. "What is it?"

Luna's pupils dilated in slow motion. "I called your father, and he's flying to Buenos Aires right now to see you." She raised her hands in front of her, looked at them as if she was confused, then stuck them behind her back.

Hanna cleared her throat.

I gawked at the two of them as they stood, Luna beside me and Hanna at the foot of the bed. "You didn't. No, you didn't."

Luna nodded her head, then said, "The doctor said you were in serious trouble and she wanted your family here."

Hanna bit her lip.

I placed my fingers over my eyes and massaged them for several long minutes. "What did you tell him?"

Luna's voice started out strong, but faded down to a whisper. "That you were in the hospital for dehydration and E. coli. You were getting fluids and a plasma transfusion, but the doctors were worried about the severity of your condition. I had to call him, chica. You need him here."

I inhaled and puffed out my breath, blowing out a fire. "When's he coming?"

Luna looked teary. She sniffed. "He'll be here tomorrow morning. He's coming to the hospital as soon as he arrives."

First, Mateo broke up with me, and now my father was coming to Buenos Aires. All my plans had blown up like dynamite. I looked at Luna and Hanna as if through frosted glass. "Oh, nothing's working out the way I planned!"

Luna patted my arm. "Look, chica. Your dad loves you. You're lucky to have someone who cares so much."

I felt like a limp doll. "I don't want to see him. I just want a new life."

Hanna sucked in her bottom lip. "Maybe that's not possible."

I pointed to my backpack on a chair. "Can you get my laptop for me? I want to call Elaine."

Luna set the computer on the table and swung it over my bed. "Clarisa sends her love. She'd be here, but she couldn't take time off from teaching. We'll be back tomorrow, but we'll leave you now so you can talk to Elaine." Hanna kissed me on the cheek, and Luna rubbed my hand on her own cheek. When they left, the room felt colder.

It wasn't going to be easy for me to see Dad after over a year. I sat for a while, wondering what I was going to say when he arrived. I opened the laptop, then turned the computer on and placed a video call to Elaine.

Her face popped up on the screen. She was dressed in a light blue blouse and navy suit jacket. “Good morning, Leonie. Where are you now?”

I rested my hand with my hospital bracelet in front of the keyboard. “I’m in Buenos Aires. It’s afternoon here.”

She peered into the screen. “Are you in the hospital?”

Trying to downplay my situation, I explained that I had just gotten a little dehydrated and ate some bad food, but I was going to be fine. Worry lines creased her forehead. “I’m ready for you to come home, buddy. You’ve been gone too long.”

I held my wrists with my hands. I didn’t feel cheery, but fixed a smile on my face. “I’m staying here. I’ve decided to go back to school to become a psychologist.”

Elaine wasn’t fooled. “Look, come home. I know you miss your mom, but it’ll be okay. I promise. I’ll help you.”

I shook my head in frustration. “Everyone’s saying that. Also, my dad is coming tomorrow and I haven’t been nice to him this last year. I don’t know what I’m going to say to him.”

Elaine smiled. “He’s going to be so happy to see you that he’ll forgive everything. Parents can’t help themselves.”

I wondered why she was dressed in a suit. “Hey, where are you going, all dressed up?”

She smoothed the front of her jacket with her hands. “I got a new job. One of the San Francisco clients of the temp agency liked my work so much that they hired me as a marketing analyst. I love it.”

“Congratulations. I’m proud of you.”

Elaine slipped her purse strap onto her shoulder. “Look, I’ve got to go to work, but let’s talk later. And get better. I’m glad your dad is going to be with you. Don’t worry.”

The rest of the day passed with me pondering why everyone seemed to think that I should go home.

CHAPTER 36

I slept better that night since my stomach was no longer raw and stormy. When I woke up the next morning, I took a shower, washed my hair, and put on a clean hospital gown. I was sitting up in bed, combing my wet hair, when Dad knocked on the door, opened it about two inches, and peeked through the crack.

His gentle earthy voice made my heart jump. "Hello?"

I pulled the comb through the last tangle and placed it on the bedside table. Clearing my throat, I bit the edge of one of my fingernails. "Hi, Dad. I'm here. Come in."

Dad pushed the door wide open, came in, and closed it behind him. He wore wrinkled navy trousers and a crumpled blue button-down shirt. His streaked-with-gray auburn hair was disheveled like he had forgotten to comb it, and bags dragged the skin down beneath his eyes. He was carrying a medium-sized black suitcase with a bright blue luggage tag buckled to the handle. He dropped the suitcase against the wall and strode up to the side of the bed, bent over, and kissed me on the forehead.

He patted the top of my wet head and brushed the side of my face. "I've been worried about you." His eyes were bloodshot.

"I'm fine, Dad. I just got dehydrated and ate some bad food, that's all."

He was so close, I could see the lines on his face. "No, the doctors were anxious, sweetheart."

"Well, I'm fine now. I even got up and took a shower this morning."

His mouth was as straight as a pencil. "Well, I'm glad I came and saw for myself. Zach just got home for Christmas the day before I left. He was worried too."

I shrugged. "I talked to Zach."

Dad rested his palms down on the bedsheets. "I know. He wants you to come home for Christmas. So do I. You've been here too long, and we miss you."

"No, Dad, I told you. I'm staying in Argentina. I'm going to live here now."

He changed the subject, and talked about picking up Zach at the airport and how the dog had jumped up when Zach opened the door. "He only has one semester left before he graduates, and has applied for a job at the San Francisco Zoo." His voice was so cordial that he could have been talking to a stranger sitting next to him on an airplane. I felt awkward too.

I wanted him to be excited about what I'd done. "Machu Picchu was an experience of a lifetime, Dad. Luna and I loved Vilma, our guide. And we met a woman named Sofia who gave us crystals. I am proud that I finished the hike."

Dad nodded, silent.

My speech was careful. "You've got to meet Luna and Clarisa while you're here. And Hanna, my friend from Sara's winery."

Dad listened and nodded like a polite co-passenger would. We were two people who didn't know each other well, making conversation to pass the time.

Dad looked at me, his brown eyes soft and wounded. A single tear welled up at the edge of his bottom eyelash and shimmered.

He touched the side of my arm with his right pinkie finger. "When are you moving in with Mateo?"

I looked at where my feet poked out of the thin hospital blanket. My toes twitched so I bent down, grabbed the end of the blanket, and threw it over them. "I'm not. Mateo broke up with me." A hiccup escaped from my mouth, and before I could control my emotions, a flood of tears trailed down the front of my cheeks. I covered my face with my hands and wept behind them, shaking my shoulders in frustration.

I could tell Dad seemed uncomfortable, like he wanted to hug me but didn't know if he should. He waited as I sobbed behind my fingers, catching my breath and wiping the tears off my face with the edge of my blanket.

"Oh, honey, what happened?"

I shook my head, feeling ashamed. "He doesn't think I'm the right girl for him. But the funny thing is, he wasn't right for me. He didn't want me to travel or go back to school. He wanted an invisible woman, and I'm not that person."

My dad didn't say anything. Just looked at me for a long time, the quiet only broken by me, sniffing up my tears. He walked to the wall, picked up his suitcase, placed his pillowy hand on the doorknob, and turned to me. "I'm going to go find a hotel, then I'll be back."

Suddenly, it seemed as if he changed his mind about leaving because he sat down at the bottom of the bed. "Honey, I don't know how to help you heal from this, but I want to. I love you so much." His face transmitted a beam of love across the room. I felt his energy surrounding me, providing support and security. "It's okay not to live near your family. It's okay to travel and explore different places. The important thing is to maintain the loving relationships with your family while you're doing it."

After a few long moments, he stood up, opened the door, and clicked it behind him.

The love he had left behind enveloped me in a cloud of security.

As I sat in my bed thinking about Dad and Zach, the outlines of the room became clearer: the corners, the tiles on the ceiling, the window, the pulled-up blinds, the edges of the bed, the lunch table, the metal stands and machines filled with lines and numbers, all of them in great detail. I imagined my mother's chair in the living room, the kitchen where she made jams and stews, and the garden where tomatoes filled vines and peppers hung from bright green bushes. I pictured Dad sitting in an Adirondack chair on the porch reading, and Zach kicking a football in the yard. In the next second, I felt renewed like a day after the rain had washed the sky so that the sun streamed down like silk strands, its light revealing the details of the plants and the earth. Sofia, the woman Luna and I had met at the sacred rock on Machu Picchu, came to my mind. She had said, "Find a place where the energy of love is strong, and you will find what you need."

I sat still.

Dad and Zach wanted me regardless of how much I'd hurt them. They didn't care if I was sad and broken. If I was a chipped glass, they loved me. What more could I want? My mother loved me. I missed her. So did Dad and Zach. We could grieve and heal together. Like a family.

Hanna, Luna, and Clarisa had encouraged me to go home. Flora and Martina had. Elaine had. Most importantly, I wanted to go back to San Francisco, to my *real* life. I had been afraid to be vulnerable, to let others see how shattered I was, how terrified I felt without Mom. I adjusted myself in the bed to sit up straighter. I had made Mom three promises and kept them. I figured out how to keep her in my life, even if it was sometimes painful. Almost everywhere I went, I found female mentors. All I had to learn was to recognize them, to realize how they could influence me, and I didn't have to live near them to keep them in my heart. And I had traveled, and someday I'd travel again—take another pilgrimage to keep myself grounded. But now it was a good time to go home. Before I went, though, I had a few things to do: see Mateo one more time, and, if I could, apologize to his mother for being rude to her when she had visited the winery.

THE NURSE CAME INTO my room, measured my blood pressure, checked my oxygen level, took my temperature, and read my pulse. When she was finished, she called the doctor, who told me, "You can go home. You're a lucky lady. Why don't you get dressed and wait for your dad to pick you up?" I reached out to shake her hand. She gripped it firmly and shook back. "Take good care of yourself. A lot of people obviously care about you."

How true that was. "Thank you."

By the time Dad returned, I was dressed in clean jeans, a pink T-shirt, and my flip-flops. I had braided my hair into a single braid, rubbed sunscreen on my face, and sat back down on the end of the bed. "Dad, I'm going home with you."

He stood over my bed for several long seconds, as if he was trying to translate what I said. "My girl. My daughter. I'm so glad. We'll heal together with Zach. Someday, you'll see, we'll feel better." He hugged me tightly. His love permeated every cell in my body.

I let his warmth soak into me. Then I lifted my head and said, "And Dad, I want to go back to school to become a psychologist. When we get home, I'll tell you more about it." He rubbed my back with his big hand. I almost felt like I was already home.

CHAPTER 37

The next morning, I called Mateo and asked him if he would meet me for a walk at the Costanera Sur Ecological Reserve again. He sounded hesitant, but agreed. After drinking coffee and eating medialunas, I set out into the humid morning to catch the metro. Once inside the park, I marched down the Camino del Medio, ignoring the bicycles, walkers, and strollers sharing the path. I didn't notice the grassy clearings with cement benches or the marshes where wild birds and turtles basked in the sun. My hands sweat with nervousness.

Near the end of the path, I spotted Mateo's long-limbed silhouette pacing in a tiny circle next to the River Plate. Behind him, the buttery round sun hung over the churning river like a glowing lantern. We found a bench near the water and sat down, leaving space between us. Our hands lay limp in our laps, and I cleared my throat, looking up at the plain blue sky for a signal.

I turned to him, searching his face for a reaction. "I'm going home to San Francisco." His eyes widened in surprise. "My dad's here. I ended up in the hospital, and he came to see me. Talking to him is what convinced me to go home." I rubbed my sweaty hands, then wiped them off on my jeans.

Furrows rose between his bushy eyebrows. "Are you alright?" His face held such empathy. I had fallen in love with a good man, just not the man for me.

"I'm perfectly fine now. I ate some bad food and got dehydrated. The hospital staff fixed everything," I said, thinking back to our walks in the vineyard and our work at the winery. Those sweet days.

Mateo scooted near and cradled me in an embrace. I could feel his heart beating and his breath flowing over my shoulder. "I'm glad you're going home to San Francisco. You're a great woman, Leonie. I will never forget you, but you'll be happier there."

My head nuzzled against his chest. "I didn't want to go home because I was too afraid to be vulnerable with my family, but my dad doesn't care whether my feelings are confused and twisted. In fact, he understands why, and he still loves me."

Mateo rubbed my arm. "Of course he does, Leonie. He's your father."

I squeezed Mateo's arm, feeling like I never wanted to let go. "I loved our time together, Mateo, even if we aren't meant for each other. And I have to be honest with you, I need to be with a man who encourages my dreams as much as his own."

A wry grin appeared on his lips, then the grin vanished. His chest rose and fell as he sighed. His eyes were watery. "You'll always be special to me. Always."

With his arm around my shoulder, we reminisced about our months at the winery and we laughed about trying to dance the tango.

"Remember the Virgin Mary?"

"Oh, yes," he replied. "I'll remember her whenever I pray."

"Me too," I said. "You know, I was afraid you wouldn't see me. Afraid you wouldn't trust me to have a conversation with you. You might have assumed I was trying to get back together."

He patted my back. "Your voice told me that you were okay. You're calmer and happier than the last time I saw you." We sat for a while and listened to the nasal notes of some warbling doraditos that were hidden in nearby grasses, then stood up and walked along the bank of the river, following the steep riverbank, watching the current percolating far out to the Atlantic Ocean.

We held hands like lovers and talked like friends. We turned right onto the Camino de Los Plumerillos, which took us back into the middle of the reserve where alder trees shaded the path and marshes were hidden in pampas grass. We searched for the lazy turtles that crawled between the weeds to avoid the heat. Wild ducks of every feather, size, and color wrote a symphony for us with their horns, strings, and percussions.

I squeezed his hand. "I have one request of you before I leave."

His voice cracked a little. "What's that?"

I paused on the path and pulled him in front of me so that he faced me directly. "I'd like to apologize to your mother for being rude to her during her visit to the winery. My insecurities overcame me, and I regret not being welcoming toward her. I realize now that I need to understand how to manage my emotions better, even in difficult times."

I saw surprise and gladness in Mateo's face. "I can call and ask her if now is a good time," he said, pulling his cell phone out of his back pocket. After a short explanation of my request, she invited both of us to her house.

FORTY-FIVE MINUTES LATER, Mateo and I were standing on Violane's porch. She had been waiting, sitting in a wicker chair with a glass of iced tea beside her. As we walked up the steps, she swept her right arm in an arch, ballerina-style, and invited us to sit down.

She looked pleased to see me. "Hello again, Leonie." She took my hand and pressed it with both of hers. "I'll get some tea for you both," she said, whirling her skirt around the frame of the open front door and disappearing into the house. In a few minutes, she came out with two more tall glasses of tea.

My voice was shaking. "Thank you, Violane." I sipped the

cold drink to wet my mouth before trying to speak again. "Mateo must have told you that we're not together anymore." I blinked.

Her hands rested in the folds of her skirt. "Yes, dear, he told me."

On my other side, I could hear Mateo breathing through his nose and sipping his tea. "I want to apologize for being rude to you when you visited us at the winery. I wasn't myself. I realize now that my grief for my mother made me feel jealous of your relationship with Mateo. I was hurting, and wasn't dealing with my emotions maturely."

Violane reached over to me and took my hands into her own. "Oh dear, grief is such a difficult emotion. Everyone mourns differently. Some people become paralyzed and can't leave home for months. Others can't eat. Others behave in ways they would never act under normal circumstances. I understand, and I forgive you for taking out your sorrow on me."

Violane's hands felt tender.

"I feel so embarrassed that I couldn't handle myself better. I didn't want to be vulnerable, and I was trying to hide my helplessness." When I finished speaking, Mateo sighed, an exhale of happiness and relief.

Violane talked about her late husband and how she still missed him, but also knew she had to continue to live a good life without him. Noticing the potted flowers on the porch, I described my mother's flower garden at home and how she'd spent hours pruning old blooms from her roses and hydrangeas and sitting in her chair outside admiring their beauty. I also shared stories about Dad and Zach and told her that, because I was in the hospital, Dad had come to see me. "I'm going home with him."

Most of the time, Mateo was silent, only adding a word or two as Violane and I talked. The shaking in my voice disappeared as Violane's hospitality comforted me, and I felt truly forgiven and accepted.

After a couple of hours of friendly conversation, I stood up to leave. Mateo said he'd walk me to the metro. Violane placed her warm hands on my shoulders and kissed me on both cheeks. "Goodbye, my sweet girl. Thank you for coming today to talk to me. You're a wonderful young woman to have such courage to apologize. I hope we can stay friends."

Courage. Yes, I had it, even though I had lost my onyx necklace.

"I hope so too. Goodbye."

Mateo and I walked to the metro station, ten minutes from his mother's house. He held my hand. "I'm glad you talked with my mother even though I think she understood why you were so upset the first time she saw you."

"You think so?"

"Yes. I've always thought my mother understood people's hearts. If I grow up to be wise like her, I'll be a happy man."

THAT NIGHT, LUNA AND I stayed up late, sitting on our beds, facing each other, spending our last night together. I said, "Thank you for being my friend. Come to San Francisco one day so we can have more soul conversations. Without our adventures, I doubt if I would have sorted out my confusion."

Luna smiled. "Thank *you*. The first moment I met you, I knew things about you that you didn't know. I saw your empathy, your courage, and your love of nature. I knew that your mother must have been an incredible woman to create such a beautiful daughter." My heart felt as warm as a bowl of soup.

As the moon rose in the sky like a pearl button, our soul conversation continued until late into the night. We shared our memories of Peru: witnessing the Incas' incredible architectural skills, star-gazing at the Southern Sky at the Cusco Planetarium, tasting the white pulp from the cocoa pod at the chocolate plantation, climbing over Dead Woman's Pass, meeting Sofia from Lake Titicaca and hearing about the importance of her pilgrimage. I had found my orbit. And Luna and I were a permanent part of each other, like I had learned my mother was an enduring part of me.

CHAPTER 38

The plane rides from Buenos Aires to Miami and then to San Francisco were long, and Dad and I couldn't sit together. I slept through most of the flights, and when we started our descent over the San Francisco Bay, I was well rested.

The plane flew over the houses and high-rises of San Jose, then over the wide expanse of the San Francisco Bay. Mount Diablo rose to the east like a solitary regal giant. Highway 101 snaked up the west side of the bay as the plane sailed over the Dumbarton Bridge, the San Mateo Bridge, and finally down to the San Francisco Airport runway. I was home again. The California sun streamed through the window, and the December sky was a cloudless bright blue.

About an hour later, after Dad and I collected our luggage and waited in the customs line, we stood outside the terminal building with dozens of other people, all of them carrying backpacks and suitcases. Next to us, a little girl about eight years old stood next to her father, waiting. She wore a blue dress, jean jacket, and black Mary Janes. She held her father's hand, watching the people around her and whistling a tune that I tried to recognize. Her whistling was so clear, the notes so pure. I recognized the tune: "Twinkle, Twinkle, Little Star." I pursed my lips and attempted to turn my breathy whistle into the song that I had known for years. The notes wheezed out of my lips like wind leaking through a broken windowpane. My shoulders fell, my heart throbbing with disappointment.

The little girl kept whistling her song, her lips pressed into a perfect circle. She looked up and noticed me. For a brief moment, she stopped whistling, reading my face. Then she resumed whistling her song, her puckered circle of lips raised up so that I could see them.

Determined, I formed my own lips into perfect circles and tried the notes of the song again, all the while keeping my gaze on her. To my surprise, my notes came out smooth and strong. I could whistle! The girl's eyes softened as she heard my notes. Joy flooded her face. A warmth that started deep in my chest spread through me. My dad turned around and looked at me in surprise.

The girl and I whistled verse after verse together as I gained confidence. Her father reached for her hand and smiled down at his daughter and up at me. People milled around us, glancing briefly when they heard the music, their smiles lighting up as they recognized the tune.

When their bus came, the girl's father tugged at her arm to go. She stopped whistling and grinned at me, then raised her free hand to wave goodbye. I waved back and watched her board the bus with her dad and disappear inside.

Zach drove up in Dad's white SUV and parked the car right in front of us at the curb. He stepped out of the car, paced to the back, and popped open the hatchback. He raised his arms and, with them, circled both me and Dad together, squeezing us, a tight knot on the sidewalk. "I'm thrilled you're back," he whispered in my ear, his voice wavering.

I released myself from the hug and stood back to look at Zach and Dad.

"I'm sorry, Zach. I was so brokenhearted that I hurt you."

He nodded and lightly socked me on the arm. I reached for him again, grasping his hands, feeling Dad's arm loop around my shoulders. I examined the crowd on the curb for another familiar face and wished with all my heart that Mom would come rushing up to us and crush into the middle of our circle.

Maybe it was the jubilation of the travelers surrounding us: a father shaking his son's hand, girls in sweatsuits screaming as they found each other, little grandchildren hugging the legs of grandparents.

Maybe it was the flawless California weather: the crystal-blue sky, the sun warming my face, a cold breeze bathing my cheeks.

Maybe it was Zach's chocolate eyes twinkling at me or Dad's pillowy hand on the back of my shoulder blade.

I heard my mother's whistle, that quartz-clear note that sang like the peal of a church bell ringing out a hymn. The whistle that my mother used in every difficult situation. She had whistled even when life wasn't perfect, even when it didn't promise happiness. Her whistle had created cheerfulness all on its own. I understood then: Happiness didn't depend on the circumstances in life; I could create it with effort, intention.

So, I whistled.

BOOK CLUB DISCUSSION QUESTIONS

1. The author includes a scene in which her mother receives chemotherapy for her breast cancer. How did that scene make you feel as you read about Leonie's mother and the other patients in the room?
2. Can you identify with Leonie's grief at losing her mother? Describe your experience or the experience of someone you know who has had a similar grief.
3. Before she dies, Leonie's mother suggests that Leonie find other women to emulate. What do you think about this advice?
4. Describe the feelings of Leonie's father when she cashes in her plane ticket and stays in Argentina.
5. Leonie meets Flora, who owns her own flower shop in Almagro, Buenos Aires. What does Leonie learn from her?
6. Leonie meets a pair of sisters in Argentina: Clarisa and Luna. What role do each of these women play in her life? Compare their relationships with Leonie.
7. Leonie works at the winery, Bodega Romero, for a little over a year. What lessons does she learn there?
8. Why does Leonie fall in love with Mateo? Would you characterize her reasons as healthy or unhealthy?

9. Leonie and Luna travel to Cusco together and spend several days acclimating to the altitude. Which of their excursions interested you the most? Why?
10. What are the lessons that Leonie learns while she is hiking to Machu Picchu? Are they significant? If so, how?
11. As Leonie travels with Luna, she becomes increasingly disturbed about how Mateo is reacting to her travel goals. What is she realizing about this relationship? Why do you think she is unhappy about this?
12. When Leonie and Luna get to Machu Picchu, they meet a pilgrim, Sofia, who has traveled all the way from Puno, near Lake Titicaca. Why do you think the author included Sofia in Leonie's story?
13. Luna calls Leonie's father when she goes to the hospital. Was that a betrayal of their friendship? Why or why not?
14. Before she goes home, Leonie wants to apologize to Violane for being rude. Why do you think this is important to her, and what do you think about her decision?
15. Does Leonie's time in South America help her grieve for her mother? If not, why not? If so, describe how.
16. What is the significance of whistling in the book? Once she learns how to whistle, has Leonie changed for the better? How exactly?

ACKNOWLEDGMENTS

The inspiration for this novel came from numerous people. First of all, my mother, Rose Marie Bronk, passed away just before I began writing this story. Her unexpected death taught me how devastating it is to lose a mother. Also, my daughter, Rachael, who lived in Argentina for over two years, was my inspiration for the fictional character Leonie. Thank you also to my friends from Peru and Argentina who taught me extensive details about their countries.

I cannot imagine having written this book without the loyal support of my writing friend, Susan Elya, who read three versions of this story. Susan gave me courage, unfailing support, encouragement, and comradery. Her friendship means the world to me.

Brooke Warner, the publisher of She Writes Press (SWP), impressed me from the first moment I met her. Her kindness, respectfulness, and positive energy light up the world of publishing. I am also grateful to Shannon Green, my SWP project manager, who guided me through the tunnels of the publishing process and kept me moving forward. Thank you also to Jodi Fodor, who edited my manuscript, especially helping me with plot development. Jessica Powers, my initial and final editor, provided me with positive encouragement, invaluable insight about plot development, and copyediting. I appreciate her unfailing belief in me and her professional and kind interaction. Also, I'm forever grateful to Caitlin Hamilton Summie, my dynamic publicist, who guided me through this journey. Her upbeat personality and professional experience inspired my creativity and steered me toward new achievements.

Thank you to Suzanne Simonetti, Debra Thomas, Rebecca D'Harlingue, and Susan Weissbach Friedman, who read my book, appreciated my story, and wrote such wonderful compliments about it. I am beholden to you and grateful for your generous contribution.

To write this story, I performed extensive research. I especially want to acknowledge the information that I gleaned from Mark Adams's book *Turn Right at Machu Picchu*. His description of his journey throughout the Amazon was delightful and inspirational.

Finally, I would like to thank the members of my huge extended family who offer unlimited ideas for topics, plots, and memorable characters. But most notably, my two grown children, Alex and Rachael, are the joys of my life. When they were born, I became a better person. They motivate me daily with their kindness, communication skills, endurance, and thoughtful decisions. My stepson, Greg, and his wife, Katlyn, have given me two wonderful granddaughters, Emersyn and Morgan, constant reminders that life should be fun and happy.

And I am eternally grateful to my husband, Robert, who listens every day to my writing saga. How blessed am I to have such a profound and wise person with whom to share my life.

ABOUT THE AUTHOR

Tess Perko grew up in Sacramento and Suffolk, England. Formerly a journalist and English professor, she is the author of several short stories and poetry. *Learning to Whistle* is her debut novel.

In addition to writing, Tess raises money for scholarships for college and vocational students, teaches essay and journaling workshops to emancipated foster youth, studies Spanish, and enjoys growing roses. She lives with her husband, Robert, in the San Francisco Bay Area.

Looking for your next great read?

We can help!

Visit www.shewritespress.com/next-read
or scan the QR code below for a list
of our recommended titles.

She Writes Press is an award-winning
independent publishing company founded to
serve women writers everywhere.